THREE WITH A BULLET

"Lyons keeps all the subplots circling nicely. . . . There's a satisfying series of revelation/showdowns—with just about everyone guilty of something. And Jake's narration views the detailed, sordid scene . . . with precisely the right mixture of deadpan drollery and true disgust, making this the best Asch outing in quite some time."

—*The Kirkus Reviews*

"A tasty confection, spiced with humor and leavened with pathos . . . Arthur Lyons keeps you turning the pages."

—*The Washington Post*

BOOKS BY ARTHUR LYONS

OTHER JACOB ASCH NOVELS

All God's Children
The Dead Are Discreet
The Killing Floor
Dead Ringer
Castles Burning
Hard Trade
At the Hands of Another

NONFICTION

The Second Coming:
Satanism in America

Arthur Lyons

THREE WITH A BULLET

An Owl Book

HENRY HOLT AND COMPANY
NEW YORK

Copyright © 1984 by Arthur Lyons
All rights reserved, including the right to reproduce
this book or portions thereof in any form.
Published by Henry Holt and Company,
521 Fifth Avenue, New York, New York 10175.
Published simultaneously in Canada.

Library of Congress Cataloging in Publication Data
Lyons, Arthur.
Three with a bullet.
(An Owl book)
I. Title.
PS3562.Y446T5   1984   813'.54   84-4598
ISBN Paperback: 0-03-008539-X

First published in hardcover by Holt, Rinehart and Winston
in 1985.

First Owl Book Edition—1986

Designer: Marylou Redde
Printed in the United States of America
1 3 5 7 9 10 8 6 4 2

ISBN 0-03-008539-X

For Brother Bill

who said it all when he said
we were lucky we only wound up
as screwed-up as we did

Acknowledgments

I would like to give special thanks
to George Albert, who was so gracious with his time
and helpful with his knowledge.

1

At any party, there comes that inevitable moment when you realize with absolute, terrible clarity that you don't want to be there anymore. That moment had crystallized for me ten minutes before—three minutes after I'd walked through the front door.

Maybe it was too many contrived Haute Punk or Narrow-Tie-Rumpled-Chic fashions from Bijan and Neo 90 and Dianne B. and Fiorucci. Or the bird-bright, coke-glittering eyes set into perfectly patinaed faces or the too-bloodred lipsticked smiles that never reached those eyes. Or the monotonic drone of the Rolling Clones or the Rubber City Rebels or whichever New Wave group was blaring from the huge speakers in the living room, amplifying a headache that was already loud enough. Or maybe it was all the Corniche and Mercedes convertibles outside or the hype that crackled in the air like a downed high-tension wire. Or maybe it was the overdue BounceAmericard statement on my kitchen counter at home reminding me that if I didn't want my credit rating to slide into the Pacific way ahead of the rest of California, I *had* to be there. I've never worked well under duress.

"When I listen to your music, I feel threatened," an anorexic-looking girl in a black-and-purple zebra jumpsuit was saying to a tall, lanky kid with blond spikes for hair.

He nodded as if trying not to look bored and popped a cocktail shrimp into his mouth. "That's what it's supposed to do. I want people to reevaluate everything. I like things that question and threaten. That's why I have so many enemies."

1

Ms. Anorexia hung on every word with rapt attention, as if he were somebody famous. Actually, he might have been. That was how much I knew about it. "You have a lot of enemies?"

"Millions."

"Who are they?" she asked, fascinated.

"I don't know," he said, warily scanning the party over her shoulder. "But they're out there."

"For sure," she said, nodding.

He could have counted me in the crowd and I didn't even know him. He moved off, leaving Ms. Anorexia looking forlorn, and I picked up a paprikaed deviled egg from the buffet table and wrestled with the idea of leaving, BounceAmericard or no. I was still wrestling with it when someone backed into me and stepped on my foot.

"Sorry, but you'll have to blame my mother. It's genetic." The man looked like a refugee from the Beach Boys. His blond hair was combed surfer-style and he kept brushing back a lock of it that continually fell across his tanned forehead. The lines around his eyes said forty-odd, but his round face still looked boyish in spite of that. He was short and looked as if he might be a little pudgy beneath his baggy Hawaiian print shirt. He also wore faded jeans and a pair of navy-blue Pony running shoes.

"That's all right."

He took a swallow of the drink he held and gave me a searching look.

"Do we know each other?"

"I don't believe so."

"Jesus Christ, you look familiar." He pushed out his hand. "Carey Stack."

"Jake Asch."

"You in the business, Jake?"

By "the business," I assumed he meant the music business. Everyone else at the party seemed to be involved in some aspect of it. "Only peripherally."

"Really? What do you do?"

"I'm Rod Stewart's gynecologist."

He smiled and said, "It's always nice to meet a man of medicine." He was about to say something else, but he looked past me and his expression changed to one of distaste. "Oh, shit."

"Carey!"

A man with a goatee and shaved head and a Mr. Clean earring in his right ear came up to us. "Hey, babe. What's happening?"

"Nothing much, Harold," Stack said. "What's happening with you?"

"TCB, babe, TCB. Hey, I saw *Bells* was three with a bullet in *Cashbox* this week. That's beautiful. I was telling Jerry the other day, if anybody deserves it, it's Carey."

"Thanks, Harold." Stack motioned to me. "Harold Jacobson, Jake Asch."

Jacobson said how great it was to meet me, then turned quickly back to Stack. "Listen, Carey, speaking of gold, I've got fourteen carats in the blender myself. A new group and you gotta hear 'em. They're dynamite."

"Another funk band?"

That remark seemed to worry Jacobson. "Yeah, but they got potential. All they need is the right tune."

"I don't write for funk bands," Stack said.

"I don't want you to write funk," Jacobson protested. "Just come over to the studio and listen to them."

"Jake here is a songwriter, too," Stack said.

Jacobson's interest in me suddenly picked up. "Yeah?"

Mirth danced in Stack's eyes. "Writes some gorgeous ballads. Commodores-type stuff."

Jacobson was getting excited now. "That's just what these guys need."

Stack turned to me. "What was the name of that song you played for me the other day, Jake? It'd be perfect for them."

"'You Don't Have to Say You Love Me, Just Wear a Rubber Suit'?"

He snapped his fingers. "That's the one."

I shook my head. "A Korean group is already recording it. Gin Seng."

3

"The Chinese Gin Seng is better," Stack said.

"They had other commitments."

Jacobson's excitement had dissipated as he realized he had been had. He tried to smile, but it wasn't working out too well for him. "Yeah, funny. I'm serious, Carey. Come over and listen."

"I'm really busy these days, Harold."

Jacobson's eyes darted around the room uncomfortably. "You see where Jerry went?"

"Silverman?" Stack asked. "Maybe he went upstairs to rip off God."

Jacobson chuckled hollowly. "Rip off God. That's great. I'll have to remember that. I'll see you around, Carey. And if you have the time, stop by the studio."

He moved off quickly, and Stack said to me, "Better count your fingers."

I looked at my hand. "I've still got five. Who is he?"

"President of Apex Records and one of the true sleazeballs of the industry." He swayed a bit and, for the first time, I noticed that he was a little drunk.

"What, may I ask, is 'three with a bullet'?"

"Chart talk," he said, smiling. "A bullet is a red dot that means a song is moving up fast."

A pale, hatchet-faced man drifted by with a girl in a baggy red 1940s dress and two-tone hair. "I've been going through a real depression lately," he was saying, "and I'm really excited about it. Some of my best work has come out of depression."

The girl nodded as if she understood completely. "I feel good myself," she said, smiling. "That's because I'm a little high."

They moved off and Carey said in a sardonic tone, "This is the only fucking business in the world in which depression is exciting. You get excited by depression, Jake?"

"Only the real deep ones," I said. "The wrist-slashing kind."

"Maybe there's something in that. I knew a guy once who used to hang himself until he almost passed out because he said it turned him on. Only the last time he did it, he accidentally kicked over the chair he was standing on and his hard-on went limp.

4

Permanently." He eyed me with curiosity. "So what do you really do? Let me guess." He tapped his chin with a forefinger as he measured me incisively. "You're a cop."

"Why would you guess that?" I asked, feeling slightly uncomfortable.

He thought a moment. "The eyes."

"What about them?"

"There's no trust in them."

"There's no trust in yours, either."

"I'm in the music business."

"What makes you think I'm not?" I asked, curious now.

"You didn't know what a bullet was. And you look too bored," he said. "Everybody in the music industry is bursting with enthusiasm. Negativism is the only capital crime. This food isn't good, it's 'incredible.' Every person in this room is 'beautiful'—at least to their faces—every song about to be released is a 'monster,' every dunce of a record producer is a 'genius.' Even depression is exciting. Hype is the fuel that keeps the music machine running and anyone who tries to break the mood is a misfit."

"I guess I'm a misfit."

"What kind of a misfit?"

"Journalist," I lied.

"For whom?"

"Free-lance."

Pat Benatar was standing a few yards away from us, wearing a leather jumpsuit so tight that she looked as if she'd been dipped in black paint. She was talking to a man who had hair like Benjamin Franklin and when she saw us, she interrupted the conversation to blow us a kiss.

"I take it that was for you," I said to Carey.

He nodded. "She's recording a couple of my songs on her new album."

"I knew I couldn't get that lucky. That's one sexy lady."

"Yeah, she can park her dagger heels under my bed anytime," he said, then turned his attention back to me. "So, you working on something here?"

"I'm thinking about doing an article on rock promoters."

"You've talked to Freddie?"

"Not yet, but that's what I'm here for."

"Well, whatever you want to know about concert promotion, Freddie can tell you. He's the biggest." He nodded toward my right and said, "Speak of the Devil. Your ears burning, Freddie? We were just talking about you."

He was tall and round-shouldered and younger than I thought he would be, maybe late thirties. He had a pouchy face and a lot of wiry black curly hair, neatly cut like a well-manicured bush. His eyes were large and dark and his brow was pronounced, delineated by thick, black eyebrows, and the pale forehead above them glistened with perspiration. He wore a brown suede jacket over a yellowish-brown checked shirt, a narrow forest-green tie, high-waisted, double-pleated khaki pants, and brown Italian loafers. It was an unassuming ensemble I imagined he had paid through the nose for at Gucci's. "How's it go, Carey? Having a good time?"

"Since I stumbled on Jake here," he said. "He's the only one in the room who isn't full of shit."

Segal turned to me and smiled broadly, but there was something tight and a bit grim in the excessiveness of it. "That's quite a character reference, coming from Carey." His handshake was firm, but his palm was warm and sweaty. "Sorry to have kept you waiting, but I got hung up with some business."

I told him that was okay and he said, "Shall we go into the den? We can talk there. Excuse us for a few minutes, Carey."

"That's okay," he said with mock forlornness. "Just cast me adrift on this sea of bullshit without a life raft. I'll just dog-paddle until I drown."

Unlike his greeting of Jacobson, Carey's manner with Segal was loose and amiable, which made me feel optimistic. Segal obviously was not the kind of man who presented a false face to the world or trusted naively. Who knew? Maybe this time, I'd wind up with a client I could like.

Segal led me away from the buffet table and down the two

6

steps into the larger lower area of the split-level living room, into the buzzing throng. From the bleached-walnut floors to the over-stuffed mohair furniture and heavy black-glass-and-chrome tables, from the genuine pre-Columbian sculpture and signed Picasso lithos to the stereo system built into the wall that looked like a control board from NASA, the place screamed of money. We made it through the room by inches, being stopped every foot and a half by someone wanting to say hello to Segal or to tell him what an absolutely stupendous party it was.

A few yards from the hallway, our forward progress was blocked by a stunningly beautiful auburn-haired woman. She had high cheekbones accented even more by the two slashes of rouge beneath them, and the catlike slant of her green eyes gave her face a sultry, feral look. "Where are you going, darling?" she asked, putting her hand on Segal's arm.

"Into the den for a couple of minutes," he said, then motioned to me. "Mr. Asch and I have some business to discuss. Mr. Asch, my wife, Denise."

We exchanged pleasantries without shaking hands and she said to Segal, "When you finish, I'd like to talk to you about a couple of things myself."

"Sure," he said. She said it was nice to have met me, then glided off through the crowd.

"You have a very beautiful wife."

"Yes," he said in a tone that didn't sound as if he were tremendously glad of the fact, then motioned me to follow.

We went down a hallway hung with more signed Picasso lithos to the second room and entered. Segal shut the door behind us. It was a large, steel-gray-carpeted study, filled with rolled-back, honey-colored leather furniture. Bookshelves filled with thick, leather-bound volumes were built above and around a large walnut desk, and the walls that were not bookshelves were paneled in a high-gloss elm burl. He signaled me into one of the leather chairs and he went to the wood-shuttered window.

The window was open and a little of the night blew into the room, along with the tangle of conversation and the clinking of glasses from the poolside bar. Segal closed the window and took the high-backed swivel chair by the desk. He had to swivel almost completely around to face me.

"You were talking to Carey Stack," he said flatly.

"A pretty outspoken guy. I liked him."

He nodded. "Carey doesn't mince words. He's also a living legend in this business."

"Really? Why is that?"

"Because he's been writing hit records for over twenty years and there aren't many people in this business who can say that." He paused and gave me a concerned look. "You didn't mention to him or somebody else why you're here or what you do for a living?"

"I told him I was a writer doing a story on rock promoters."

"Good. Not that I don't trust Carey. He's probably one of the few straight-shooters in this business. I just think until we determine how we're going to proceed, it'd be better to keep things quiet." He seemed to catch the drift of my thought and said, "I realize a party with two hundred people may strike you as a strange place to discuss a confidential matter, but I have to leave town in the morning for a few days and I didn't want to let things wait."

"Let what wait, Mr. Segal?" I asked. "All I know is what you said on the phone, that you had a security problem."

"That's right," he said. "I'm being sabotaged. Someone is trying to destroy me."

He did not look particularly paranoid. There was tension in the face, around the mouth, and the eyes were a little skittish, but he didn't look as if he were seeing submarines in his bathtub or anything. Then again, you could never tell. I once dated a girl for a week and a half before I found out the reason she would always wait, no matter how long, for me to open doors for her was not that she was a stickler for protocol, but because of the "germs." "Not all germs," she had told me in a calm, expository voice as if what she was going to say next would make it all clear. "Just TB germs." I never looked at door handles the same way after that.

I waited for him to go on.

"It started three months ago," he said. "Limousines supposed to deliver groups to concerts have been called up and canceled or sent to the wrong addresses. Acts have been phoned and told wrong starting times so that the shows went on late. Orders for lighting have been changed by people claiming to be from my office." He paused meaningfully. "It culminated last month at the Stevie Wonder concert at the Forum. A gang went through the crowd outside. One kid was stabbed."

"I heard about it."

"I'm pretty sure that whoever is behind it is being helped by somebody inside my organization. The information they're privy to is too exact. Pickup times of the limos, the hotel room numbers where the acts are staying, the catering companies I've been using. It has to be on the inside."

Always one to take first things first, I said, "Why would somebody want to ruin you, Mr. Segal?"

He blew out some air and slouched back in his chair. His head retracted into his shoulders like a turtle trying to get into his shell. Then he took a deep breath and gave me a vexed look.

"Things have changed drastically in the promotion business in the last couple of years. It used to be a promoter could make good money because he paid groups a flat fee to perform; but then all the groups and their managers started to scream rip-off, and pretty soon everybody started demanding a fee plus a percentage of the net. The percentage varies. Sometimes it's sixty-forty, with the group getting sixty, but with superstars, it can go up to ninety-ten. A giant act like Bowie might want a guarantee of a million dollars against a ninety-ten split.

"What all this means is that the profit margin is so small nowadays, a promoter has to do a hundred, two hundred concerts a year to make it. And in order to do that many concerts, you've got to control the venues."

"Pardon me?"

"You've got to have the town sewn up," he explained. "That's the only way you can make it today because the managers have to

9

give you their big acts because they need you to play their shit acts. Understand? That way, you've got some bargaining power. You can scream at a manager and say, 'Look, how the hell can you talk about only coming up with five grand for your big act after I played that crap group of yours and lost six?' You've got to have a lock on the town."

"And you do?"

He nodded. "But it took a lot of years and a hell of a lot of aggravation to do it. The one thing you've got to have in this business is a good ear, and I've always had that. I was always able to listen to a band and know if they were going to make it or not. I built relationships with acts when they were small, so when they got big, they stuck with me. Any of the heavyweight groups go on the road and plan to make dates in L.A., they call me. They know who they're dealing with and that I'll get the job done for them. Until now, that is." He leaned forward. "You ever deal with rock musicians, Asch?"

I said I hadn't.

He smirked. "Count yourself lucky. They're animals. They all call themselves artists, but maybe one in twenty has any talent at all. Most of them just luck out and hit with one record and suddenly their heads start to swell and they start to demand more and more. You know what a rider is?"

"You mean a contractual rider?"

He nodded. "If the group wants a baby-grand Steinway or pink spots because the drummer thinks it covers up his acne, or the use of a limo while they're in L.A., or moo shu pork and Orange Julius for sixteen people at three in the morning, it goes into a rider. Ever heard of the Rollons?"

"Some New Wave group, aren't they?"

"The biggest right now. I just booked them for a two-night concert stand at the Santa Monica Civic. One of the riders on the contract was that they wanted Chinese food catered for themselves and their production crew after each show. My people hired Wan Fu, the most expensive Chinese caterer in the city. Right before Wan Fu's people were supposed to set up, somebody

10

called and changed the address. Wan Fu wound up sending his people to some fucked-up address and Pizza Man arrived at the Civic with pepperoni for seventeen. Mel Hamms, the leader of the group, got really pissed off and called me up in the middle of the goddamn night to call off the rest of the concert. He thought I'd done it on purpose just to show him what a swellheaded little prick he was. I got it straightened out, but it was touch and go for a while. All this may sound ridiculous to you, but I nearly lost that group because of that one little incident."

The thought that the future of L.A.'s biggest rock promoter rested on a very shaky bed of fried rice struck me as funny, but I didn't laugh. Instead, I said, "So you think somebody is trying to break your hold on the town so they can get their foot in the door."

"Right."

"And you want to find out who they've got inside your organization."

"Right," he said. "And you've got to find out fast. This is a crucial time for me, Mr. Asch. Concert attendance is down ten to fifteen percent in the major markets from last year and as much as twenty-five percent in the secondaries. As a result, promoters are having to go to balanced tour packages and return major artists to three-thousand-seat halls for higher ticket prices. A lot of promoters are having to pass on major acts they booked before because they can't handle the guarantees for the big halls. That means I've got to do a number convincing managers they should cut me enough slack to put together the right kind of shows and put their acts in smaller halls. That's tough enough when things are going smoothly, but if much else goes wrong, it's going to be impossible."

"You said on the phone, Mr. Segal, that Ed Blackburn recommended me."

"That's right."

"Blackburn your attorney?"

"A friend," he said. "I don't have much call for a criminal attorney."

"Strange he should recommend me."

"Why?"

"I've done some work for Ed, but not in quite a while. He must have other investigators he uses more frequently."

He cleared his throat uncomfortably. "To be perfectly blunt, Mr. Asch, Ed gave me a list of names. The first two were tied up with other matters."

I rankled a bit at that, but thought about Paris's advice to Hector about gift horses and BounceAmericards and said nothing. "How many people in your office, Mr. Segal?"

He tugged at his tie knot, loosening it. "Thirteen."

"The first step would be to sweep your office for bugs. There's a chance it's nobody in your employ at all, but somebody outside, listening in. If that turns up zip, I'd give polygraph tests to all your employees—"

"Lie detector?"

"Right. Also, I'd background everybody in the office. What that consists of is having them fill out a standard form listing past schools, bank accounts, credit card numbers, past residences, car license numbers, then checking out what they've written down. It's amazing what people lie about and why. It may be a little thing like embarrassment over a lack of formal education, or it may be trying to cover up a conviction for grand larceny. Or it may be because they're working for somebody else on the side. It may take a few days to track down, it may take a few weeks, depending on how good a liar the saboteur is and how nervous."

He said a bit impatiently, "You're the detective. I don't care how you do it. Just do it."

"When I'm working straight time, my rate is two hundred a day, plus expenses and mileage. When I'm working with a polygraph, I charge by the test, mainly because of the time involved. Fifty dollars per."

I thought he might balk at that, but he waved a hand in the air and said, "I don't care what your rates are. If your rates were five hundred a day, it'd still be cheap if you get results. Another couple of major fuck-ups and I'll be lucky to book the Holiday Inn lounge."

12

He opened the desk drawer and took out a checkbook. When he'd finished writing, he ripped out the check and handed it to me. It was for six hundred dollars. "That should get you started."

I folded it and slipped it into my inside breast pocket so it could be next to my heart. I told him I'd be at his office the next day and asked him the address on La Cienega. "Before I start, you have any particular suspects?"

"No."

"Anybody who came into your employ around the time the incidents began?"

He shook his head. "No. Everybody has worked there for quite some time. My most recent employee is Julia, my secretary, and she was hired at least six months before this started."

"There are only three reasons why someone would engage in this kind of thing, Mr. Segal: money; because they're working for somebody else; or revenge. Can you think of anybody inside your operation who would have it in for you? You have any conflicts with anyone, any major differences of opinion?"

He thought for a moment, then shook his head again. "No."

"Anybody ask for a raise lately and didn't get it? Anybody express the opinion that they're underpaid?"

"Everybody in my office gets top salary," he said, a little indignantly.

I nodded and stood up. "You have a key to the place? I'd like to get in before anybody arrives. It'll be easier to check for bugs."

He took a metal ring of keys from his pocket and pulled one off. He handed it to me and said, "I'm leaving early in the morning for Phoenix and I won't be back until Friday. I'll tell Julia what you'll be doing. She's outside."

I pocketed the key. "I hope I'll have your saboteur by the time you get back."

He stood up and said grimly, "Let's hope so."

"By the way," I said, patting my pocket where the check was. "This entitles you to call me Jake."

He put his hand on my shoulder and his smile relaxed a little. "Yeah, I imagine it would."

We went out into the maelstrom. We weren't ten paces into the

13

room when Segal's hand dropped from my shoulder and he stopped abruptly. His eyes were riveted on a couple a few feet away and his face was dark with anger.

The man was wearing a white silk shirt with baggy sleeves, skintight black leather pants cinched by a wide belt, the ornate silver buckle of which was probably not quite as big as a Viking breastplate, and black boots with Cuban heels. He was tall and piano-wire thin and was strikingly handsome in a feminine kind of way, with shoulder-length brown hair, large, long-lashed eyes, and a full-lipped, sensual mouth. He weaved unsteadily on his feet as he half-listened to a black-haired girl in a red skirt suit and black gather jacket. The girl was obviously disturbed, punctuating her speech with muted gesticulated pleadings, and the man was grinning as if he were enjoying her distress. His grin got wider when he saw Segal coming toward him. "Freddie!"

I followed cautiously. It looked like trouble and it was probably none of my business, but my curiosity and the check in my pocket obliged me to tag along.

The eyes of the black-haired girl were wide as Segal stepped up, and she made a helpless gesture with her hands. "Mr. Segal, I—"

Segal was not looking at her. "What are you doing here?" he asked the man. His voice was hard, taut.

The coldness of the greeting did not seem to bother the good-looking man. He just kept grinning. There was something vicious in that grin. "Tsk, tsk, Freddie, that's no way to talk to your guests."

"You're not my guest."

The man licked his lips, as if his mouth were dry. It might have been. His eyes looked like glazed doughnut holes. He was obviously blasted on something. He waved a hand at the black-haired girl and said, "Your secretary here won't put any of my calls through and you won't return them, so I thought I'd come up and see you."

"Get the hell out of my house," Segal said. The tension coming from him was almost palpable and I stepped in a little closer, just in case things got physical.

14

The handsome man did not seem to be bothered by that prospect. He kind of smirked and asked, "You get the stuff I sent over?"

Segal's eyes burned holes into the man's face. "I got it."

"How'd you like it?"

Segal's forefinger stopped about two inches from the man's nose. "Listen, you whore, if you think you're going to intimidate me—"

"I'm back, Freddie. Like Lazarus from the dead. That's going to be the title for the new LP, by the way—*Lazarus*. Like it?"

"I think you took one hit of acid too many, Cooney. You're hallucinating again. Hasn't it sunk in yet? You're the fucking plague. Nobody in this business would touch you with a ten-foot pole."

The man seemed oblivious to what Segal was saying. He smiled patronizingly and said, "The songs are ready. I talked to Arista and they're real interested. I called Johnny Brandt and we'll be putting them to music this week. He's getting the boys together. We'll be ready for a concert tour by the end of the month."

Segal's lips compressed and he said through clenched jaws, "I told you after that last time, you'd never work any stage I booked and I meant it. Save yourself the heartbreak and get a job as a busboy or something."

The man seemed to consider that thoughtfully. "Naw. If things didn't work out with you, I'd probably just go back to photography. Maybe work for *Rolling Stone* or something."

Segal was trembling with anger and his face was suffused with color, drawing it from his bloodless, clenched fists. Some people in the immediate vicinity seemed to have noticed, because conversation around us died suddenly, and heads turned to watch what was going on.

The other man smiled confidently. "I owe you, Freddie. That's why I'm giving you the first shot. Hey, I know I screwed up before. But things will be different now."

Segal inspected the man's condition and said disdainfully, "Yeah, I can see how different things are."

15

The man swayed unsteadily, as if moved by a sudden wind, and nodded as if Segal had just said something profound. "Fuckin'-A right. The new stuff is dynamite. Pure fucking dynamite." He wheeled around and scanned the room. "Where's the bar? I need a fucking drink." He lurched away and wove through the crowd.

Segal turned to the black-haired girl and demanded, "Who let *him* in here?"

The girl gesticulated helplessly. "I don't know, Mr. Segal. I tried to get him to leave, but he wouldn't."

"Never mind," Segal said. "Asch, this is Julia Roth, my secretary. Julia, Mr. Asch is going to be doing some work for me. He'll be in the office tomorrow. I want you and the rest of the staff to cooperate with him and give him anything he needs."

"Yessir," she said. She was short, even in her three-inch spikes, and that was probably what pushed her from pretty into cute. Her short black hair was combed straight back from her forehead and looked wetted down. She had a small pucker of a mouth, a tiny nose, and dark, heavily made-up eyes, all arranged adequately on a pale, oval face. She still looked shaken by the confrontation, even more shaken than Segal, whose face was slowly returning to its normal color.

"What was that all about?" I asked.

"Nothing. Just a party crasher," Segal answered, then turned to the girl. "Julia, come with me. Asch, make yourself at home. I'll be right back. I want to find out who let that sonofabitch in here."

They went off together and a voice behind me repeated, as if a refrain from a song, "What in the hell is Cooney doing here?" It was Carey Stack.

I'd known the handsome man had looked vaguely familiar; now it fell into place. "*Phil* Cooney? That's who that is?"

He nodded. Phil Cooney had been the lead singer and major force behind a group called Overman a few years back and his songs at that time seemed to be perpetually at the top of the charts. His wild and well-publicized antics, however, and a series

16

of arrests for public drunkenness, drug possession, indecent exposure, and lewd conduct during several concerts had resulted in a downward spiral in the group's popularity, until Overman had finally broken up and Cooney had faded into oblivion.

"I wouldn't say he was Mr. Popularity," I said. "Segal didn't seem too happy to see him either."

"He has good reason," Stack said, his eyes fastened like barbs on Cooney's back. "Cooney fucked up a couple of big concerts for Freddie. Got arrested at one for taking off his pants and pissing on the stage. Another time, he arrived so messed up on whatever that he couldn't perform and Freddie had to refund the gate." He paused, but just for a breath. He had a roll going. "I've seen dozens of Cooneys come and go in this business. Record companies manufacture them. Some jerkoff comes along and gets lucky with one hit and the company head gives him anything he wants and his manager strokes him and tells him he's a genius and pretty soon he starts to believe it. He gets hung up on the power that comes with the adulation of the crowd. He starts to think he's some kind of amoral superman. It's fitting that Cooney named his group Overman. Straight out of Nietzsche."

"I never cared for his music," I said. "It was always a little dark for my tastes."

"He had talent," Stack said grudgingly. "As a lyricist anyway. He just blew it on drugs and booze. He swallowed the image the media and the record company had created for him. I've heard people call Jim Morrison a Dionysian god. That's bullshit. He was just a fucked-up paranoid bound for self-destruction. Cooney will go the Morrison route."

"You really think so?"

"With the public adulation people like Cooney get comes a lot of power. People who come in close contact with them can get infected by that self-destructiveness. It's like a dark magnet, drawing them in. I've seen more than a few people who have gone down in flames just by getting involved with people like Cooney."

His eyes grew watery, remembering, and I got a feeling for the

17

first time of softness beneath that tough crust. It hardened again, however, when I said, "From what I overheard, he seems to be contemplating a comeback."

He gave me an empty smile. "There are no comebacks in the Land of Rock and Roll. Not from as far out as Cooney has been. He's trod on too many toes. Look at him. He can't even fucking walk. His old fans can wait until Doomsday for the rock to roll away from his cave. There will be no Ascension for Phil Cooney."

"I don't understand why Segal doesn't just have him tossed out if he doesn't want him here," I said.

He shrugged. "Maybe he thinks it'd be more trouble than it's worth. You never know what that asshole will do once he's provoked. He's a walking volcano. I once saw him take a restaurant apart when he was asked to leave."

The Motels blasted concussively out of the stereo and it was probably my imagination, but the smoke in the air seemed to pulsate with the beat. "Fuck this," Stack said, glancing irritatedly at the ice cubes melting in the empty plastic glass in his hand. "He's not worth the conversation and it's too noisy in here and too smoky. I need some smog. Let's go outside and get a drink."

I had intended to go home, but Segal had left so suddenly, I had not had a chance to find out if he wanted to tell me anything else, so I agreed.

We pushed through the smoke and throbbing music, around the edge of a group of pogoers who were jumping up and down and bashing into one another with looks of religious ecstasy on their faces. The music spilled out of the doors, and reverberated around the patio, but after the trapped air in the room, the night tasted cool and clean. A red-jacketed bartender poured us two double vodka-rocks and we took them to the metal railing that ran around the pool decking.

The house seemed to be cantilevered on steel stilts out over the chaparral-covered side of the canyon. The supports were underneath us and invisible from our vantage point.

Stack looked down at the ground twenty feet below. "I feel like I'm in some goddamn Vulcan city in a Flash Gordon serial. But that's appropriate, I guess. After all, look where we are. 'You want a swimming pool in the air, sir?' Why not? This is Hollywood, where any dream can become reality."

I gestured at the city lights that smoldered like an endless, fiery grid below us. "You don't believe in the Hollywood Dream?"

"I did when I came here," he said, sighing. "But then I discovered that Hollywood was just another small town in America, with a cop, a judge, a fag, a whore, and a little Timmy who got run over in the second grade. Those pretty lights are just the gaudy neon signs on run-down movie theaters and liquor stores with dirty floors. Most of the people here will wind up dead, in jail, or barbecuing steaks in the backyards of middle-class tract homes in suburbia."

Down the hill, a couple of coyotes yipped.

"They sound close," I said.

"They come down out of the hills and prey on the rich people's poodles. You know, every time I begin to doubt the existence of a divine plan and wonder how God could have created a creature as disgusting as the poodle, along comes a coyote and restores my faith in the orderly universe."

I was getting to like him more all the time. Not only did he share my opinion of poodles, but he was one of the few people I'd met with an attitude more cynical than my own.

He looked at me and smiled sardonically. "I hope my outlook doesn't taint what you're writing."

I shook my head. "I'm not even sure what I'm writing at this stage."

"Freddie give you what you need?"

"A start. He said you were a living legend in this business."

He lifted an eyebrow, saying without braggadocio, "Yeah, I guess I am."

"Why is that?"

He stared out at the lights. "Because I've survived. That's a rarity in this business." He held up a finger. "At what cost, though; that's the question. Sometimes I feel like a fucking dinosaur, completely out of my own time. This business used to be

19

fun, but no more. It's gone corporate. In a business that's supposed to deal with the street, it's being run by a bunch of jerkoffs
driving Corniches who think that 'the Street' means Rodeo Drive.
I'm not going to last much longer. I'm just going to pack up one
day and disappear. Go live in the desert where the coyotes and I
can sing to each other."

He fell silent and we finished our drinks, then I straightened
up and yawned. My headache still throbbed, and as much as I
liked his company, I wanted to get out of there. "I'm going to
split," I said, "but first I have to find Segal and a couple of aspirin
before my head falls off."

He nodded. "Let's have lunch sometime. That's the standard
bullshit line, isn't it?"

"I'd like that, no bullshit." I went through my wallet until I
found somebody else's business card and wrote my name and
number on the back.

"Now let's go find Freddie for you," he said, putting the
card away.

Inside, Stack asked some heavyset woman if she'd seen Segal,
and she said she'd seen him a couple of minutes ago in the back
den. The St. Vitus Dancers were jumping around to some rock-
abilly number and we moved around them to the hallway, which
was crowded with people talking and laughing. At the third door,
Stack stopped and knocked, then went in.

It was a small sitting room done in forest green. French doors,
open now, looked onto the backyard. A thin, twittery blonde girl
wearing black leather gloves sat with three men on two green
couches that faced each other. They were watching a Space Pa-
trol Punkette tap small piles of white powder onto the glass top of
the coffee table from a two-gram bottle. She wore a pink spandex
jumpsuit with Buck Rogers shoulders and lime-green boots. Her
hair was the color of rocket exhaust, except for the green at the
top. She looked up. "Close the door. Otherwise, every asshole and
his brother will be in here wanting some of this shit."

Her face might have been pretty if it weren't for what she'd
done to it. Her eyebrows had been plucked and drawn back on at
savage angles, her cheeks were hollowed with two dark slashes of

20

rouge, and her eyes had been blackened to give them a wanton, drugged-out look.

Stack shut the door and asked if anyone had seen Segal. A dark-haired man holding a cane told him he had just left and should be right back. Stack watched the Punkette chop the piles of powder into lines with a razor blade and asked, "Mind if we join you?"

The man with the cane smiled. "I'm sure Freddie wouldn't mind. This is his shit. He just broke it out and left."

Stack turned to me. "How about you, Jake? A little blast? Might straighten you up for the ride home."

"No, thanks."

"Sure? The coke and the food are the only two things that are good at these parties. Not the usual crap that's been stepped on with procaine so many times that it's only good for root-canal work."

"No, thanks."

"Suit yourself. I'll just toot a quick line and we'll go find Freddie."

The door opened and Cooney lurched into the room, grinning drunkenly. The faces of everyone in the room fell when they saw him, except for the Punkette. She glanced up from the table, mumbled an inaudible greeting, then went back to the task at hand. Cooney looked at what she was doing and leered. "Don't mind if I do."

"Who asked you?" Stack snarled.

Cooney's gaze focused on Stack. "Ah, the master songwriter. Have I ever told you that you write trivial shit, Stack?"

Stack tensed as if he were going to go for him, but I put a restraining grip on his arm. "Relax, Carey. It's not worth it."

The smile never left Cooney's face and he brushed by Stack as he went to the table. The man with the cane handed the Punkette a hundred-dollar bill and she rolled it into a tube and inserted it in her right nostril and snorted up a line with it. Then she did the other nostril and Cooney took the bill out of her hand. He bent over the table and did a line, then straightened up and handed the bill to the man with the cane. A black-haired man

21

wearing a red shirt and a black tie went next, and Stack was reaching for the bill when I noticed that Cooney had gone dead-white. His head dropped onto his chest and he gagged, as if something were caught in his throat. He said something about feeling sick, and stumbled through the French doors.

"I guess he finally went over his limit," Stack said with a self-satisfied smile as we could hear Cooney retching violently outside.

But I was watching the man with the cane. His eyes were glazed and his face had a bluish tinge.

"Is it hot in here?" the man in the red shirt asked in a slurred voice. "My goddamn shoulder is numb."

The Punkette was yawning. I moved Stack away from the table and picked up the bottle and smelled it. The odor was strongly acidic. I turned to the blonde girl and the Latin-looking man who hadn't inhaled any of the stuff and said, "Go find Segal. And find out if there's a doctor here. Quick!"

They looked fearfully at the man in the red shirt, who had fallen onto the floor now, doubled over convulsively, and hurried out of the room.

"What is it?" Stack asked. "What's happening?"

"I don't think this is cocaine."

"What is it?"

"I'm not sure, but I think it's heroin."

"Heroin?!" He dipped a finger into the bottle and pulled it out. He stared at the white residue on the end of his finger and started to put it into his mouth.

I grabbed his arm. "Are you nuts?"

"That's what cops always do—taste it."

"Only on television," I said. I waved a hand at the others. "Go ahead, if you want to wind up like them."

He quickly wiped the powder on his pants and I bent down to examine the Punkette, who was slumped on the couch and showing definite signs of cyanosis. Her skin was cold and clammy and her respiration shallow, but her pulse at least was strong and even. I looked up at Stack. "We've got to get these people to a hospital. In the meantime, round up some men with

22

strong backs. We've got to keep them awake and as uncomfortable as possible."

"That sonofabitch," Stack said, as the thought hit him. "I was about to put that shit up my nose."

"Think about that later. Right now, we have bigger problems to deal with."

He left and I got the Punkette's arm around my shoulder and hoisted her to her feet. Her head lolled loosely on her shoulders and I kept slapping her face. "Aweeezimecanl . . ."

I began walking her. If she weighed a hundred pounds, she weighed a lot, but by the fourth circuit around the room, she felt more like 350. Segal came into the room, looking more bothered than anything else. "What is . . ." The annoyed look turned to one of concern. "What's wrong with them?"

"I'm not sure, but my guess is acute heroin poisoning."

"Heroin? Where would they get heroin?"

"From you," I said.

He put a hand on his chest and said in a stunned tone, "Me? What the hell are you talking about?"

I pointed at the bottle. "You gave that out, didn't you?"

He looked at it and was about to say something when Stack came into the room, trailed by four husky types. "You fucking bastard," he snarled at Segal. "Are you nuts, handing out fucking heroin to people?"

Segal threw his hands out in a frustrated gesture. "I don't know anything about heroin. That shit on the table is pure Peruvian flake. I know. I paid enough for it."

"I told you to deal with that later," I said to Stack, who looked as if he were going to take Segal's head off. "Is there a doctor here?"

"Don't think so."

"Then show me where your bathrooms are," I said. "Ones with a shower and preferably a bathtub." I turned to Stack and his crew. "You guys get Cooney and the others and come with me."

"I'll get Cooney," Stack said tiredly, "although I really don't know why I'm bothering." On the way past the table, he stopped and picked up the bottle. "What about this? We leave it here and

23

somebody else might think it's coke and do a line."

"Right," I said. "Bring it."

A crowd had gathered outside the door in the hallway and Segal had to do some shoving to get them to move aside. "Please, it's okay. Everything is under control. Just a little too much to drink. Stand aside, please."

He ran interference for us down the hallway and went through a huge green bedroom where a gigantic king-sized bed was covered with coats, into a dark-green-tiled bathroom about as big as the living room in my apartment. There was a stall shower with a frosted glass door and a large sunken tub at the far end, next to a glassed-in atrium.

"We have to make them throw up," I told the others. I stuck the Punkette's head in the toilet and put my fingers down her throat until she'd worked into the dry heaves. While the others were taking turns with their patients, I lowered her into the bathtub and began running the cold water. The man in the red shirt seemed to be in the worst shape, so I told the big man holding him to put him into the tub, too. The man with the cane was put into the shower.

Stack came in a couple of minutes later, alone. I stopped slapping the Punkette's face long enough to ask, "Where's Cooney?"

"I couldn't find him."

"What do you mean, you couldn't find him."

"Just what I said. He's gone. He's not outside and nobody out by the pool has seen him."

"He can't have gone far. Not in his condition."

"I'll get some people out looking." He dug into his jeans pocket and pulled out the bottle. "What do you want me to do with this?"

"Put it on the sink for now." He did, and I said, "We're going to need ice. Lots of it."

He said he would get it and went past Segal, who was standing in the doorway looking nervous. "They're going to be all right," he said, as if to assure himself.

I clamped my mouth shut, reminding myself of the check in my pocket, and went back to work, slapping and dunking. The man in the red shirt didn't seem to like that much. His eyes snapped open and his arm thrashed out at me, which didn't bother me a bit. You had to be awake to fight. It was the Punkette I was worried about. Her coughing had turned raspy and her color was bad. "You'd better call the paramedics," I said to Segal, who was really sweating now. The drops glistened beneath his eyes and above his upper lip.

He stepped forward shakily, his eyes wide with panic. "If I did that, the police would be involved. It'd get in the papers—"

I whipped around and said in a tone as nasty as I felt, "You've got good reason to sweat, Segal. If any of these people die, that's murder."

"Murder?" His mouth gaped.

"You said in front of five witnesses that you bought the shit they snorted. That makes you responsible."

His eyes were glassy and his head snapped back and forth jerkily, as if he had Parkinson's. "They'll be all right. They can't die. Not from coke. I swear to God that's all it was—"

The door opened and Stack and another man came in, lugging a large white plastic trash can full of ice. I told them to empty it into the bathtub and when they did, the Punkette woke up. She came roaring out of the water like the Creature from the Black Lagoon, and it took three of us to hold her down. There was a lot of strength in that wiry little frame, and fortunately the heroin had drained most of it. Within a minute or two, her fury had subsided into writhing and incoherent whining, but that was a good sign.

I was taking a breather to wipe off my face, which was dripping sweat and ice water, when the door opened and Mrs. Segal came in.

Her face registered surprise when she saw the congregation. I didn't blame her. She probably thought she had walked in on the latest S-and-M swinging party. Everybody gets stoned and soaked down in the tub while the others slap him or her silly. "What is this? What's going on?"

"Nothing," Segal snapped at her. "A little accident, is all. Nothing to worry about."

"Accident?" Her face grew troubled.

25

"Szzzmecando," the Punkette said.

"It's all right," Segal said, his voice very sharp. "Get out of here and close the bedroom door on your way out. Everything is being taken care of."

She motioned to the two in the tub. "Is this why the police are here?"

"Police?" Segal blurted out.

She nodded. "They say they got a report of a disturbance. They want to come in."

He grabbed her arms. "You didn't let them in, did you?"

She winced. "You're hurting me, Fred."

He let her go as if she had burned his hands. "I'm sorry. What did you tell them?"

"I told them to wait, and I shut the door," she said, rubbing her arms. "They're still waiting."

"Go tell them I'll be out in a minute," Segal told her, and she shot him an angry glance and went out. He went to the sink in two steps, picked up the bottle, and emptied the contents into the toilet.

I yelled, "Hey!" but it was too late. The junk was already gone in a swirl of Blueboy. I said angrily, "That wasn't too bright. We don't know for sure this was heroin. The hospital lab might have needed a sample for analysis."

He turned on me. "You don't think I'm going to leave that stuff lying around for the cops to pick up, do you?"

"The cops can't come in here if you don't let them in. And if they force their way in, they can't use what they find anyway."

He looked at me desperately. "Jesus Christ, what do I tell them?"

"That you don't want to upset your guests by the presence of the police and good night."

He touched my arm and said pleadingly, "You're more experienced in these things, Asch. You know how to deal with them. Come with me. Please."

The man had not been scoring a whole lot of points with me in the past twenty minutes, but he was my client. I made a mental note to charge a half-day's pay against his retainer and told Stack to take over my bathroom duties.

The jaws on the two LAPD patrolmen on the front porch were grimly set and the impatient edge beneath their superficial courtesy said they didn't like to be told to wait or have doors closed in their faces. The spokesman for the duo, a cherubic-looking Aryan type, launched into his explanation about a disturbance call and asked if they could come in. Segal told them the caller was mistaken, that there was no disturbance, and that he would keep the noise level down, but they couldn't come in. I did not know if it was a ploy, or just because he picked up on Segal's nervousness, but the patrolman said, "The caller said there are narcotics here. Do you have any narcotics on the premises, Mr. Segal?"

"Narcotics?" Segal squeaked. "Why, uh, no. Of course not."

"Then you wouldn't mind if we came in and looked around?"

From behind Segal I said, "Sure, fellas. Come on in." Segal's head snapped around like Linda Blair's in *The Exorcist*, and the two cops started to step inside. "As long as you have a warrant."

They stopped dead in their tracks and the Aryan glared at me. "Who are you?"

"Conrad is the name," I said. "Joseph Conrad." I didn't say it was *my* name. "I'm Mr. Segal's legal adviser."

The Nazi Youth Corps graduate looked suspiciously at my soaked hair and clothes, but then he probably looked at his own kid's pet turtle with suspicion, wondering what it was harboring underneath that shell. "You have an accident, Mr. Conrad?"

"The Wethead is not dead." His partner kept trying to see around us. Before he saw something he could deem "reasonable cause," I said, "You *do* have a warrant?"

The Aryan frowned. "No warrant."

I smiled. "Good night, gentlemen. Sorry you had to come all the way up here on a crank call."

They were still looking at me suspiciously when I closed the door. I waited for the doorbell to start ringing furiously, but it didn't. The party did not seem to share my concern. Like some indestructible autonomic organ, it continued to beat at its own

27

uninterrupted tempo. I let out my breath slowly, and looked at Segal, who asked excitedly, "Who in the hell would make that kind of a call?"

I figured he would know better than I, but I asked anyway: "Any of your neighbors got it in for you?"

"No. I'm on good terms with all of them. This whole thing stinks," he said. "I'm being set up, I tell you. How did they know there was dope here?"

I waved a hand at the pogoing, skanking, moonwalking room. "I wouldn't say it was a long-shot guess. Who knows? Maybe they were just saying that to get in."

"Do you think they'll be able to get a warrant?" he asked desperately.

"They won't even try."

That seemed to calm him a little. He wiped the perspiration from his brow and flicked it off his fingers. "Jesus. I feel like I've been through a wringer."

He felt like he'd been through a wringer? I felt like a worn radial tire whose steel belt was starting to wear through the side. I looked at the sopping sleeves of my gray tweed jacket, which I had brilliantly not taken off, and made another mental note to tack on the cost of a new jacket to his bill. For what it had cost me, the goddamn thing probably wasn't Sanforized, and I'd wind up with munchkin sleeves. I could always shred them and go punk.

Stack and company were walking the dripping, shivering three around the bathroom when we got back. Their color was better and they were able to answer questions coherently, but the Punkette's eyes were still glassy. When I asked two of the walkers if they could drive them to the hospital, Segal cut in, "Hospital? Why? They're okay now. . . ."

He was starting to sicken me, check or no check. "They aren't out of the woods yet. With heroin poisoning, you can have relapses. They go to the hospital."

"All right, all right," he said, caving in with a wave of his hand and walking away.

I went out and back down the hall to the small den. It was empty and the night cooled the room through the open French doors. I went through them and outside.

The lawn ran away from the house for a few yards, then turned into an ivy bed that sloped gently down to the street. A path had been trampled out of it and I followed the path to the street, but there was still no sign of Cooney. I went back up to the house and on the way in, I ran into a glum-looking Segal. "Carey and the others ran them to Westside Community. You find Cooney?"

I shook my head. "You know how he got here? Did he drive?"

"I don't know."

I asked him for a local phone book with a Yellow Pages, and he pulled one out of the cabinet by the phone stand. Stack and company had not made it to Westside yet and Cooney had not checked in there, either. I called the ER's of four other hospitals close enough for him to have made it to and got the same answer.

I looked up at Segal. "You know where he lives?"

"Cooney? No."

"If he did somehow make it home, he could be in a bad way. If he dies, your neck is in a noose."

He swallowed and started to look worried again. "What do we do?"

"Know anybody here who might know where he lives?"

"I—" He thought of something and snapped his fingers. "Wait. Maybe. The girl who came with Andy Brubeck used to date Cooney. I'll ask her."

I waited. The walls of the room vibrated from the bass of the stereo and the happy party sounds wafted through the open French doors. At least some people were having a good time. I thought about a drink. My nerves were frayed and God knows I could have used one, but I knew that if I took one now, I'd come unraveled like a ball of yarn. Segal came back in holding a piece of paper. "She didn't remember the number of the house, but she drew a map."

The name of the street was Prospect, off Laurel Canyon, and the girl had written on the paper, "third on left, long balcony."

"Does she have a phone number?"

He shook his head. "She said she threw it away. Cooney isn't the most popular guy with her, either. I thought she was going to spit when I mentioned his name."

Of course, he wasn't listed. I put down the phone book and told Segal I was going to go over there, and he said in a contrite tone, "I want to apologize for acting like a stupid asshole tonight. It's just—I don't know, I've been living on the edge lately, with all this crap raining down on me, and I just blew it. I'm grateful you were here to take charge of things. Thanks."

Maybe the man was not so bad after all. I told him I would call him later and left.

2

Mulholland Drive twisted through the dark hills as if trying to shake off the houses that clung to its sides and, after a while, it succeeded. I rolled the window down and let the cool air blow against my face and, as I drove, I suddenly realized that my headache was gone. Nothing like a little emergency-room crisis to make one forget one's trivial discomforts.

Every once in a while, my headlights would flash on a car parked on a gravel turnout, lovers who had come up to gaze at the grid of amethyst lights.

I punched in a Steely Dan cassette and thought about all the other things I would have rather been doing and wondered why in the hell I'd volunteered for this expedition. Stack was probably right. If not tonight, Cooney would just O.D. the next week or the week after, and two German shepherds would show up for the funeral. But let him die with his own hands, without a little help from his nonfriends. At least not from my client. I was bone tired and annoyed at myself for the profession I was in.

I slowed for the red light flashing over the Laurel Canyon intersection and turned and started the descent into Hollywood. Houses poked out of the dark scrub, shake-roofed houses overhung by eucalyptus and shaggy palms, and high above the roadway, others were cantilevered on steel legs over the side of the hill, like obscene gestures of defiance at the San Andreas. They were similar to Segal's house and I didn't like the feeling of foreboding they gave me. Defiant gestures have a funny way of com-

31

ing back at you; and when the Big One finally hit, every one of those man-made works would be racing its neighbors to the bottom of the canyon. I just hoped it wouldn't be tonight.

After a few miles, a small cluster of stores appeared on the left. That was it. I made a left onto a narrow street shaded by palms whose thick trunks were choked with vines. I went slowly. On the left, narrower streets ran up the hill and disappeared into the thick foliage. My lights flashed briefly on the sign for Prospect and I turned.

The street dead-ended fifty yards up. It was not wide enough for a garbage truck, which was perhaps why all of the garbage cans in front of the houses were overflowing, and it gave me a claustrophobic feeling. On the right was a thick wall of dark trees, their branches dripping with vines, and on the left the houses had been built on the slope of the hill, so that they seemed to hover, brooding, over the street. Most of them were the same architectural style—Spanish stucco with terra cotta roof—and most of them could have used paint and patchwork. The third one, aside from having a few more of its roof tiles missing, was the only one with a wooden balcony overhanging the street. Light shone through the curtains that had been pulled across the set of glass doors leading into it.

A sign across the street from the house said, "NO PARKING AT ANY TIME." I decided to be daring. I got out of the car and locked it, then stood there, listening. Traffic whispered on Laurel Canyon below and crickets rubbed their legs together in the bushes. Other than that, nothing. I looked up the block. Cooney's was the only light on. Not even the gray-blue tinge of a television screen. I checked my watch. Quarter-to-one. Everybody was in bed, asleep. Anybody with any sense.

A peeling stucco retaining wall ran beneath the house and the only way I could see to get to it was a flight of broken cement steps that had been stuck on the side of the hill. Through labored breath, I counted twenty-one of them to the front door of Cooney's place.

A large century plant flanked the arched front door and I gave it wide berth to avoid its sharp spikes. There was no bell, so I used the wrought-iron knocker. When I got no answer, I tried the tongue latch. It was unlocked. I pushed open the door and stepped inside. "Cooney?"

The furniture was a mixture of cheap and expensive, and none of it fit in with the textured plaster walls or the arched Spanish doorways in the house. A worn Persian carpet occupied the center of the wooden floor and on it, surrounding a littered black laminate parson's table, was a couch and two deco pretzel-armed rattan chairs. Ceiling-to-floor bookshelves packed with books flanked the arched doorway leading into the kitchen. At the opposite side of the room, crammed into a tiny arched alcove, was a heavy round oak dining table with clawed feet, and four tired-looking cane-back chairs. I called again: "Cooney?"

Nada. The mess on the parson's table stopped me on my way through the room. There was an almost-drained bottle of Jack Daniel's, an empty cloudy glass, a crumpled pack of Merits, and an ashtray full of dead cigarette butts, quite a few of which had lipstick on them. I was thinking about that when I heard something in the kitchen, a muffled, clicking sound.

The kitchen had dirty walls. Half a dozen dirty glasses stood in the coffee-stained sink, and on the white tile countertop beside it was a brown paper bag that held a jar of Taster's Choice, a quart of milk, and a pack of Merits. The ants that marched around the bag were not interested in milk or Merits; they were going straight for the crumbs in the empty Dolly Madison doughnut box beyond. Being more curious than they, I reached inside and felt the milk. Still cold.

There was a door on the other side of the refrigerator and I opened it and stepped outside. A stone pathway led between Cooney's house and his next-door neighbor's, and I followed it around to the front. There was nobody on the stairs, nobody anywhere. It had been a long night and my imagination was starting to play PacMan with my mind. But I was not imagining the sound of the car starting down the hill. I kept peering at the bottom of the stairs, in case it drove by, but the sound of the motor grew fainter. I waited until it became indistinguishable from the Laurel Canyon traffic, then went back inside, through the front door.

A narrow hallway ran from the living room to the back of the house, and I went down it. There were three doors, two on the right and one on the left, and all of them were open. The one on the left was a green tile bathroom and the one across the hall from it was a small bedroom filled with an assortment of guitars, amplifiers, wah-wah pedals, and other musical accoutrements. Cooney was in the third room, lying diagonally across the king-sized bed in a red velvet bathrobe, and unless he *could* rise like Lazarus, he wouldn't be making a comeback this or any other year.

His face was dark blue and his mouth was open. I didn't have to feel for a pulse to know I wouldn't find one, but I did it anyway.

His long hair was spread over the pillow in wet strands, and the robe and bedclothes were soaked with sweat. From the way the sheets were twisted, it looked as if he'd gone into convulsions before he died.

On the cigarette-burned nightstand by his head was a yellow spiral notebook. The first twenty or so pages of the notebook were filled with verse written in pen in a scrawling backhand. I read the first:

> Love is death and death is near
> It rides on the wings of a swan
> From the deserts of the north
> Death is the end of us
> But so is love
> Embrace death as a lover.

Real upbeat stuff. I read on:

> From the winds of the mind we arise
> Like dust devils in the desert

We must have water to cross
To reach the Great Sea.

There is no help.

I wondered if this was Cooney's great new material. I was no judge, of course, but it didn't sound like solid gold to me. I somehow couldn't imagine a room full of teenyboppers skanking the night away to songs about embracing death, but then I couldn't imagine skanking, period.

I put the notebook back and went through the glass-topped chest of drawers. All it told me was that Cooney didn't like to fold his clothes. It was sometime while sorting through polka-dotted boxer shorts that I realized I was doing this solely out of habit. I had no idea what I was looking for or even if there was anything *to* look for.

I pulled open the drawer of the nightstand. A bottle of Visine, some Q-Tips, a bottle of Vaseline, and three prescription bottles, two with labels and one without. The labeled bottles were for Quaaludes and Tuinals. The third was half-full of a white crystalline powder that did not look like either coke or heroin. I closed the drawer and used the phone on the opposite side of the bed to call the cops. After that, I called Segal. He answered and when he heard who it was, he pounced: "What's up? Where are you?"

"At Cooney's. He's dead. The cops will be here any minute, so just listen—"

"Dead?"

In the background the party was still throbbing. Death didn't affect it. The only thing that would kill it would be a power failure. "That's right. If I were you, I'd get hold of an attorney immediately. Blackburn is good, by the way, if you want to use him. Whoever you call, though, tell him everything that happened at the party. Don't hold anything back. I'll volunteer as little information as I can to the cops—"

"But, but—"

"Just do it, Mr. Segal," I said. I was not in the mood to deal with any more of his anxiety attacks. "I'll call you later this afternoon."

I hung up and went out to the kitchen and in one of the cupboards found a glass that looked halfway clean, rinsed it out, and returned to the living room. I sat in one of the rattan chairs and poured myself a double shot of Cooney's Jack Daniel's. I didn't think he would mind. I took a good slug of the bourbon and tried to work myself into an upbeat mood for the cops. After all, I had to show them that everything was up and exciting in the wonderful world of rock and roll.

3

After telling my story to the arriving patrolmen and then twice more to two homicide detectives, who arrived later and grumbled constantly about being rousted out of bed for something as passé as yesterday's fad, I found my own enthusiasm waning.

I'd been dispatched to Cooney's house by Mr. Fred Segal who'd been worried about Cooney after the latter had disappeared from Mr. Segal's party not looking at all well. Upon finding the front door unlocked, I had entered and found Cooney in his present—and from now on, forever—state, dead, upon which I had immediately phoned the police.

I was more than a little vague, but they didn't seem to mind all that much. They had already found the bedside stash, plus assorted goodies in the medicine cabinet, so they were ready to put it down to another O.D. brought on by decadence and rock and roll. Then, luckily, some representatives of the press had begun to show up and the detectives were too busy making sure their names were being spelled right to waste a lot of time with me. Yesterday's fad, after all, was more news than no fad at all.

After checking my story out with Segal by phone, the police took down my numbers and cut me loose. It was nearly 4:30 by the time I got to my apartment. I poured myself a triple vodka, ate a slice of Bran'nola bread to placate my growling stomach, and fell into bed. Most of the vodka was still in the glass on top of my digital alarm-radio when I woke up at 7:10.

I lay there for a moment, trying to grasp why I would want to

37

wake up at 7:10, when insistent knuckles rapped on my door. I put on a robe and careened into the living room.

"Who is it?" I asked through the door.

"Plumber," a female voice said.

"I didn't call a plumber."

"Telegram, sir."

"Telegram?"

Hesitation. "Uh, Candygram."

I didn't say anything.

"Land shark."

Sturgis stood on the porch, dressed in a sleeveless down vest over a white ribbed sweater, jeans, and black leather boots. Her frosted shag looked a little limp in the weak morning light and her big green eyes were bloodshot. "Sorry. Did I wake you?"

"I hope I don't look like this all the time."

She showed me at least thirty of her thirty-two straight white teeth. "I was just in the neighborhood and thought I'd stop by."

"The neighborhood," I said dubiously.

"Yeah. Hollywood."

"Hollywood is nine miles away."

"So I went a little out of my way. You should feel flattered." She paused and looked me over. "You look like you spent the night in a cement mixer."

"I feel like it. It was a rough one."

"Cheating on me again, eh? Serves you right." She looked past me. "Am I interrupting something, I hope? A cheap interlude, perhaps?"

I probably should have told her to leave, but I knew it would be useless to try to sleep now; the damage had already been done. Besides, when Sturgis worked herself into one of these moods, it was like trying to negotiate position with a moving train. I sighed in resignation and told her to come in. She went directly to the kitchen and looked shockingly at the stove.

"No coffee? Jesus, what kind of a place are you running here?"

The hand motions were exaggerated and the New York Jewish accent was particularly thick, a pretty good barometer of how "on" she was this morning. Although Sturgis was, in fact, Jewish and from New York, she thickened the accent for comedic purposes. It was part of her stock in trade and she had landed a couple of minor parts on sitcoms because of it. Sydney Sturgis was an actress. We had gone out a few times a year or so back and I'd canceled the show when she'd started talking about moving in. Ever since that time, she would show up on my doorstep periodically, usually between boyfriends or commercials, and always at odd hours, just to remind me what I had passed up. What I had passed up was an attractive, very bright, and very funny semi-manic-depressive who would have worn me to a frazzle in two weeks with her frenetic neuroses, which she tried to cover up with her sharp and often caustic sense of humor.

"I'll make coffee," I offered.

"Never mind," she said, spying the vodka bottle on the counter. "I'll have a Bloody Mary."

"What are you running on?" All her movements had an even more manic quality to them than usual.

"Oh, a pinch of this, a dash of that. Rhonda and I went out celebrating last night. I bagged a shoe commercial yesterday. They wanted a tall girl with big feet."

I looked at her feet. They didn't look particularly big. In fact, I thought they were quite in proportion to her big-boned, five-ten frame, and I told her so. She was too busy waving her hands disgustedly at my refrigerator to listen to me. "Of course, no Bloody Mary mix. Not even any tomato juice. Look at that. It's like the goddamn Gobi desert in there."

I put the kettle on and moved behind her, feeling obligated to defend my territory. "Whaddya mean? The basic food groups are all represented in there. There's bread, and milk, and tuna fish—"

"Great. A new drink. Vodka and tuna fish. What would we call that? A Bloody Tuna? No, we'd still need tomato juice. How about something romantic-fishy, like a Blue Lagoon?"

I shook my head doubtfully. "I don't know. The smell . . ."

"You're right. I've got it. A Blue Slough." That settled, she promptly abandoned the idea, twisted the cap off a Henry Weinhart's and sipped the beer as she conducted an inspection tour of my cupboards. "I don't believe this. There's absolutely nothing here."

I shrugged helplessly.

"Tell you what I'm going to do," she said. "I'm going to go down the street to that little market and pick up some things and come back here and cook us breakfast."

"Just spare me the Sego waffles," I said. "I'd rather have a Blue Slough."

"Sego waffles," she said, disgustedly. "You really don't have much faith in my domestic abilities, do you?"

"You know the floor plan of the Jewish American Princess's dream house—ten thousand square feet, no bedroom, no kitchen."

She looked at me quite seriously. "I'm surprised at you, a half-Jew, swallowing all those JAP myths. The only difference between Jewish girls and non-Jewish girls is that Jewish girls are overt ball-cutters and non-Jewish girls are *covert* ball-cutters. All the rest of that stereotype stuff is—"

"Just what I've been looking for my whole life—a tall, overt ball-cutter with big feet."

"With the help of a little Demerol, you'd love it," she said, and went out.

I was working on my second cup of coffee when the phone rang.

"Jake? Ed Blackburn."

"Hello, Ed."

"I just got off the phone with Fred Segal. He told me about last night. How did it go with the police?"

"I was pretty skimpy with some details, but they were too distracted to notice. They will, though. Then they're going to want to talk to me again."

"I'd like to hear the details before they do. Fred is going to be in my office around ten. Think you can make it?"

"I'll be there. Thanks for the referral, by the way."

40

"Sure. See you then."

I drained my cup and poured myself another and took it into the bathroom. Half an hour later, I was shaved, showered, and in one more cup of coffee would be ready to enter the affray. When I went to get my coffee, Sturgis was in the kitchen, mixing butter and flour in a bowl. Bacon was sizzling in the frying pan on the stove. She had made a fresh pot of coffee and I filled my cup. "What are you making?"

"*Pâté brisé.*"

"Oh. Of course. I should have known."

"It's a French piecrust made for holding moist fillings."

"What is it going to hold?"

"Quiche Lorraine."

"Don't you know that real men don't eat quiche? If word of this got out, I'd be the laughingstock of my profession."

"Your profession is already a laughingstock," she said. "And I've had a craving for it since four this morning. It'll be ready in an hour. Why, are you starved?"

"No. But I have to be in Beverly Hills in an hour, which means I will have to go quicheless this morning." I bent over the frying pan. "I'll just take a couple of strips of bacon and some toast."

Her hands stopped mixing. "You mean to tell me that I went out and crapped around at the market, which in your lovely neighborhood is a life-jeopardizing undertaking in itself, bought all this shit, and have started making *pâté brisé* for nothing? Why didn't you tell me you had to be somewhere?"

You could have cut the New York Jewish accent with a knife, but there was no humor in it. "The call came while you were gone," I explained. "Anyway, it's not for nothing. You've got a craving for quiche, right? So make quiche. I'll have a piece later."

"You know what I like about you?" Sturgis asked after a moment.

"What?"

"You make me hate men so much I can go out and do anything I want and not feel guilty about it."

"I can relate to that," I said, and forked a strip of bacon from the pan.

41

4

Ed Blackburn looked like an experiment from the island of Dr. Moreau. He had the nose of a pig, the eyes of a ferret, and the ears of an elephant; but in a courtroom, only the best instincts of those animals came out. He was a relentless digger, incisive and ruthless, and never forgot a word, and for those reasons—and because he always collected his fees in advance—he was a highly successful and much-sought-after criminal attorney who could spurn the drunk drivers and miscellaneous misdemeanor cases that make up the bulk of most criminal attorneys' caseloads.

He sat behind a mausoleum-sized desk, about the only pretentious piece of furniture in an office that might have been considered austere for its posh Century City address. He yanked on the vest of his three-piece, gray pin-striped suit, cleared his throat, and said, "Fred has retained me to represent him, just in case the D.A. decides to prosecute. He's convinced the same person or persons who have been trying to sabotage his operation switched drugs on him last night. I want to retain you to investigate the case."

I glanced over at Segal. He was slumped down in his chair and he looked like hell. There were dark smudges under his eyes and his face was drawn and grayish. I wondered if he'd been sniffing some of his own stuff. "Mr. Segal has already retained me."

Blackburn smiled and plucked a pen from the Greenland marble penholder in front of him and sat back holding it in both hands. "That was last night. Things have changed, obviously. You being retained by me instead of Fred gives us certain distinct advantages. As Fred's attorney, I can't be forced to hurt my client by divulging information to the police. As my agent, they couldn't force you to talk either."

Since I was not particularly anxious to talk to the cops anyway, I said, "That's fine with me."

The door opened and Blackburn's secretary came in with three cups of coffee. The cups were styrofoam and the cream was that horrible nondairy powder they started using in coffee only after it didn't work out in Vietnam as a defoliant. I sipped it, made a face, and asked Blackburn if he'd heard how the others were who had been taken to the hospital.

He tugged a lobe of one of the elephant ears and said, "They're all fine."

"The cops know about them?"

"I don't know if they've put it all together yet, but they know. What exactly did you tell them at Cooney's?"

"Not much. I said Cooney had left the party sick and Segal had sent me over to check on him, to make sure he was all right."

Blackburn took a yellow legal pad from the desk and leaned back with it in his lap. He wrote something on it, then turned to Segal. "That's good. That shows concern on your part."

"Yeah," I said, "but concern for what? The cops might just see it as Mr. Segal's concern for his own ass. Especially after they talk to a few people who were at the party."

"What's that supposed to mean?" Segal asked.

"You argued with the man in front of witnesses. It's not going to take Sherlock Holmes to find out you hated the man's guts."

He threw out his hands. "So what? I could name you at least twenty other people at the party who hated him as much as I did."

"But they didn't give him the dope that killed him. You did. Why didn't you have him thrown out of your house?"

"Because I thought he might have been on dust or some goddamn thing and thrown a fit. You never knew with Cooney. He'd

43

done that sort of thing before. I thought it'd be easier to let things alone." He paused and anger flashed behind his eyes. "Hold on. Are you trying to imply that I slipped him that junk on purpose?"

I held up my hand like a crosswalk guard. "Take it easy, Mr. Segal. I'm on your side. I'm only trying to anticipate what the cops are going to ask you. They get paid to be suspicious."

"He's right," Blackburn said.

Segal sat back and grunted scoffingly. "Hell, if I'd wanted to murder Cooney, I wouldn't have been likely to do it in my own house in front of two hundred witnesses. I wouldn't have been likely to do it at all. As far as I was concerned, the man was already dead. He buried himself in the shit he pulled on me. He was a washed-up zero who couldn't buy a gig in this town. I made sure of that. So you see, I've already had my revenge. I didn't have to kill him."

"From the gist of your conversation that night," I said, "I take it Cooney wanted you to set up some concert dates for him."

"Who knows what he wanted. He was nuts."

"He asked you if you'd gotten the stuff he'd sent you. What was it?"

He looked away and waved a disparaging hand. "Who knows? Some crappy lyrics to some new songs he'd written."

"Was the stuff any good?"

"Who knows? I threw them away."

I looked over at Blackburn, who seemed preoccupied with his scribbling.

"Do you throw many parties, Mr. Segal?"

"A couple a year."

"Is there always coke at them?"

"Look, in this business coke is a social necessity. Half of the people in the industry run on it. It keeps them happy."

One more word about being up and happy, and I was going to throw up. "So anybody who was invited would have known there would be coke around?"

"Probably."

"Where did you keep the stuff before you put it out?"

"In a safe in the den."

44

"Who has the combination?"

"Just my wife and myself."

"How much was there?"

"When I bought it? A 'Z.'"

"When did you buy it?"

"A week or so ago."

"Who from?"

He glanced at Blackburn, who nodded. "Tom Taylor. But I've been buying from him for years. He wouldn't sell me any shit like that. Besides, some friends were up at the house a few days before the party and tooted some then."

"Nobody got sick?"

"Of course not."

"Then it was switched after," I said. "How long was the stuff out at the party, before people started taking sick?"

"Twenty minutes, maybe."

"Did anybody snort any before people started getting sick?"

"I don't know. I put the stuff out and then somebody called me away, and I left the room."

"If it was the same people who have been dirty-tricking you, I doubt they intended to kill anybody. And if there is an inside man, I'd bet he's probably good and nervous right now. It'd be a good time to put your people on the lie box. Are you going to your office today?"

He nodded tiredly. "As soon as I leave here."

"I should be able to round up the equipment I need and be over there by two."

Blackburn had stopped writing. He stood up and came around the desk with his hand extended. "I'll have a check made out for you to make this thing official."

That was a signal for me to follow. I told Segal I would see him later and went out with Blackburn. When the door closed, he said, "What do you think?"

"I'll let you know this afternoon. If there is an insider, we'll smoke him out. That I don't have too many worries about. Do you think they'll try to indict?"

He put his hand on my shoulder and walked me toward his

secretary's desk. "With the obvious publicity possibilities this case has? Does a shark shit in the sea? That's why it's important to move as fast as we can to squelch it. The more publicity it gets, the worse it's going to be for Fred."

Blackburn signed the check his secretary had made out, and I told him I would call him as soon as I found out something.

5

The offices of Segal Productions were on the second floor of a two-story red brick building on La Cienega, in the middle of a block dominated by posh interior designers.

Three men and a woman were crowded around the receptionist's window when I entered the small, walnut-paneled waiting room, jockeying for pole position. When I saw the Minicam on the floor by their feet, I knew who they were, and thought it funny how the image of vultures came instantly to mind. Not too many years back, I would have been right there with them, clamoring for an interview.

The telephone seemed to be ringing on schedule every three seconds, and the frizzy-haired receptionist was trying to decide whether to keep answering it or cope with the reporters hanging through the window. I excused my way through them a bit forcefully and said, "Mr. Segal is expecting me—"

"I'm sorry," the girl interrupted in a harried tone. "Mr. Segal is not making any statements to the press at this time."

"My name is Asch."

"Oh, yes, Mr. Asch. I'm sorry. You can see things are a little crazy here." The phone rang again and she signaled with her eyes to the door on her left. I picked up the polygraph and she buzzed the door open. One of the reporters tried to follow me though, but I turned and put a hand on his chest and shook my head ruefully. "You heard the lady. Mr. Segal is not making any statements at this time."

"Who the hell are you?" he snarled angrily.

47

"The Catman of Paris. You don't want to see me sprout claws, do you?"

He backed up and I shut the door. The large room I was in was filled with desks. Young people, most of them casually dressed in jeans and sweaters, bustled back and forth between the desks, carrying papers and talking on phones. The receptionist slammed the window shut and stood up. "Jesus Christ, this is insanity. Those people are goddamn animals. They don't know the meaning of the word no."

I spent the next half hour checking for bugs. When the receptionist found me, she led me into a small, sun-washed office whose curtainless windows offered a splendid view of the drapery store next door. I swung the suitcase onto the desk top and said, "Looks like they've really got you going today."

She pushed her dark hair off her forehead. "Normally it's not this bad, but all those reporters out there are making me crazy. Then Julia called in sick, which doesn't help things—"

"Mr. Segal's secretary? What's wrong with her?"

"I don't know. She called in and said she'd fallen and hurt herself." She hesitated. "You were at the party last night, weren't you?"

I said I was.

"That was horrible, what happened to Phil Cooney." She glanced warily at the suitcase. "Is that what you're going to test us about?"

"Not really. I might ask a question or two about it, but that isn't my primary reason for being here."

The phone rang again and she said, "Excuse me. I'll tell Mr. Segal you're here."

After watching her miniskirt all the way back to her desk, I turned my attention to the suitcase. I used to sub out my testing until I finally got ill seeing someone else rake in all that money, and decided to learn the technique. I made up the $2,500 I spent for the machine in four months.

I got out the blood-pressure cuff and finger rings and was positioning a chair on the opposite side of the desk when Segal came in. He looked anxious. "You all ready to go?"

48

"Pretty much."

"How long will it take?"

"The average test runs an hour and a half."

"For each person?"

"That's right. I have to run a pretest to get a response level, then the test, then analyze the results."

"That'll take days."

"Maybe," I conceded. "Or maybe we'll hit the culprit on the first shot."

"I didn't realize it would take so long. The cops came by a little while ago. A couple of detectives. They know about the people in the hospital. They've already talked to a couple of them, I guess. How could they find out so fast?"

"Hospitals report drug overdoses to the cops as normal procedure."

"I wouldn't talk to them without Ed. He's going to go with me to the Hollywood station at four to answer questions." His eyes darted out the door. "I feel like I'm surrounded by wolves. Did you see that fucking pack in the outer office? They can taste my blood already."

"They taste blood all the time. It's a permanent state with them. Don't worry about it."

He tossed his hands in the air. "Don't worry about it? Shit, I can see the headline now: 'Promoter Assassinates Rock Star.' That'll inspire a lot of confidence. The big acts will flock to me in droves, just begging me to book them."

"Your secretary who didn't show up today—Julia—how long has she been working for you?"

"A little less than a year, I guess."

"What exactly does she do here?"

"A little of everything. Sets up my appointments, makes accommodation arrangements for the bands, screens all my calls." He looked at me curiously. "Why?"

"Did you see her last night after all the shit broke loose at the party?"

His expression grew thoughtful. "Come to think of it, I didn't."

"Did she talk to you when she called in this morning?"

"No. She talked to Mitzi."

"I'd like her home address and phone number."

"It's in the Rolodex up front. Mitzi can give it to you." His brow furrowed. "It'd be really hard for me to believe that Julia would be the one. She was with me for months before the trouble started. I really trust her."

"I'm not saying she's the one. I just want to talk to her." I pointed at the dark-haired receptionist in the miniskirt at the front desk. "We might as well start from the front and work back. You want to tell her to come in?"

Segal went out and told the girl, and she stood up and came in, smiling nervously, I told her there was no need to feel nervous, and that turned out to be a truthful statement. She passed with flying colors. I only managed to test one other before 5:30, primarily because I kept getting reactions to the questions dealing with cocaine, but I was eventually able to sort out their personal habits from events at Segal's party and clear them of complicity in any sabotage or Cooney's murder.

It was prime traffic-snarl time and I was in no hurry to do battle on the freeway, so I decided to kill time paying Julia Roth a visit. On the way over, I wondered how Segal had fared with the cops. He hadn't returned to the office or called in, and I wondered if they were still raking him over the coals. After talking to him, one thing was sure: they were going to want to talk to me again, after they realized there were holes in my story big enough to drive a squad car through. I just hoped I could brick up a few of them before the homicide boys got around to serious interrogation.

Julia Roth lived on Sweetzer in West Hollywood, a street where modern behemoth apartment buildings with banners across their fronts saying "NOW RENTING" were putting the squeeze on the smaller, older buildings between them. The number I wanted was one of the squeezes, an old stucco bungalow court built like a U, with an ivy-covered archway connecting the two halves of the building. I parked and went under the archway and through a tiled courtyard filled with banana plants and neatly tended flower beds to number 9 in the back. I pressed the buzzer and when nothing happened, I knocked. Finally a woman's voice asked through the door, "Who is it?"

"Jacob Asch."

"Who?"

"I'm working for Mr. Segal. We met last night."

A lock clicked back and an eye and a strand of disheveled hair appeared at the crack in the door. The eye looked red and swollen, as if she had been crying. She also looked as if she were having a hard time focusing on me. "What is it? What do you want?"

"I'd like to talk to you for a couple of minutes."

"What about?" There was a sharp, nervous edge behind the slur in her voice.

"Mr. Segal is in some trouble because of last night. You know Phil Cooney died last night after he left the party."

"I—yes." She started to say something, but it caught in her throat. The eye closed, then opened again. "I don't know anything about that. Please go away. I'm not feeling well."

I was beginning to feel disconcerted, staring at that one blinking eye. She had not cracked the door half an inch more since she had opened it.

"I heard you fell. I hope you didn't hurt yourself too badly."

"I'm all right," she said, her voice belligerent now. "Look, I'm not feeling so hot, so if you'll excuse me—"

"Just one more question and I promise to get out of your life," I said, flashing her a diffident smile. "Do you happen to have a cigarette? I'm completely out and I'm dying for a smoke."

There was an exasperated sigh and the eye disappeared. "Just a minute."

She left the door cracked. I pushed it open and stepped quietly inside. The living room was small and whoever had decorated it had been in an Oriental mood at the time. She stood with her back to me in the middle of the room, dressed in a baggy purple sweatshirt and jeans, fumbling frantically with a pack of cigarettes. She had not heard me come in, thanks to the squealing

51

tires in the "Kojak" rerun on the tube and to her obsession with the task at hand. She weaved a bit, then swore, as she poked around inside the pack for a cigarette. Part of her problem could have been from the half-empty fifth of Smirnoff on one of the red lacquer coffee tables in front of her, but finally she managed to extricate one and straightened up triumphantly. Her triumph turned to surprise, then anger, when she saw me. "Hey, goddamnit! Shit! Who said you could come in here? Get out!"

I could see why she would only want to present the right side of her face to the world. The left eye was blackened and swollen shut and the left side of her jaw was purplish and puffy. Her sweatshirt had "HEAVEN" written across the front of it. She started toward me angrily.

"Cooney give you the shiner last night during a seizure?" That stopped her. She turned the bad side of her face away from me self-consciously. "What are you talking about? I fell down, that's all. Now please leave. You have no right to barge into my house like this."

"You drove Cooney home last night," I said. I took a step toward her and she cringed and her hand flew up to her face to protect it. Sure she fell. I plucked the cigarette from between her fingers and said, "You left a couple of these there."

"A lot of people smoke Merits," she said weakly.

"Sure. But only one person has your fingerprints. You had to have left them all over the place. The cops haven't matched them yet, but once they have you to compare them with, they will."

"You're crazy," she said, turning her back on me.

"I might be crazy, but you were at Cooney's last night. I saw you."

She whirled around. "You couldn't have. No one else—" She cut herself off, realizing she was nailed. "All right, all right," she whined, "I took him home."

"Why try to hide it?"

"I was scared, that's why," she said in an emotional voice. "I didn't want to get involved. I thought people would think that somehow I was responsible. People have terrible minds. They al-

52

ways think the worst. Look at that girl who was with John Belushi. She had to run to Canada."

She picked up the pack of Merits from the table and poked a shaky finger inside. To save her the trouble, I handed her the one in my hand. "Here. I don't smoke."

She took it with a trembling hand and put it between her lips. I picked up the book of matches from the coffee table and lit it for her, just to save her from lighting her nose.

"Thanks." She brushed an unruly strand of dark hair from her face and moved unsteadily over to the couch, where she sat down heavily.

I pulled up a black lacquer chair opposite her, and gave the room a quick scan.

The furniture and arty knickknacks—porcelain Buddhas and Mandarins, ornately painted jars and framed rice-paper paintings—looked like expensive stuff for a secretary's salary, but whatever she had paid for it, she had not spent a quarter since on maid service. The place smelled stale; dust and cigarette smoke had taken their time settling into the cushions and the salmon-colored carpet.

She took a drag from her cigarette, then made a face and mashed it out in the ashtray. She picked up the glass from the table and took a sip. "Want a drink?" she asked, but the courtesy sounded forced.

"No, thanks." I spied a brown prescription bottle behind the metal Japanese lantern on one of the tables and picked it up. It was for Percodan. "You shouldn't drink and take this stuff at the same time," I told her, as if she needed a reminder after the night before.

"They're for the pain," she said, but her gaze was focused inward.

"How did that happen?"

She bit her lip, then dropped her eyes to the table. "I fell trying to get him up the stairs."

"How did you happen to elect yourself to that job?"

"I was outside when everybody got sick at the party. Phil stumbled out the door right in front of me, vomiting. He was in a bad way. I could see that, and I asked him if I could help, but he just kept saying he had to get home, and he got up and stumbled off. I knew he was in no shape to drive, so I followed him. I kept telling him he should go to the hospital, that I'd drive him, but he just kept saying he was okay, that this had happened to him before and he'd be all right. When I insisted he go to the hospital, he started to get violent, and I gave up trying to convince him, so I told him I'd drive him home. I knew he wouldn't make it if he drove himself."

Tears glistened in her good eye, and she snatched up a used ball of Kleenex from the table and daubed at her eyes. She turned away and blew her nose.

"You knew Cooney well?"

"Only from the office," she said quickly. "He'd been coming around lately, wanting to see Mr. Segal, but Mr. Segal wouldn't talk to him."

"You were talking to him at the party when Segal and I saw you."

"I was trying to get him to leave before Mr. Segal saw him. Mr. Segal hated Phil Cooney with a passion. I was afraid of what would happen if he saw him."

"What happened after you left the party?"

"I brought my car up and somehow managed to pile him into it. He was really out of it. He kept babbling and I thought he was going to pass out, so I drove with the windows rolled down. By the time we got to his place, he seemed better. He was still unsteady, but he was sitting up and at least semicoherent. He was really mad at Mr. Segal, though. He seemed to think he'd tried to kill him on purpose."

"Why would he think that?"

Her eyes started playing hide-and-go-seek again. "I don't know."

"He must have said something."

"No," she protested, almost fearfully. "He wasn't making all that much sense. He just kept saying that Mr. Segal had tried to kill him, but that he'd cheated him and lived his trial by fire. He seemed almost happy about it. He kept saying over and over, 'Whatever doesn't kill us, makes us stronger.'"

"Nietzsche," I said, pulling the quote from somewhere in the recesses of my mind.

She nodded. "Phil was a big Nietzsche fan."

For someone who knew Cooney only through a couple of brief office encounters, she knew quite a bit about his philosophical inclinations. "What happened then?"

She sniffed, wiped her nose, and began twisting the tissue around her finger. "He wanted some coffee, so I went in the kitchen to look for some, but there wasn't any. So he told me to go to the market and get some, that he'd be okay. I thought he would be; I mean, he didn't seem to be in any immediate danger, y'know? If I'd have known he was going to have a relapse, I wouldn't have gone. I had to go all the way down to Sunset—that was the only market open that late—and when I got back, he wasn't in the living room. I went back to the bedroom. He was lying there, real still, and I knew something was wrong." Her gaze grew glassy and distant. "I called his name, but he didn't answer. Then I went over and touched him and I knew he was dead." Her eyes focused again momentarily and her head turned slowly toward me. Her voice was blank, dead. She was having momentary lapses when the hysteria was breaking through the anesthetizing effect of the painkillers and alcohol.

"I panicked and ran. I know I should have called the police or an ambulance or somebody, but I couln't think about anything at that time except getting out of there. I thought somebody would blame me. And I couldn't stand the thought of staying there alone, with his, his . . . body." She blinked tearfully and said in a voice barely audible, "He shouldn't have been there."

I leaned forward to catch the words. "Pardon me?"

Pain contorted her features. "It's my fault he's dead. I never should have left him alone."

"There probably wouldn't have been anything you could have done if you'd been there."

Her head wagged back and forth. "I shouldn't have listened to him. I should have driven him to the hospital."

I did not fully understand her willingness to assume the load of guilt she was shouldering, but it was undeniable that her leaving Cooney alone gave Blackburn a crack he could drive a wedge into in court.

"Did you snort any of the coke at the party?"

"No." She wiped her nose with the crumpled tissue. "I can't understand why Mr. Segal would do something like that, give his guests something that might kill them. It doesn't make any sense."

"He thinks it makes plenty of sense. He thinks somebody switched the coke for heroin later. The same person or persons who've been trying to sabotage his operation."

Her eyes darted away and stayed away.

"You think that's what happened?" I asked.

"I—I don't know. It's possible, I guess. Things have been going wrong lately. Too many things."

"Mr. Segal thinks whoever it is has an inside man. Any idea who it might be?"

""How would I know?" Her voice cracked. Her eyes, like two flies, were landing on everything in the room and taking off again. Landing on everything but my eyes.

"Will you be at work tomorrow?"

"I think so."

"Would you be willing to submit to a lie-detector test?"

Her head snapped around and her good eye widened. "Lie detector? You don't mean Mr. Segal suspects me?"

"As a matter of fact, he doesn't, but I'm running tests on everybody in the office, just to clear away the clouds of suspicion. Would you be willing to take a test? I promise the questions will relate only to the issues at hand. There will be nothing of a personal nature asked."

Her jaw stiffened and her tone turned petulant. "If Mr. Segal doesn't trust me, maybe I should quit."

"I wouldn't do anything rash," I said. "Mr. Segal trusts you. He

56

told me so himself. It's just that he's in a tight spot right now, as I'm sure you can realize. And it wouldn't be fair to test some people in the office and not others."

"What if I refuse to take it?"

"That's between you and Mr. Segal. Anyway, you can make up your mind about it tomorrow. You might feel different about it then."

I apologized again for disturbing her and went out into the dusk. She was lying, about that I was certain. About what and why was something else again, something I could deal with when I got her wired up, which was why I hadn't pushed her too hard. I didn't want to spook her yet, not until I could arrange for her own little trial by fire.

6

Traffic on the freeway was still a snarl, and it took me almost an hour to get to the beach. Cooney's death was on the radio, but they were not releasing a cause of death yet, nor any other details, except that the body had been discovered early in the morning, by a "friend." I wondered if my body was going to be discovered by someone who had been as good a friend to me as I'd been to Cooney. I tried to think of a friend, period. By the time I got home, I'd given up trying to come up with a name.

I made myself a stiff vodka-soda and called the answering service. To my surprise, the cops hadn't called. Three reporters from various papers had left names and numbers I didn't bother to take down; Sturgis had called twice, and Blackburn and Segal once each. I was going to call them, but my stomach was making obscene noises, so I took care of first things first and heated up the quiche Sturgis had left in the refrigerator.

Halfway through my second helping, the last day and a half caught up with me and I stretched out on the couch, thinking I would just close my eyes and let my mind settle out a bit before I called Segal. The phone woke me up.

I fumbled with the receiver for a while, before managing a hello. Over a background of loud music and voices, a man said, "Is this Jake Asch, the intrepid free-lance journalist?"

I paused, waiting for more than three neurons to fire at once. Finally, they did. "Carey?"

"The One and Only. You know how disappointing it was to find out that the only nonbullshitter at that party was a bullshitter too?"

"Sorry about that," I said groggily. "At the time, Segal thought a cover was necessary."

"I know. Freddie filled me in, which is why I'm calling you now. I'm at the Rainbow, on the Strip. How long will it take you to get here?"

"Why would I want to get there at all?"

"Aside from my scintillating company, I ran into somebody here you should talk to. Cooney's ex–bass player. He has some things to say about the dearly departed that might interest you."

My watch read 9:35. "I'll be there in forty-five minutes."

Things were slow in the Rainbow parking lot as I pulled in, and the valets didn't have much to do except move to the reggae that blasted out of the doors of the Roxy, the live rock club next door. The music playing inside the Rainbow was canned Hendrix, appropriately out of date.

The Rainbow had originally been put together in the early Triassic by a group of rich rock-and-roll heavyweights who wanted a place they could go for a drink or dinner or just to socialize with their friends, and fifteen years or so ago, you might have sat at the bar on any given night and rubbed elbows with Peter Townshend or David Crosby or Stephen Stills. But it did not take long for the egalitarian ethic of rock and roll to take over, and as the groupies and gapers inevitably began to find their way in, the stars and record company biggies began to drift away to more exclusive watering holes, leaving the Rainbow to the seventeen-year-old guitarists looking for a connection and the burned-out acid rockers whose last hit had been in 1971 but who still wanted to feel part of the scene, and the hollow-eyed Dorothys who had given up the Yellow Brick Road for the Great White Way and snorted coke in the heads.

A procession of chattering young girls with spandexed thighs moved down the stairs from the upstairs dance club and I excused my way through them and went into the bar.

The walls in the lounge were covered with dark paneling and

the lighting was dim. Most of the stools around the circular bar that took up much of the small room were empty, and the sparse crowd that was there looked more middle-of-the-road than rock and roll. A middle-aged man in a sweater vest leaned against the end of the bar, trying to look like a Mafioso. A few stools down from him, two gays held hands on the bar and stared longingly into one another's eyes. Stack was seated at one of the video game tables in the back, beneath some lighted fish tanks, and he stood up when he saw me coming. He was wearing a shirt with different tropical flowers on it, but I thought the same jeans and running shoes.

"Good to see you, buddy," he said, shaking my hand. "Jake, this is Johnny Brandt."

The man sitting opposite him pushed back his chair and stood up, offering his hand. He wore wire-rimmed spectacles and had dark, scraggly hair, and the part of his face that was not covered with a heavy beard was bony and had an unhealthy, bled-out look. He was about six feet and very thin and his brown leather jacket hung loosely on his stooped shoulders. He could not have been thirty, but he exuded an aura of dissipation.

We sat down at the Space Invaders game, and Stack signaled the cocktail waitress who was standing at the end of the bar, sharing a joke with the bartender. She came over and I ordered a vodka-soda. Stack ordered a vodka for himself and a beer for Brandt, then said, "It's a fucking shame about Freddie. I called him today to apologize. I sort of flew off the handle last night. When I thought about it, though, that wasn't something Freddie would do. I told him I thought somebody was doing a very nasty number on him and that I'd do anything I could to help him find out who." He nodded at Brandt. "I just ran into Johnny here by accident. Tell Jake what you told me."

Brandt shrugged. "I guess it can't hurt anything now. A couple of weeks ago, Phil called me up and asked me to come over to his crib. It was sort of a surprise, 'cause we haven't been in touch much since the group broke up. We'd talk on the phone every couple of months, but that was about it. He was too fucked up most of the time and I didn't like being around him when he was like that. He got too crazy, you know what I mean?" He had one of those too-calm monotonic voices that were the product of taking too much acid way-back-when.

"Anyway, when I got over there, he gave me some lyrics and told me he wanted me to put them to music. Then he said he wanted me to get the boys back together, 'cause he was going to get Segal to book us on the Rollons tour. I thought he was talking through his ass or stoned or something, and I asked him what he was on. I told him Segal wouldn't book us into a pay toilet, never mind the Rollons tour, not after the fucking-over Phil gave him, and he said not to worry, that he had Segal in his pocket and that it would be taken care of."

"What did he mean by that?"

"He said he had somebody close to Segal working on him, and that we'd have a gig by the end of the month."

"Did he say who?"

He nodded. "Segal's secretary."

"Julia Roth?"

"Yeah, that's the chick. I guess she was the latest one to fall under the Spell."

"What spell?"

"Phil's. The man had something, I'm not sure what, but women really fell for it. A certain kind of woman, anyway."

"What kind was that?"

"Self-destructive. Thrill seekers. Phil was like the burning bush to them, y'know? It was amazing to watch. Hell, he'd use 'em, abuse 'em, humiliate 'em, beat 'em, and they'd come back begging for more."

The waitress came over with our drinks and Stack told her to put it on his tab. I tried to protest, but he waved me quiet and shooed her away with the same hand.

"Is that how it was with Julia Roth?" I asked Brandt.

He spurned the glass the girl had brought and took a swig of beer straight from the bottle. "I don't know. I guess so. If they stuck around for any length of time, the pattern was usually the

61

same, and from the way Phil was talking, she'd been around for a while." He shook his head. "I hated the way he treated his women. We had arguments about it, which was why I didn't see much of him in the past year or so. He'd always say it was necessary, that it was part of the purification process, but I didn't like it."

His face hovered like a sickly, bluish moon over the screen of the video game. "You gotta understand, Phil thought of himself as a modern-day Dionysus. All the drugs and booze and sex were part of that trip. Overindulgence, man. Tantrism. He was constantly trying to overload his senses to create chaos, so unity could emerge, he said. That was what all his music was about, if you've listened to it, taking people one step further, pushing them beyond the boundaries of conventional morality so they could become amoral supermen. The Overman. Phil believed that the only way anyone could be truly free was to throw off the shackles of society; and he'd convince the chicks he was with that the fastest way to do that was through self-debasement. He even made up a name for it: entering the Abyss."

He smiled strangely. I couldn't see his eyes; his glasses were two gray-blue disks. "The idea was trial by fire. They'd enter the Abyss and be purified by fire."

"How?"

"It varied. Whatever kinky thing popped into his mind at the time. It didn't really matter; it was all a power trip with him anyway. He'd start out slow, just him and the chick, and get her to fall for him. He could be a real charmer if he wanted to be. Then maybe he'd talk her into a threesome or a dyke scene, or maybe a little S and M or golden showers. He loved to have people over and relate in detail what he'd made the chicks do. In front of the chicks, of course."

"That must have gone over big with them."

"Hey, man, I felt really embarrassed seeing some of those chicks humiliated like that. But Phil would tell them that they couldn't be fully evolved until they didn't care. He'd set up these scenes and then he'd take pictures and then he'd wait until company came over and pass the pictures around in front of the chick. It was really weird the sick shit he could get those queenies to do. One time, he invited a couple of the guys over for a drink and while we were sitting there, he told this one little groupie chick to fuck this dog in front of us. I couldn't believe it when she did it."

Hendrix went off the sound system, replaced by Robin Trower's tinny guitar. "He sounds like a regular Charles Manson."

Brandt shook his head. "Phil could get pretty far-out, but he wasn't into violence."

"That's not what I heard," I said. "Carey was telling me about a few places he took apart. Isn't that right, Carey?"

Stack was staring balefully at a dark corner of the room where three orange cigarette tips glowed in a line. He didn't seem to be paying any attention to what we were saying.

"That was when he was dusted," Brandt said. "Phil could never handle PCP. One time when we were on tour in Omaha, he took some and wound up crawling through the halls of the Holiday Inn naked, howling like a wolf. They weren't quite used to seeing that kind of stuff in Nebraska. They asked us to leave the hotel, so Phil proceeded to tear all the wallpaper off the walls of his room. It cost him five grand."

I glanced over at Stack. He had transferred his attention to a lithe girl in a slinky, low-cut, black 1940s dress that was hiked up so high that the tops of her purposely run, black nylons showed. She had very watchable legs and I didn't blame him for preferring to squander his attentions on her over us. I turned back to Brandt. "So did Julia Roth get a grand tour of the 'Abyss'?"

"I don't know. Like I said, I hadn't been in touch with Phil lately. He did say that she'd taken him further than any chick he'd ever been with, and Phil had been pretty far-out." He paused thoughtfully. "You know what I think it was about him that reeled them in? I think it was the darkness, the destructiveness they sensed in him that titillated them, the thrill of flirting with danger. It was like a dark ride on a roller coaster that could fly off the tracks at any time. Only most of them didn't make it to the end of the ride. They either flew out or stood up at the wrong time and got their heads taken off. Like that little chick who was living with him."

"What little chick?"

"Lisa something. I can't remember her last name. She wanted to be a singer in the worst way, but she didn't have the stuff. Phil kept telling her she did, but he was just keeping her around because he said she gave the best head in town. He really screwed that poor chick's head up. Turned her on to dope and had her do freak scenes with that little groupie who used to hang around the Whiskey. What in the hell did she call herself? Oh, yeah. Star. Star E. Knight."

"That wasn't her real name, I take it?"

"All those queenies make up names, man. In her case, it should be Herpes. She'd fuck anything with a cock and a guitar. But Phil didn't care. He would've stuck his cock in cancer. It didn't matter to him."

"What happened to Lisa?"

"She got hooked on pills and O.D.'d."

"When was that?"

"About two months ago."

"At Cooney's place?"

"No. They found her in Topanga somewhere. She hadn't been staying at Phil's for a while. He tossed her out. Said he caught her trying to pawn some of his stuff to feed her habit, but I think he just got tired of her." He shook his head slowly. "I really felt sorry for that chick. She was a pretty nice kid, but she just couldn't hack it. I've seen the same thing happen to a lot of people. They get obsessed with somebody like she was with Phil, and the other person doesn't respond or treats them like shit, but they can't escape. So they find a new lover—heroin, barbs, anything to loosen that other person's control. They're so fucked up all the time, the other person can't touch them anymore. Only after they stop chipping and realize they're hooked, the honeymoon is over and it's the same thing all over again. They just sit around and think about their new lover and wait up for calls."

"Karma," Stack said suddenly. The girl was still at the bar but he looked a little more relaxed now. He took a drink and looked at us.

"Huh?" I said.

"That Cooney died the way he did."

"Maybe," Brandt conceded. "Phil could be a vicious mother-fucker. But then, he could turn around and be the sweetest guy in the world. I know that might be hard for you to dig, after what I told you, but it's true. He'd go out of his way sometimes to do things for you. Little things, big things, it didn't matter."

"If he was such a sweetheart," Stack asked him, "why did you quit Overman half a dozen times before the end?"

He smiled sheepishly. "The thing was, Phil was totally unpredictable. You could never tell who he was going to be from day to day. That doesn't make for a very good working relationship. But when I was with Phil, we were on the top, at least for a while. The fucker was like a comet. He burned out fast, but he blazed, and I blazed with him. What the fuck am I doing now?"

"I wouldn't feel too bad about it," Stack said. "Cooney's dying was probably the best career move he made in the last three years. For all of you. He's got his big comeback. Everybody will be at Tower Records, tomorrow, buying up all the old Overman albums."

"I never thought of that," Brandt said, then smiled, probably tallying royalties in his head. He glanced at his watch. "Hey, look, Carey, I gotta split."

"One more question," I said, as he pushed back his chair. "Any idea where I might find this Star E. Knight?"

He stood up and stroked his beard. "As a matter of fact, I saw her last week at the Starlight. She's been hanging around the punk group that was playing there—Jiz. She's been fucking the drummer. At least she was last week. Find out where they're playing and you'll probably find her." He glanced nervously at Stack. "Uh, Carey, you will take care of that, huh? I mean, you'll get the word along?"

Stack smiled easily. "I told you I would, Johnny. Relax."

Brandt's head bobbed up and down and he sighed. "Thanks."

He walked away and Stack explained, "I'm supposed to get word to Freddie that he helped out with that information. He's got a shot with a new group and he wants to get off Freddie's shit list. That's the reason he emptied the vacuum cleaner bag on Cooney."

Stack signaled the waitress for the check and when she came over, he laid a twenty on her and told her to keep the change. I told him I appreciated both the drink and the information.

"Anything I can do to help out Freddie."

"This could be quite a big help," I said, as we stood up. "At least we know that there are quite a few females floating around with a motive for killing Cooney."

"You think whoever switched the stuff at Freddie's was after Cooney, and not Freddie?"

"Maybe. At least it has muddied the waters a bit."

"Except Cooney wasn't even invited. How would the killer know he was going to be there?"

"Maybe he *was* invited."

His eyes widened as he looked at me. "Julia?"

I shrugged. "It's one question, along with a few others, that I intend to ask her."

He pushed the door open and we went outside. "But what kind of a sicko would do in three other people, just to get one?"

"Just that, a sicko. Or a very bright person not encumbered by something as mundane as conscience. They're around. A few years back, a guy blew up a whole jetliner just to get his mother, who was on board. It was a great smokescreen."

"Couldn't have been that good," he said. "They found him out."

"And I'll find this one out, if that's what happened."

We gave the valets our tickets and they stopped reggaeing long enough to run for the cars. "Why all the questions about that Star E. Whatever?"

"You think in karmic terms. My mind isn't quite so cosmic. I just ask questions and let Carl Sagan take care of the cosmos."

He looked out at the traffic on the Strip and said, "Well, that was a hell of a coincidence, anyway."

"What?"

"The bit about her fucking the drummer from Jiz."

"Why?"

He gave me a surprised look. "Didn't you know? That chick in the Star Wars outfit, the one who snorted up at the party, she's the lead singer for Jiz."

"I didn't know. What's her name?"

"Wanda Fleming."

I gave him a look.

"I didn't make it up," he said defensively.

"Where can I get hold of her?"

"I don't know where she's staying. She's playing at the Starlight through the week."

"You know her?"

"We know who each other is, let me put it that way."

"Like to bop on over to the Starlight and tender an introduction?"

"Tonight?"

"Tonight I want to have a little chat with Julia Roth. How about tomorrow night?"

He gave me a disbelieving look. "Are you serious?"

"Of course I am. You are an influential man in this business. I'm sure an introduction from the great Carey Stack would go a long way."

He wavered, then took out a piece of paper and scribbled on it with a pencil he borrowed from a valet. "I don't know yet what my plans are for tomorrow night, but you can call this number any time tomorrow. My service will tell you how to reach me." He held out the paper and as soon as my fingers touched it, he said, "But if I do go with you, you're going to owe me, buddy. It's against my religion to sit through a set of the kind of shit that those guys lay down."

They brought his car up first. It was a nasty-sounding, fire-engine-red Mustang with a white convertible top. "What year?" I asked as he got in.

"Sixty-five," he said, and grinned. "A time when a boss Mustang was the most important thing."

I liked him better all the time; his car was two years older than mine, even if mine was beyond the stage where twenty coats of lacquer would do any good. "Sounds hot."

"I've done a few things to her."

He waved and took off into traffic while I waited with sad expectation for the valet to bring up my own classic.

7

All the way over to Julia Roth's apartment, nasty possibilities whispered over my shoulder. I found a space down the block from her building and walked back. A warm wind carried the faint scents of jacaranda and citrus blossoms. The soft, soothing sounds of a romantic symphony played behind one of the doors. I went around the banana plants to her door and knocked. The door moved.

There were no lights on inside, no sound. "Julia?" I called. Nobody answered. Crickets sang along with the string section of the orchestra. I was beginning to have an attack of *déjà vu* and didn't like it.

I pushed the door open farther and stepped inside, feeling along the wall for a light switch. I found it and flicked it up, but nothing happened. A breaker must have blown. She'd probably left the door open while she had gone to see about it. I was wondering where the breaker box would be when suddenly my toes were scrabbling for traction as I was off the floor, being propelled backward, and a hand was trying to make Silly Putty out of my face. My backward motion was stopped by the door, so hard that my teeth rattled loose, and then a wrecking ball slammed into my rib cage and I collapsed like a condemned building. I was doubled up on the floor, gasping for breath, and he yanked open the door, hitting me in the back with it. Brilliant tactician that I was, I'd fallen in front of the door, blocking his exit.

I wasn't about to let him get out of there that easily. I wanted him to leave there knowing he'd administered a *real* beating. Feet began kicking me in the stomach. Not wanting him to wear out a set of knees on my account, I rolled out of the way, then nobody was kicking anymore and the door was yanked open and heavy footsteps pounded on the walkway outside. I rolled over as fast as I could and managed to get a glimpse of a smooth black head rounding the corner of the building.

While I lay there, listening to my breath trying to make the rounds in my chest, an engine revved down the street and tires peeled rubber. I knew how those tires felt. I fingered my ribs gently and my brain sent back a message that spelled P-A-I-N, but I didn't think anything was broken. I talked myself to my feet and almost instantly regretted the move. I seemed to hurt everywhere, and not just when I laughed.

I did a geriatric hobble out to the car and fished a flashlight out of the glove box and the tire iron from underneath the seat where I always kept it. If I was going to become a speed bump again, at least whoever ran over me was going to know they'd gone over a big one.

I went back to the apartment and poked my flash through the door. The room looked about as it had this afternoon. A little more messy, perhaps, but there were no signs of violence. The Smirnoff bottle was gone from the table, but the pills were still there, along with a tattered *TV Guide*. A disemboweled box of Kentucky Fried chicken sat on the kitchen dinette, its waxed-paper innards spilling out. A woman's brown velour jacket lay across the back of one of the chairs and on the seat was a brown purse. "Julia?"

The night breeze murmered languorously in the banana leaves, whispering of far-off places and tropical nights. That sounded fine to me. Maybe I'd go to travel agent school. Anything was better than this. I shook the tire iron to test its weight, took a deep breath, and stepped inside.

Nothing charged out of the darkness at me, no malevolent eyes glared at me from behind the furniture. A green, round-bellied Buddha watched my movements from the corner with a mocking smile. I went down the hallway to the bedroom.

The light switch was by the door, but I got a zero there, too. I waved my flash around the room and breathed a sigh of relief when I found it empty. My light stopped on the floor beside the unmade queen-sized bed. A drawer from one of the teak night-stands flanking the bed had been pulled out and stood on its end on the floor. I found that curious, but decided I would rather think about it in the light, so I slid open the closet door and began looking for a breaker box. I found it behind a red dress.

There were only five switches on the panel, and I started throwing them from the top down. The lights went on when I kicked the third one, but the switch held for only a couple of seconds, which meant there was a short someplace. I went back down the hall and stopped in front of the bathroom door. I poked my flash in there.

The room was yellow—yellow tile walls, yellow lowboy toilet, a yellow tub across which frosted-glass sliding shower doors were pulled shut. The sink was littered with makeup bottles, cold cream jars, bobby pins, false eyelashes, and a Gotcha Gun hair dryer, which lay on its side, pointed at me. I was about to throw up my hands and surrender to the forces of Hair Care, when I saw the cord. It was plugged into the wall socket near the sink and the shower doors were closed against it. I stepped over and unplugged it, then pulled open the shower door.

The cord belonged to a clock radio that was submerged in the water by Julia Roth's side. Her eyes were closed and her head rested against the porcelain edge of the tub. A few tired wisps of bubble bath clung to her naked body, which was a nice one. I went down and felt her throat for a pulse, but gave up after a bit. I pulled a couple of pieces of tissue paper from the box on the sink, fished out the clock radio by the cord, and looked at its dripping face: 10:10. I lowered it back into the water. By her head, there was a glass half-filled with a clear liquid, but I didn't touch it.

I went out into the living room and closed the front door, then went back to the bedroom and threw the breaker again. This time it held.

I bent down and inspected the drawer on the floor. There was nothing in it but middle-of-the-night stuff—Kleenex, nose spray—and the same held for its mate on the other side of the bed. But anybody could determine that without pulling it all the way out. I thought about that, then used one of the pieces of Kleenex from the drawer to hit the rewind button on the telephone answering machine beneath the rattan lamp on the gutted nightstand.

There were no messages on the tape, but the machine was a Computa-phone with a memory that stored the last number dialed. I picked up the receiver and punched the "Dial" button. I tried to count the clicks as the machine automatically began dialing the number, but couldn't quite get them all. It rang six times; I was about to give it up when a female voice answered: "Morninglory Productions."

"Pardon me?"

"Morninglory Productions."

"What kind of a company are you?"

It was her turn to say, "Pardon me?"

"What does Morninglory Productions produce? Movies? Records?"

"Musical concerts."

Bingo. I felt a little adrenal rush. "Can you tell me who is in charge there, please?"

"This is the answering service," the girl said. "There won't be anybody in the office until nine. Would you like to leave a message?"

"I'll call back in the morning, thanks."

I hung up and stared at the phone as if it would answer my questions. Concert promotion. A rival of Segal's? Was Julia Roth the saboteur, the inside man? That didn't make much sense. If she had been using her influence with Segal to help Cooney, why would she try to throw a monkey wrench into his operation?

I gave the drawers of the dresser a quick toss, and from the way their contents had been sloppily shoved around, I was willing to bet somebody else had, too. I went back out into the living room and used the piece of tissue to open the purse. Among the usual

72

crap I came up with three items that rated closer inspection—a brown two-gram bottle, a small red address book, and a checkbook.

The bottle was filled with a white powder and was identical to the one at Segal's party. I unscrewed the cap carefully to make sure I didn't wipe off any prints that might be on it, and put it under my nose. The contents did not have the same acidic smell of the junk at the party. I put a tiny bit on the end of my finger and rubbed it on my gums. The freeze said cocaine, and pretty good cocaine at that.

Cooney's number was in the address book, along with the number of Morninglory Productions, only it wasn't listed under the M's. It was under the W's, and it was one of two numbers under the name J. D. Walton. I took down the name and the other number and went on to the checkbook.

The last check in her check record—number 281—had been written the day before, to Von's Market for $13.91, leaving a balance of $698.50. Five months ago, her balance had been as low as $162.45, and two months after that, it had reached a high of $781.30. Aside from a regular deposit of $413.92 every two weeks—her paycheck from Segal, I assumed—there were no particularly unusual entries. Von's Market, Mastercard, a few to clothing stores, an occasional check to "Cash," but no large deposits or withdrawals that stood out. What stood out wasn't what was there, it was what wasn't. For as long as the check record went back, which was about a year, there was not one entry for rent, or any checks made out on a regular basis to any corporation or real estate office.

I put everything back in the purse and called the West Hollywood sheriff's station. The deputy I talked to there sounded about as excited as if I'd ordered a spinach soufflé when I told him I was sharing an apartment with a dead body. He took my name and told me to wait there, that company would soon be dropping by.

While I waited I drifted around the room aimlessly, looking things over. My mind was still working on the questions and was still not coming up with any answers. I stopped in front of the stereo wall unit and glanced over the titles of Julia's album collection on the shelf above the Marantz tuner. There must have been a hundred LPs and at least ten of them were Overman. To keep myself amused more than anything, I pulled them down and looked them over.

Death and madness seemed to be the reigning themes of all the albums, but one jacket, for an LP called *Across the Abyss*, really caught my attention. On it, Cooney, dressed in a black shroud, ferried the rest of the members of his band across a brackish, mist-laden river in a boat the prow of which was encrusted with human skulls. Brandt was in the back of the boat, looking apprehensive. I didn't blame him; if I was putting my fate in the hands of Cooney, I'd look apprehensive, too. He probably had a feeling even then that the boat would soon sink and he would be washed up on the shores of the Rainbow, waiting for a gig and talking about what once was. I started to put the album back on the shelf, but stopped. I took another album off the shelf and tested its weight in my other hand. The *Abyss* album seemed to be a lot lighter, and when I looked, I found out why. There was no record in the jacket, just a large manila envelope. I pulled it out.

The six-by-nine envelope was still sealed and was addressed to Phil Cooney at his home address. It had been sent registered mail on the third, three weeks ago, and the return address was the same address on Prospect. Across the front of the envelope was hand printed: "Photographs Do Not Bend." I promised whoever was listening that I wouldn't bend them. There were three five-by-seven color photographs inside. In one, two men were loading cardboard boxes into the back of a white van parked in front of a dirty stucco building. The sign over the top of the building read: SOUND TEK ENGINEERING. They were turned away from the camera, but not so far that I couldn't recognize one of them as the man with the red shirt who had shared the tub with the Punkette at the party. In another picture, he and the other man, whom I didn't know, were standing in the doorway of the same dirty stucco building, talking to a short, stocky, gray-haired man in an

74

apron, whom I also didn't know. The third photograph was a grainy blow-up of what the man from the party was holding in his hand. It was an LP jacket, which had been blown up so much that the quality of the picture was bad and part of the title was obscured by his hand.

MARICO

IN CONC

I put the albums back on the shelf and took the envelope out to the car and locked it in the glove box, just in case the cops got the urge to search me, then came back. I left the apartment door open to let the breeze work on the place. The sounds of the symphony drifted in with it. The movement was an adagio, but it sounded like a dirge to me.

8

Momaday was large. He was at least six-four and 260 pounds, with a yard of shoulders and a sizable paunch that hung over his huge silver-and-turquoise belt buckle. His nut-brown face was well-weathered and there was a shock of white in the front of his otherwise shiny black hair. He wore a rumpled brown suit, with a rumpled white shirt, a string tie with a silver Indian thunderbird clasp, and brown shoes that looked like scuffed cello cases.

He looked down at me and sort of smiled. "Well, well. Sam Spade in the flesh. How long has it been, Asch? Two years?"

"Closer to three, I think."

"You were working for the attorney who defended that creep Festinger."

"Right."

He nodded. "That was *over* three years ago," he said, shaking his head.

"See how time flies when you're having fun? You get your degree yet?"

"Last quarter," he said.

"Congratulations. Should I call you doctor now?"

"Under these circumstances, sergeant will do."

The other cop came out of the back room. He was younger and almost as tall, but stringy. He wore a gray tweed jacket with a brown suede patch across the shoulders and a white Stetson with a feather in the front of it. A cowboy and an Indian. Cute.

76

"What do we have?" the Indian asked him.

"Broad wanted to see how her radio played underwater, so she took it in the bathtub with her. Looks like she was boozing and knocked it into the tub. Name's Julia Roth. She lived here."

"Accidental?"

The cowboy shrugged. "That's what it looks like, but I don't know. This guy called it in. He's a private dick by the name of—"

"Asch and I know each other," Momaday said. "He's okay. Asch, this is my partner, Jeff Rhodes."

Rhodes favored me with a curt nod. He had a craggy, un-friendly face to match his disposition, with a typical macho-cop mustache, and a long wolfhound nose. He turned his narrow, suspicious eyes on Momaday. "Asch says he dropped by around eleven-thirty to visit the Roth woman and found the door open and the lights off. The radio had kicked the breaker, I guess. When he stepped inside, the roof fell in. Somebody else was in the apartment, somebody who was in such a hurry to leave, he used Asch here for a doormat."

"Description?"

Rhodes consulted his notes. "Black, six-one or two, weight two-twenty or so. Shaved head."

"That's it?" Momaday asked.

"It was dark," I added, then winced from a twinge of pain in my side.

Momaday turned to Rhodes. "Check the neighbors?"

Rhodes nodded. "So far, zilch. Nobody saw or heard anything unusual."

"What else is new?" Momaday asked in a bored tone, then looked at me. "You usually go out visiting this late, Asch?"

"That depends."

"On what?"

"On whether the person I'm visiting goes to bed early."

"You know the woman well?"

"Not well," I said. I was not sure just how much I wanted to tell him about my reasons for being there, and to buy myself a few minutes to decide, I said to Rhodes, "Tell him about the drawers."

Momaday looked questioningly at his partner, who said, "We found one of the drawers from one of the nightstands in the bedroom pulled out and on the floor. Asch says it was like that when he came in. We're lifting prints from it now. Some of the bureau drawers look as if they might have been gone through, too."

"Burglary?"

Rhodes shrugged. "Maybe. But if it was, he was either stupid or in a hell of a hurry. Her jewelry box was untouched and her purse was out in the open with money in it."

"Where's the body?"

Rhodes jerked a thumb down the hallway and Momaday told me to stay put. They went down to the bathroom where Julia Roth was holding court for the photographer and evidence boys and a couple of men from the M.E.'s office.

I thought about the last time I'd seen Abel Momaday. We had been working opposite sides of a homicide case. I'd found him to be a thorough, patient investigator and a good cop, but even then, his real passion had been in solving mysteries that had been on the books a lot longer than any tucked away in the homicide files. Momaday's dream job was a teaching position somewhere where he could sift through the soil with those huge paws, searching for bits and pieces of lost Indian civilizations. He had been going to school nights, working toward a Ph.D. in cultural anthropology. It was fodder for a bad television series—the full-blooded Kiowa cop trying to crack the case of the Lost Tribes of Powhatan.

He came out of the hallway with Rhodes just as two men from the M.E.'s office wheeled a gurney through the front door. He stepped back to allow them to pass, and I asked, "You're really leaving the force then?"

He nodded and rubbed a chin that would have made a female pelican swoon. "I officially retire in three weeks. Moving to Tucson. Got a job teaching at a little JC down there. Should be some good digs down there." His mind seemed to be there already and he smiled, but then his eyes drifted back down to the hallway and his expression soured. "Which is why I want to get this cleaned up fast. I don't like the idea of leaving unfinished business behind." He took out a small spiral notebook and sat in the chair opposite. "Okay, enough bullshit. What are you doing here?"

I had already decided against trying to lie to him; it wouldn't buy much except a little time. And bringing Julia into it might in the long run buy us more time, by giving the D.A. one more thing to check out. I laid it out for him briefly, fuzzing over some details and leaving out others, particularly those that would have fingered me for evidence tampering. When I'd finished, he asked, "So Cooney and the Roth woman were having an affair. So what?"

"So maybe nothing. That's what I was coming over here to ask her. She lied to me about how well she knew Cooney, but that could have been to protect her job. If Segal knew his secretary and Cooney were an item, it might not have set too well with him."

His eyes looked sleepy, but that was only because of the heavy fold of skin on the upper lids. Those black, watchful eyes never missed a trick. He dipped a hand the size of a catcher's mitt into his coat pocket and brought it out a fist. There was a loud cracking noise and he unclenched it and began picking through the remains of three or four walnuts. I had seen him do that three years ago, but it still had a mildly disconcerting effect on me. I could imagine the effect it would have on a suspect during a serious interrogation. "What time were you over here this afternoon?"

"A little before six. I left about ten-to."

"How was she acting then?"

"Upset. And she was pretty well smashed."

"You told Rhodes the bruises on her face were there when you saw her earlier."

"That's right. She claimed she fell helping Cooney up the stairs to his place."

"Sure there weren't any new ones since you saw her?"

"I don't think so."

Rhodes sighed and said to his partner, "I don't see any need to postpone your retirement for this one, Abel. The broad was all busted up over her boyfriend taking gas, so she goes home and starts eating Percodan with Smirnoff chasers and winds up in the tub with Paul McCartney. No big mystery here."

"What about the black guy? Where does he fit into that picture?" Momaday asked.

Rhodes pulled a tin of Copenhagen out of his pocket and while he took a pinch and stuck it in the corner of his mouth, said, "Maybe she liked black meat and he was dropping by for a little trim. Or maybe he came to toss the place, got partway into it, then found the broad in the bathroom and got scared. Maybe he figured he'd get blamed for it. Nigger found in the apartment of a dead white girl. Hell, he didn't know how she'd died. She could have been murdered, for all he knew. When Asch showed up, he freaked."

"It does fit some of the facts," Momaday conceded.

Rhodes smiled proudly. The chewing tobacco made him look as if he had an impacted wisdom tooth. "Sure it fits: Look, according to the clock on the radio, it went into the tub at ten-ten. Asch got here at eleven-oh-five. If the guy killed her, you think he's gonna stick around the apartment for an hour? What for? He couldn't watch 'The Jeffersons.' The electricity was off. It stands to reason he only was here shortly before Asch showed up."

Momaday sighed and shook his head, then looked around for a place to deposit the walnut shells in his hand. He wound up putting them into his pocket. "Asch, you think you could I.D. the guy if you saw him again?"

I shook my head. "I only saw him from the back for a few seconds as he ran away. In here I was too busy being a basketball to see anything."

One of the lab boys stuck his head out of the bathroom door and shouted, "One of you guys want to come in here a minute?"

Rhodes looked at Momaday, then shrugged in resignation and got up. When he disappeared into the bathroom, I said to Momaday, "I don't think your partner wants to file this as a homicide."

"I can't blame him. We're working on six right now we haven't got a rat's ass chance of solving. He's not real hot to make it seven."

"I got the feeling he doesn't like me too much."

"Don't take it personally," he said, smiling. "Jeff doesn't like anybody. Especially when he's tired and frustrated. But you have to admit, what he was saying makes sense."

"As far as it goes."

"Meaning?"

"Segal claims that someone has been trying to sabotage his operation from the inside and that someone switched heroin for coke at his party. Suppose Julia Roth was the inside man. And suppose whoever was paying her wanted to make sure she didn't tell anyone."

"What are you talking about?" he asked disbelievingly. "A hit?"

"It's possible," I said. "When I talked to her tonight, she kept saying she was responsible for Cooney's death. She said, 'He shouldn't have been there.' At the time, I didn't pay much attention to it. I just put it down to her being distraught. But it makes sense if she was the one who switched the stuff, not imagining Cooney would show up."

His dark look was doubting. "You're reaching."

"Maybe. But it's worth checking out, isn't it?"

His tone became patronizing. "Don't worry, Asch. We'll check it out. Just because I'm going to retire, it doesn't mean I'm intentionally going to become deaf, dumb, and blind for the next three weeks. Go on home. We'll call you if we need you."

"Look, if Julia—"

"We can take care of it," he said, holding up a hand. "Go on home."

I looked at the hand. With a few white letters, it would have made an impressive Stop sign. It was hard to imagine it tinkering with fragile bits of pottery. "Somehow I can't see it."

He scowled darkly. "What?"

"You leading the contemplative life. Don't you think you're going to miss all this?"

He looked around questioningly. "All what?"

"The action."

"What action is that? Hanging around with stiffs in bathtubs? I've seen babies with their brains bashed out by their adoring parents, I've seen mothers stabbed to death by sons, I've seen people blown away by strangers for not signaling before they made a left turn. I've seen 'em burned, poisoned, impaled, and cut up on band saws, and you know something? I don't find anything funny about it. And once that happens, you're finished as a cop. The only way you can make it through in this job is to maintain a sense of humor. I woke up one morning awhile back and realized I'd lost mine. No, I think I'll survive without the action, thanks. Digging up arrowheads rather than mutilated corpses sounds just fine with me."

He signaled the cop at the front door to let me out and went down the hallway looking as if he'd just won a weekend for two at Sand Creek.

9

After a night of being pursued by a spectral Julia Roth with electric sparks for eyes, I woke up dog tired. I went into the bathroom and splashed cold water on my face, but that didn't do much to wake me up. I just kept glancing at the tub to make sure there wasn't a body in it.

The morning was typical beach weather for this time of year, dull and overcast. I sat at the breakfast table with the paper and drank successive cups of coffee to the "20 Minute Workout," which was about all I had energy for this morning.

There was a follow-up story on Cooney on page three entitled "Heroin Overdose Cause of Rock Star's Death," and I was sure it was not going to make Segal's day. The autopsy showed that Cooney had died of "acute morphine poisoning," and although the reporter did not come right out and say it, it was clear in the article where he thought the drug had come from. He had managed to dig up the other three hospital admissions from the party—Dean Cuthburton, Ross Stillwell, and Wanda Fleming—and although none of them was willing to comment on the events of the evening, a hospital spokesman confirmed they had been treated for heroin poisoning. One anonymous partygoer was quoted as saying he had seen Segal handing out the heroin to the people who had gotten sick. The LAPD detective in charge of the case, an investigator named Exley, confirmed the police were looking into the possibility that Cooney and the others had "ingested the toxic drugs at the same place," and that evidence was being gathered for a "possible indictment," although he did not say who was going to be indicted or for what. There was nothing on Julia Roth's death.

I called Segal at home. "Oh, my God. How did it happen?" he wanted to know when I told him about Julia.

"The police think it was an accident."

"You don't?"

"I'm not sure. It could have been. She certainly was screwed up yesterday afternoon when I talked to her. She was all broken up over her lover's death."

I waited to see if he would bite. He did. "What lover?"

"Cooney."

"*Phil* Cooney?"

"The one and only. You didn't know about them, then?"

"Hell, no. I had no idea. You think the deaths are connected in some way?"

"I don't know. There's a connection in time. And there certainly was a connection between them when they were alive."

"You think they were the saboteurs?" he asked excitedly.

"What would be the motive for that?"

"Cooney knew I would never book him on a Southern California stage. Maybe he saw me as an obstacle to his so-called comeback and wanted to knock me off."

"So he had Julia switch heroin for coke at the party, then wandered in and snorted some? Just to be sociable?"

"It might have been a mistake," he said feebly. His view of the universe was definitely egocentric.

"I'd like it better if the two of them had been fighting, and she saw an opportunity to slip him a dose of smack and get even."

"A lover's quarrel?"

"Maybe. Anyway, it'll give Blackburn some smoke to blow in the D.A.'s face." There were some things I didn't like about that theory, either, but there was no reason to recite them to him. "You know of an outfit called Morninglory Productions?"

"Sure. That's J. D. Walton."

"He a rival of yours?"

"Not really. He's a black promoter. Handles only black acts. R & B funk bands."

"Think he has any interest in expanding his operation?"

"How do you mean? Putting together shows with white acts?"

"Yeah."

"He couldn't."

"If you were out of the way?"

"He couldn't anyway. He couldn't deal with the managers."

"Why?"

"He's black, for one thing, and he doesn't really have a feel for the kinds of concert packages he'd have to put together. The managers and groups would feel that, even if it weren't true. Hell, it's taken me years to build up the relationships I've got with these groups. They wouldn't be likely to just allow some strange black dude who doesn't have much experience as a promoter to start booking them into halls. Especially one who has a rep like Walton's."

"Which is?"

"A marginal crook."

"How so?"

"Know anything about publishing?"

"Not really."

"What a publisher essentially does is buy song copyrights from writers, then get them to the right groups and get them recorded. For that, the publishing company gets about three cents a cut on every album, which is then supposed to be split between the publisher and the writer. It doesn't sound like a hell of a lot, but it can be an incredibly lucrative business if you know what you're doing. It only takes six bucks to copyright a song and once you have a copyright number, for the next fifty-six years anyone who wants to record your song has to pay the owner of the number. You can see the possibilities, which is why almost every A & R man has his own publishing company and tries to tie up the writing talents of the artists he's recording. Usually, it's a provision in the contract.

"That was the way Walton made it. He latched onto a couple of groups from the ghetto and talked them into making him their manager. Sally and the Satins, and the Moonbeams. Along with his fifteen-percent management fees, both groups wrote a lot of their own material, so he made sure he tied up the publishing rights, too, and when they took off, Walton cleaned up. He also made a couple of smart moves buying up black catalogs that some singers like Ronstadt revived. But then a couple of the writers he had tied up began bitching that they were getting cheated. Both Sally and the Satins and the Moonbeams fired him as their manager. He still has the rights to a lot of their old stuff, so he still makes some good bucks from them, but not like before."

"*Was* he cheating them?"

"Could be. Most writers probably get screwed by their publishers."

"How?"

"Easy," he said. "New writers are vulnerable—they get swept away by the glamour. Most of them are so goddamned thrilled to get a song done, they don't give a shit about anything else, and when they finally start making money, it's usually more than they've ever seen anyway, so getting screwed means nothing. They never expected to make a hundred bucks, so when somebody hands them ten thousand, it doesn't matter that they should have gotten fifty. It usually takes them a few hits under their belts to wise up, then it's finger-pointing time.

"Older writers are just as vulnerable. Say a hot new kid wants to cut a song published by somebody else. The producer will go to the publisher and demand a fifty-percent cut on the copyright assignment. Think the publisher is going to absorb that himself? Shit, no. He'll go to the writer and say, 'Look, we've got a chance to make a few bucks here. Don Henley wants to record one of your old songs, but we gotta kick back sixty percent.' The song's been dead for years and it's like found money anyway, so nine times out of ten, the writer will go for it, even if he thinks he's being scammed."

"Sounds like a lovely business."

"Why are you so interested in Walton?"

"His name and phone number were in Julia Roth's phone book. And his was the last number she called before she died."

"How do you know that?" he asked, intrigued.

"I'll tell you about it later. Right now, you can do something for me. I need to know where I can get in touch with Wanda Fleming."

"Jiz is out here from New York," he said. "I can find out where they're staying. Julia knew. She sent out all the invitations to the party."

Maybe we should hold a seance and ask her, I thought. "Can you find out for me?"

"No problem. Call the office later."

I picked up the paper. "Who was the man I put in the tub with her? The guy in the red shirt? Was that Cuthburton or Stillwell?"

"Dean Cuthburton," he said. "Why?"

"What does he do?"

"Production engineer. One of the best."

"You got his number?"

"Why do you want to talk to him?" His voice sounded strangely tense.

"I want to talk to everyone who was in the room that night," I said vaguely. That seemed to satisfy him and he told me to hold on a minute and put down the phone. He came back on and read off Cuthburton's home number and I told him I'd call the office for the other information later.

I tried the number he'd given me and let it ring eight times before giving up. I was more successful with the Altaloma Apartments, where Julia Roth had lived.

The manager was named Mardian and he was very cooperative after I identified myself as Sergeant Fuller of the Los Angeles sheriff's office. He said the woman had always been a good tenant who never caused any trouble and always paid her rent promptly on the first, which was how most apartment managers rated anyone's worth as a human being. The rent had always been paid in cash, never by check. As he had told the other detectives last night, she didn't have many visitors. He had never seen a black man with a shaved head around the place. He had seen her with a black man once, he remembered, getting into a white Mark V, outside the building, but the man's head had not been shaved. He was tall, had a short Afro, was sharply dressed. The manager was sure he would not be able to identify the man if he saw him again. They all look alike, you know.

I poured myself another cup of coffee and drank it leisurely while I watched the rest of the "Today" show. After bidding adieu to Jane and Bryant, I tried Morninglory. A woman picked it up and when I asked if this was the answering service, she replied no. I'd reached the office, and to whom did I wish to speak?

"Yes, uh, this is Regal Cleaners down the street from you. Maybe you can help me. A man was just in here and dropped off some dry cleaning and he left your business card, but stupid me, I forgot to get his name. He's black, has a shaved head, big—"

"You must mean Legrand."

"Is that a first or last name?"

"First. Ball is his last name."

"Then it's all right for him to charge to Morninglory Productions. I mean, he does work for you?"

"Oh, yes. He's Mr. Walton's driver and bodyguard."

"Thank you very much and I'm really sorry for the inconvenience. His suit will be back on Tuesday."

Legrand Ball? She'd sounded serious. I had to admit he had waltzed me around the room pretty good. Now it was my turn to lead.

The overcast had burned off by the time I got to Hollywood and was replaced by a gray soup of smog that made my eyes tear and my sinuses smart. Even at this early hour advance scouts of Hollywood's army were already congregated on the street corners, waiting for buses or other connections. Clumps of miniskirted whores and seventeen-year-old male hustlers with boys' bodies and sharks' eyes watched traffic for possible tricks. They probably thought they would get a jump on the day while the others were still sleeping off the effects of the previous night's score.

Morninglory's address was on Ivar, just around the corner from LAPD's Hollywood Division. The building was two-storied, not old and not new, with a brick bottom half and gray vertical louvers across its second floor to shade out the sun. I drove around the corner and found a meter about half a block from the police station and walked back. A young male hustler wearing blue eye shadow stood in front of the Hollywood Division with his thumb out and he smiled at me as I walked past. I had to hand it to the kid—what he lacked in brains, he made up for in chutzpah.

There was a small parking lot alongside Morninglory's building and a white Mark V with a gold vinyl top was parked in the fourth slot from the street. I took down the license number and went around front.

Morninglory was upstairs, and, according to the lettering on the door, J. D. Publishing occupied the same suite of offices. The waiting room had rust-colored grass-cloth walls and rust-colored carpet and was filled with cream-colored furniture. The receptionist, a pretty mocha-skinned girl with colored beads in her corn-rowed hair, gave her nails two last swipes with her emery board and smiled at me with a lot of very white teeth. "Yes?"

"I'd like to see Mr. Walton, please."

"Do you have an appointment?"

"No, but it's really important that I see him."

She put the emery board down on the desk. "What is it concerning?"

"Julia Roth."

There didn't seem to be any recognition in her eyes. "Who?"

"Julia Roth. Tell him I'm a friend of hers."

Her beads clicked like castanets as she shook her head. "I'm sorry, but Mr. Walton is a very busy man and unless you have an appointment—"

I leaned on the desk and smiled at her gently. "Why don't you tell him what I just said and if he doesn't want to see me, I'll go away and no harm's done. If he does want to see me, however, and you turn me away without finding out, he might get annoyed, or even angry, and none of us want that, do we? I'll leave it up to your good judgment, dear. Whatever you think is best."

She bit her lip and thought about it, then said, "Your name?"

"Moody," I said. "Clifford Moody."

"Wait here, please." She stood and went through the door to the left of the desk. Then she came out shortly and told me to come in. I went through the door and down a carpeted hallway, into an office with salmon-colored walls and a lot of windows. Walton was sitting behind a modernistic laminate desk that looked like an inverted manta ray. He looked up from the contract he was going through, but did not smile. "Sit down, Mr., uh, Moody, is it?" I sat in a round-backed chair in front of the desk and he nodded the girl out of the room.

He had a long, smooth, sculptured face, like an African mask. His skin was dark and satiny, and his jeri-curled hair glistened in the light from the window behind. His eyes were narrow and he sported a neatly clipped mustache that ran along the line of his upper lip and down to his chin. He wore a pale yellow three-piece suit with a pale yellow tie and a gray shirt. His diamond horse-head stickpin and matching cuff links were not big enough to be considered ostentatious, but that couldn't be said about his rings. There was a diamond pinkie ring on each hand that must have been three carats each, a gold ring with a green stone that could have been an emerald, and a five-carat aggregate of smaller stones piled into a volcanic cone.

One corner of his mouth lifted, the result being a kind of superior sneer. "I hear I want to see you." There was nothing of the street in his voice. It was deep and soft and devoid of any kind of black accent.

"I am—correction, *was*—a friend of Julia Roth."

His face was a blank. "That supposed to mean something to me?"

"I was hoping."

He shook his head. "Sorry."

"You don't know her?"

He tried to look as if he were thinking, stuck out his lower lip, and shook his head. "I don't believe I do."

"That wasn't what she said. She said you two were tight. She said you were paying her rent, as a matter of fact, for certain services she was rendering."

"I have no idea what you're talking about. What services? Who is this Julia Roth?"

"Fred Segal's personal secretary," I said, and tried to maintain a uniformly bored expression as I looked the room over. The walls were covered with framed black-and-white eight-by-ten glossies of Walton with his arms around various black men and women I assumed were celebrities. On the wall to the right of the desk were two framed gold 45-rpm records. "What are those for?"

"A couple of songs I produced a long time ago," he said, with an edge in his voice now.

"Sally and the Satins or the Moonbeams?"

He looked at me curiously. "The Moonbeams. How did you know about those groups?"

"That's not really important. What's important is that I know about Julia. I know she called here last night before she stepped off. The cops don't know that yet, but they have her address book, and your name and number are in it. You try this playing-dumb act with them, and they'll tear you a new asshole."

"Wait a minute," he said, his eyes widening in astonishment. "You trying to say the woman is . . . *dead*?"

"You do surprise very well," I said. "Where's Legrand?"

"Running some errands. Why?"

"Better get him the word to go in the hole. The cops are looking for him. Or at least they will be after I tell them that he was the one in Julia's apartment last night who did his Mills Brothers routine on my kidneys."

His eyes narrowed. "Legrand was with me all last night."

"Then I guess that puts you right at the scene, J. D., because Legrand was *there*. I saw him, I *felt* him. I even know his shoe size, 'cause in his haste to get out, he left his footprints all over me. What happened? Julia try to put the bite on you? Or you just got nervous 'cause she was starting to come unraveled?"

He put his forearms on the desk and leaned on them. "What the fuck are you talking about? Man, you gotta be fucking crazy

91

to come in here and try to lay this line of shit on me." Suddenly he didn't sound white anymore.

"Julia confided in me," I said. "Everybody needs somebody like that in life, I guess, somebody you can tell things to. She told me a lot of things. Like about the heroin."

Something rippled across his face, just for an instant. It started in the eyes, like a rock dropped into a pond, and the ripples spread over his entire face before the surface became glossy again. "What heroin?"

"The heroin you gave her to switch for coke at Segal's party."

He was trying to make his smile look amused, but it didn't come off. "Now why would I do something like that?"

"To knock off Segal so that you could get a toehold as a promoter in this town. It was just one more rat-fuck, but it got botched. I don't figure you meant to kill anybody, just get some people pissed off at Segal, but things got screwed up, the smack was too pure or Julia put too much in the vial she switched at the party or whatever. Accidents happen. Only this accident could send you away for a tenner or so, and Julia was not the kind of person with whom I would have wanted to entrust ten years of *my* life, especially in the emotional condition she was in." I paused. "It's kind of ironic that she wound up icing her own boyfriend, but then the world's full of ironies."

"Boyfriend?" The surprise seemed genuine this time.

"You didn't know about her and Cooney? Seems to be the best-kept secret around. Sure. That's why she was coming apart at the seams. She was being eaten up by guilt. She killed him."

He sat back and rubbed his chin. He stared at the top of the desk, lost in thought.

"She called you last night and you could hear how unstable she was, so you sent Legrand over to calm her down. Hell, I don't blame you, J. D. You had to protect yourself. I mean, hell, the stupid bitch had suddenly become a dangerous liability. With Segal facing a homicide charge, you're home free—unless she cracks. No, I can't really blame you at all. She had to go."

His expression turned nasty and he pointed a ringless index

finger at me. "You listen to me, motherfucker, and you listen good. I don't know what kind of cheap jive-ass game you trying to run, but you start fucking with me, motherfucker, and I'll make a fucking TV dinner out of your white ass. You dig?"

"Cannibalism a part of your family tree?" His finger was still pointed at me and rage flared behind his eyes, but I took away his initiative by saying, "You know the thing about pointing fingers, J. D.? You point one and there are four pointing right back at you. So you can spare me your bad-ass shit."

The index finger curled and joined the rest of the fist and I thought for a moment he was going to launch himself across the desk. To short-circuit any ideas he might have had in that direction, I donned my own nasty mask and leaned forward aggressively. "I am not playing a fucking game here, J. D. This is life. *Real life*. And it certainly is not cheap. Right now Segal is as good as buried, but if I start telling people what I know, it's going to be Musical Coffins and you're going to take his place in the box. *You* dig?"

He continued to glare, his eyes malevolent slits. "What's your *real* name, anyway?"

I shrugged. "What's in a name? What's important is what I want, J. D."

"What would that be?"

"I'm talking about a five-figure package, J. D. That seems fair, doesn't it? And you don't even have to pay my rent. For ten thousand, Segal gets buried, you get your ass out of hot water and get your shot at sewing up the town, and I leave town, never to be heard from again."

He grinned and his manner became suddenly and falsely amiable. "You talking extortion, my man."

"Shocking, isn't it?"

"It's a crime, is what it is."

"Yeah," I said, and pointed to the yellow phone on the desk. "Why don't you call the cops? I'll wait until they get here. I'll even give them a confession." He glanced at the phone, then back at me, but said nothing. The grin was gone, as suddenly as it had appeared. I stood up and said, "You'll want to think about it. I can understand that. I'll be in touch later. You don't have to give me your home number. I've already got it. Later, my man."

I took the front stairs by twos and maintained a brisk pace to the corner. A sniffling bag lady in a moth-eaten sweater and a stocking cap shuffled down the sidewalk toward me, dragging a wire basket with wheels, but I doubted she was following me. You never know, though. She might have been concealing a .38 in all the garbage can refuse in the basket. Confessions of a Mafia Bag Lady. She talked to herself as she went by me, and I kept my eyes on the building to see if anyone came out. Nobody did, unless it was Claude Rains.

I thought about Walton's reaction to what I'd said. An honest man might have taken me up on my offer and called the cops or come across the desk and taken a poke at me, or at least told me to get out. The fact that Walton hadn't done any of those things didn't mean he wasn't honest, but I somehow doubted that Diogenes would be making any stops here in the near future. Anyway, all I could do now was let him stew, then hit him again and see what happened.

Interrupting the conversation of two patrolmen standing outside Hollywood Division, I asked the location of the nearest phone booth and they pointed me to one down the block. I dug out a handful of change and spread it on the coin tray and started dropping dimes.

The answering service had three calls: one from a Detective Exley, who left his number and said it was important, one from Sturgis, and one from Ed Blackburn. The first two were probably just chew-out calls—Sturgis for my not calling her and Exley for my leaving a few minor details out of my Cooney statement. I ignored them and called Blackburn at his office. His secretary told me he was in conference for another half hour or so; I left my name and told her I would call back. The girl in Segal's office told me that Jiz was staying at the Hollywood Holiday Inn and gave me Wanda Fleming's room number; but when I called there, the hotel operator said Ms. Fleming had left instructions not to put any calls through until one. I tried Cuthburton's number again, but got no answer there. The entire world was out, unconscious, or too busy to talk to me.

One o'clock. That meant I had two hours to kill, and there is nothing like a little breaking and entering to while away a spring morning.

10

Prospect was almost like a sylvan sanctuary from the hot soupy smog that squatted on the hills around Laurel Canyon. The street's thick foliage filtered and purified the daylight, turning it green and cool, and the smells of hibiscus and eucalyptus, which the smog was doing its best to smother, were there.

Cooney's house looked seedier in the light of day. Its sides were covered with gray blotches of plaster that had not been painted, making the house look as if it were suffering from some skin disease, and the paint was flaking off in handfuls from the wooden balcony. I got my set of picks from the glove compartment and locked up the car.

A leathery-looking woman wearing a red bandanna and walking a Lhasa apso on a leash was coming down the stairs as I went up, and I smiled and said hello. There seemed to be a note of reluctance in the hello she gave me back and perhaps a hint of suspicion in her eyes, and I wondered where she lived and how long she intended to walk her dog. I wouldn't have minded if she decided to walk the goddamn animal back to Tibet, but I'd settle for fifteen minutes. She looked like the nosy-neighbor type.

I must have been getting used to the climb, because I wasn't breathing nearly as heavily when I reached the top as I had the other night. There was no yellow tape on the front door, which meant they had taken everything they needed as evidence to the coroner's office.

The neighborhood was almost as quiet in the daytime as it had been at night, except for a dog barking somewhere. I bent down and looked at the lock on the kitchen door.

It was a standard Schlage, no dead bolt, and it took only a minute or so to pick it. The air inside was pent-up and stale. Sunlight streamed in through the curtainless window, overflowed the sink, and spilled onto the scuffed linoleum floor. The same dirty dishes were in the sink, but the bag with the coffee was gone. The cops had probably taken it for prints.

The living room was dark except for a sliver of light that slipped through the drawn curtains. I turned on the lights and went over to the shelf by the stereo and started going through Cooney's album collection. Every one of Overman's LPs except *Across the Abyss* was there, which led me to guess that Julia had taken it when she'd left.

It took me just a couple of minutes to toss the small desk in the guitar room. There was nothing much in the drawers except past-due bills and threatening letters from several collection agencies, and nothing taped to the sides or backs. There were clothes in the bedroom bureau and medicine in the bathroom medicine cabinet. The closet was an environmentalist's nightmare. There were lizard-skin boots and snakeskin belts and leather pants and coats of suede and sheepskin and kangaroo, and I felt like some ghoulish poacher going through their pockets. The label inside one fur-collared overcoat said it was made from unborn pony. Cooney certainly wasn't growing on me.

After the pocket search came up with nothing but some old valet parking stubs and some odd coins and a half-used packet of spearmint Certs, I turned my attentions to the shelf above the clothes racks. An electric blanket, a Pan Am flight bag, a zippered leather camera case, another cylindrical zippered case, and two cardboard shoe boxes. I pulled down the camera case first.

It contained a 35mm Pentax, unloaded. There was an Albion telephoto lens in the cylindrical case, which Cooney had probably used to take the Sound Tek pictures. The flight bag was empty and one of the shoe boxes contained a pair of old Bally loafers. A rubber band held on the lid of the other shoe box; I pulled it off and lifted the top. Inside were two five-by-seven color snapshots, a tarnished turquoise-and-silver bracelet, a tarnished silver crucifix, and a couple of cheap silver rings, one of which had the name Lisa spelled out on it. The pictures weren't porno. In one of them, Cooney was standing in front of a hotdog stand with his arm wrapped around the shoulders of a girl who looked no more than seventeen. She had a face that was cute, if a bit babyish, with a tiny bud of a mouth and an upturned pug nose that was lightly dusted with freckles. They were both smiling broadly, but their eyes contained a kind of manic gleam that made the happiness in their faces look almost demented. The middle-aged couple in the other photograph were smiling, too, and also had their arms around each other, but their eyes lacked the mad, glassy glint of the other two. The man was tall and kind of gawky-looking, with a weathered face and receding hairline, while the woman was shorter and heavier, with short, gray hair. They stood in front of a rose garden and the woman held a red rose in her right hand, as if she were quite proud of it.

I put the photos back into the box. My thoughts tried to imitate the particles of dust that eddied aimlessly in the rectangle of sunlight that fell across the bed. Lisa. Brandt had said the name of the O.D. case who'd lived with Cooney was Lisa. Things were breaking fast; I'd just confirmed something I'd learned the day before. Maybe if I held the crucifix for a while a last name would come to me in some blinding, psychometric flash. I didn't even know why I was interested. The likelihood that this teenaged casualty had anything to do with Segal's predicament was pretty slim. Still . . .

I looked at the freckled face of the girl in the picture again. She seemed like someone from a Rockwell painting, too innocent to be into the kinds of scenes Brandt had described, but in this day of kiddie porn, you never could tell. I pocketed the pictures, put the shoe box on the shelf, and resumed my search. Fifteen more minutes of that failed to materialize any dirty pictures of Lisa or anyone else. Assuming Brandt had been telling the truth and Julia had been one of Cooney's photographic subjects, maybe she had taken them to keep anybody else from finding them.

I had another hour to go before Wanda finished with her beauty sleep, but I had her room number, and I didn't need clearance from some yo-yo desk clerk. After all, time was money—Segal's money—and I'd kept her awake before. Hell, I was goddamn responsible for the fact that she could wake up at all; she should be *overjoyed* to have my smiling kisser as her first vision on that fine morning.

I let myself out the kitchen door and went around front. The woman with the dog was just coming up the stairs and she gave me the same suspicious look. As I passed them, the dog growled, tugging on the leash, and I wondered if they had coyotes around here. The thought was comforting, anyway.

I drove down to Hollywood Boulevard. Everybody on the sidewalks looked as if they were suffering from a bad case of jet lag that morning, although I doubted many of them had been farther than a mile away all night. The advance scouts for the Mole People—the hustlers, the self-styled sly, those who live in darkened rooms and who transact business by night—were beginning to stumble out of apartment doorways, squinting into the daylight with watery, bewildered eyes.

On the way to the hotel, I stopped at a record store on Hollywood Boulevard and combed the alphabetized stacks for a group that could fit the "Marico-" in the photograph. The album was *Maricopa in Concert* and Cuthburton had been the recording engineer. So what was so special about an engineer walking around with a copy of his own album? I decided to buy it anyway.

I took it up front and, just to be making conversation with the cute young thing at the cash register, I asked how the album had been selling.

"Real good," she said, reeking enthusiasm. (It had even infected the retail end of the business.) "It's only been out about a week and we've had to reorder it once already."

I pulled hard on the reins. "You mean, this record has only been out a week?"

"That's right," she said.

I thanked her and left the store, my scalp tingling. As the record's engineer, Cuthburton would more than likely get advance copies. But then why would Cooney bother mailing those pictures to himself? It might have meant nothing, but I was not about to count on it, and I was filled with that old electric feeling as I went to the car.

The Holiday Inn was on North Highland, a twenty-three-story white cliff with a turret restaurant on top that rotated at night so that diners could be entertained by the glamorous glitter of Hollywood while they supped. Twenty-three floors was about right; any closer to the street and some appetites might be lost.

The hotel had valet parking out front. In a sudden upwelling of concern for my client's money, I drove around the block to look for a meter. Two nose-to-nose black-and-whites and a phalanx of blue uniforms cordoned off the street, keeping at bay the small group of rubbernecks who were trying to get a look at something by the back entrance of the hotel. I passed the barricade and turned right at the next street and homesteaded a space being vacated by a truck, half a block up.

The crowd had grown in my absence. I edged my way through to the front, countering the grumbles of protest by saying, "Make way for the press, make way for the press," until a beer-bellied cop with a drinker's nose held up a hand and asked with great originality where I thought I was going. I held up my old press card, keeping my thumb over the seven-year-old date, and said, "Asch, *Chronicle*."

The crowd to my left surged forward a little, distracting him. "Keep back, there," he shouted at them, and I put the card away before he had a chance to inspect it more closely. He turned back to me and said in a voice as excited as a clay pot, "Some chick decided to do a triple gainer off the seventeenth floor."

"Got an I.D. yet?"

The crowd surged forward again and he shot them an irritated glance. "*You*," he shouted, pointing his nightstick at a young ducktailed kid who looked like a regular from Sha-Na-Na, "Get back and stay back."

"They're pushin'," the kid protested.

The red-nosed cop glared at him, then said to me, "What'd you say?"

"I asked if they have an I.D. yet."

He looked faintly surprised. "I.D. that mess? Maybe after they scrape some fingerprints off the sidewalk."

I looked over his shoulder where an hysterical woman in a blood-spattered dress was trying to be calmed down by a uniformed cop and another civilian male. A coroner's wagon, two more squad cars, and an ambulance were bunched in the middle of the street; most of their occupants seemed to be congregated behind a new Ford station wagon parked in front of the canopied entrance to the hotel. None of them looked as if they were feeling too well. "That where she came down?"

He nodded. "Lucky she didn't kill that woman over there. She was coming out of the hotel when the body came down. Hit about five feet in front of her."

"When did it happen?"

"Twenty-five minutes ago, maybe." He pointed his nightstick at the kid again. "I'm not going to tell you again, goddamnit!" He muttered to himself, "Assholes. Up to me, I'd let 'em all in to take a look, except then we'd have to clean up the puke."

"Bad?" I asked.

"I haven't seen too many good ones, but this one was especially nice." He put the side of his hand to his mouth and said loud enough for everyone in a radius of ten feet to hear: "She must have been screaming, 'cause she came down with her mouth open, right on the license plate of that station wagon there. Cut her head right in half at the nose." A self-satisfied smirk crept across his lips as some would-be gawkers stirred behind me and beat a nauseated retreat to the rear, and the cop next to him snickered.

"What color hair did she have?" I asked.

He watched the crowd. "Huh? Blonde."

"Not red?"

"Now it is," he said, eliciting another snicker from the cop next to him.

"But before, it was blonde?"

"That's what I just said, ain't it?" His eyes narrowed suspiciously on my face. "What paper you say you were with?"

"*Chronicle.*"

I thanked him for the information and got the hell out of there before he asked to take another look at my press card. The jumper probably had nothing to do with me, but all I needed right now was to be placed at the scene of one more death—it didn't matter whose.

I walked around to the front of the hotel. The lobby was crowded and there were cops at the end of the hallway that led out to the back entrance, but nobody tried to stop me from coming in. I walked through shocked mutterings of "Horrible," and "That poor girl," and "How could anyone?" to the house phones. The operator buzzed me through to 1714 and a husky female voice answered, "Yes?"

"Miss Fleming? Miss Wanda Fleming?"

"Who is this?" Her voice sounded tense.

"Jacob Asch."

"Who?"

"I was at Fred Segal's party the other night. I was the one who—"

"Look," she cut me off, "all hell has broken loose here. I can't talk now." The room behind her was filled with a chaotic din of voices.

"Before you hang up, are you *Wanda Fleming*?"

"Huh? Yeah, yeah. Look, call back later, will you?" she said and hung up.

Whoever the jumper had been, it was not Wanda Fleming. There was really no reason she should have been, except that from what I'd seen, rock performers hadn't been faring too well of late. My throat was parched and I could have used a beer, but I didn't want to have to listen to the inevitable topic of conversation in the hotel bar, so I went back outside and began hoofing it back to the car. While walking, I found myself talking out loud, asking the same questions I would have heard in the bar: "Who was she?" and "Why did she jump?" Not that it mattered. When you're strawberry Jell-O on the sidewalk, it doesn't matter much to you if you stepped off because of the right boy or the wrong boy, a bad case of acne or a worse case of boredom. There were plenty of them out there, God knows, precariously perched on other ledges and ready to take the plunge, too sick or too tired or too sad for one more roll of the dice.

I got my beer at a little joint on the Strip called the Hideaway Lounge. I used the pay phone in the back to call Carey Stack. There were some questions I wanted to ask him. He wasn't in, but his service gave me a number where he could be reached. Before I dialed it, I tried Cuthburton again. He wasn't in, either, but when I told the girl who answered that it was very important that I get in touch with him, she said I might be able to catch him at Golden Sound studios after seven, that he was doing a recording session there that night.

Stack's forwarding number turned out to be the Polo Lounge of the Beverly Hills Hotel, and after I did a short stint on hold, he got on the line.

"So that's where you hang out to pick up your messages," I told him. "Life must be really tough."

"What can I say? We are all born to affliction. Actually, I only come here like everybody else, to have myself paged. Where in the hell are you?"

"The Hideaway Lounge."

"What are you doing there?"

"Hiding away. What else would you do in the Hideaway Lounge?"

"You eaten lunch yet?"

"No."

"Good. Get your ass over here and we'll have it together. I'm starved."

"I'll be there in fifteen or so," I told him.

I settled my account at the bar, tipped the bartender a bit too generously, and managed to make it to the car without any bodies falling on me.

The Beverly Hills Hotel rose like a pink stucco castle out of its setting of lush gardens and palm trees, and next to it, every other luxury hotel in L.A. seemed impossibly sterile. It was a monument to another era, an era of glamour and gaiety, an era of Gable and Lombard and Bogie and Bacall, an era in which I'd always thought I should have lived. I let the valet park my car this time, and went inside.

The Polo Lounge, or "Polio Lounge," as its frequenters like to call it, was busy, its dark green corners inhabited by the usual assortment of Beautiful People—movie stars, producers, dealmakers, and emotional cripples who come to soak up the leftover glitter—and it took me a couple of minutes to find Carey. He was sitting by himself at a table in the garden room, staring out of the glass wall that looked onto the patio. He pulled out a chair when he saw me. "Squat, son, squat."

His face was suffused with a ruddy color and his eyes were unnaturally bright. The pupils were very dilated. He shoved a menu at me. "How about some lunch?"

I was surprised to realize I was famished. "Only to make you eat your words about 'Let's have lunch' being the standard Hollywood bullshit line."

"Consider them eaten." He signaled to the waiter and told him to bring him another vodka and me a Michelob. At a table outside on the patio, two young, healthy-looking couples dressed in tennis whites munched club sandwiches. Both the people and the sandwiches looked good, so I decided on the club.

The waiter arrived with the drinks and we ordered lunch and Carey sat back and beamed. "We're having some fun now." His smile looked curiously strained, his face slightly feverish. "You'll have to excuse me if I seem a little jacked-up. If I start to walk on the ceiling, just pull me down."

"Is ceiling-walking normal for you, or did something specific bring this on?"

He nodded and took a sip of his drink. "I've been in meetings here all morning with some execs from Columbia who flew in last night from New York. It's a deal I've been trying to swing for a year—a six-figure package over the next three years—and we finally came to terms."

"Congratulations."

"I don't even care about the money. I mean, I'm not going to bitch about it, but this is more important than money. It's a chance to branch out into other areas, be more creative. It's something I've wanted to do for a long time."

"Great," I said through a forced smile.

Carey had stopped talking and was looking at me strangely. "What's the matter?"

"Nothing. I've just had kind of a rough morning, that's all. I don't mean to rain on your parade."

Concern tugged his eyebrows. "What happened?"

I told him about the jumper and he looked sad and started shaking his head. "Jesus Christ. Who was the girl?"

"I don't know."

"Any way to find out?"

"Wait for the papers to come out tomorrow."

His eyes widened in surprise. "And you can still eat lunch? If I saw something like that, I wouldn't be able to eat for a week."

"It's called getting case-hardened."

He looked out at the table of young tennis players, who were joking and laughing. "Youth," he mused. "I'm glad I survived it. Did you know, Jake, that if a male cat lives past its first couple of years, the chances of it living to be a very old cat skyrocket?"

I said I thought I'd heard it somewhere.

He nodded and kept his eyes on the table of youth. "It's all in the glands. Every goddamned commercial on the tube, every magazine we pick up, tries to sell us that youth is the answer. They don't quote the suicide and accident mortality statistics. It's in the glands."

He drained his drink and signaled the waiter for another, then sighed and smiled at me. "Well, whoever your jumper was, at least she went down in flames. She might even rate a page-two column in the *Times*, which is more than most of us will get."

I shrugged. "Julia Roth didn't even rate a mention in the Metro section. Somehow, I don't think she cares much."

He gave me a surprised look. "What happened to Julia?"

"You didn't hear?"

"No."

I told him about how I'd found her, but nothing else; and when I'd finished, he shook his head sadly. "That poor fucking kid. You think it was an accident, or suicide?"

"I'm not sure it was either."

His eyebrows knitted and he leaned forward. "You're not saying she was murdered?"

"Nope. I just said I'm not sure what happened."

"Who would want to kill Julia?"

"Good question." He made a thoughtful face and I looked out the window. The tennis players were finished and were getting up. One of the girls had great stems. Carey seemed momentarily distracted by them, too, and I took the opportunity to change the subject. "What do you know about record counterfeiting?"

"I know it's probably costing me a small fortune in royalties every year." He raised an eyebrow. "Why?"

"Just curious. There's a big traffic, then?"

He shrugged. "Maybe four hundred million dollars a year, give or take a few mil."

"Jesus. I didn't realize."

He nodded, drained his drink, and held up the glass to the waiter standing by the doorway. "About one out of ten LPs on the market, and one out of every four tapes, is counterfeit. It has literally bankrupted some companies. The general public doesn't realize, but eight out of ten records are stiffs. Only a company's hits keep it afloat. Siphon off the bread from its hits, it's *Titanic* time. And counterfeiters don't copy stiffs."

The waiter brought Carey's drink at the same time another arrived with our food. Carey continued to talk while he dove into his chef's salad. "It all started back in '78, when record sales went through the roof. *Saturday Night Fever*. The Eagles' *Hotel California* album, and Fleetwood Mac's *Rumours* smashed every goddamn sales record and the companies couldn't keep up with the

106

demand, so they went outside their normal production channels and parceled out work to independent pressers. People only started realizing what was happening when the bottom dropped out of sales two years later and companies started going down the chute right and left."

"That's how a counterfeiter would work? Go to an independent presser?"

"That's one way."

"Another way?"

"Say you own a pressing plant and Warner's comes to you to press five thousand Eagles albums. You press two hundred fifty thousand and sell the surplus."

My mind was starting to speed up. "Say I wanted to get set up in the business and I didn't have a pressing plant. How would I go about it?"

He said through a mouthful of salad, "You know how records are made?"

"I take it they don't come in a package like Aunt Jemima pancakes."

"Not quite," he said. "The first step is tape. That's what the engineer does at the studio. After that, the sound is laid on a lacquer disk, which is then silvered. That's called a 'negative.' Off the negative, you do a positive, which is called the 'master.' The completed master is made from that. That's called the 'mother.' After chemical treatment, another positive is made, which is the completed mother, and from that you get your stamper. The stamper is what makes your record. Follow?"

"Sounds complicated," I said. "So what would I need?"

"All you would need would be a master and some pressing equipment and you'd be in business.'

"How would I get the master?"

He shrugged. "Bribe somebody at the record company, steal it . . ."

"Couldn't I just tape off an existing record?"

"You could, but the quality wouldn't be nearly as good. You could tell then it was a fake."

"You couldn't if you had the master?"

He shook his head. "Some companies are experimenting with laser-detectable codes and identification marks and shit like that, but if a counterfeit is good, even the quality control people can't tell the difference."

"So who's behind it? Organized crime?"

He snickered. "Yeah, if organized crime is headquartered in Oklahoma City. Oh, there are probably some mob boys with their hands in. There always will be when there's that kind of money to be made. But nobody's got any monopoly, not when you can dupe an album for a dollar-fifty and sell it to a retailer for two-fifty to three dollars. The same record would cost the store four to six dollars. If he bought from a record company. Tapes are even better. You can make a tape for seventy-five cents."

He squinted at my face, as if trying to see inside it. "Is that what all this is about? Counterfeiting?"

I stared at the sandwich on my plate and realized I was not hungry anymore. I forced myself to take a bite, though, knowing my mind was playing tricks with me and that if I didn't eat something I'd be starving as soon as I got to the parking lot. "I don't know what all this is about," I said truthfully.

I could tell he didn't believe me. "Then why all the questions?" He held up his hands before I could answer. "I know. 'Just curious.' "

I managed to get down half of the sandwich before deciding I couldn't eat another bite. The lunch crowd had departed, leaving us alone in the room. I ordered another beer and asked, "Who would I talk to at Capitol, for example, to determine where a certain record was pressed?"

He flashed me a knowing look. "Capitol, for example? Or Capitol, period?"

"Capitol, period."

He grinned. "M and E. That's Manufacturing and Engineering. The plant manager would have that information."

"Would he talk to me if I called?"

"Cold? Probably not." His smile deepened. "But you, dear boy, are with a man of influence. If you have a dime—I'm completely out of change—I'll go use some of it."

I gave him a dime and he went away. He came back five minutes later and sat down. "You're lucky you know me, you know that?"

"I count my blessings seventeen times a day."

He gave me a gratified nod and handed me a piece of paper he'd scribbled on. "That's the plant manager's name and number. He'll tell you whatever you want to know."

"Thanks, Carey. I really appreciate it."

He waved a hand at me. "Forget it. I don't know what you're into, but if you've stumbled onto some kind of counterfeiting operation, I'm doing myself a favor. Maybe the bastards are counterfeiting some of my songs."

The waiter brought the check and I tried to grab it, but Carey snatched it away from him. I tried to argue him out of it, but he just shook his head ruefully and gave the waiter some plastic. He tut-tutted me when I offered to get the tip and I didn't give him much of a fight about it.

While we waited for the cars to be brought up, I asked, "We still on for the Starlight tonight?"

He made a face. "Meet me at the Rainbow at nine-thirty and we'll go from there. And I meant it about you owing me for this."

"I'll put you in my will tomorrow."

The attendant brought up his Mustang and he got in and cranked up the Bob Seger tape on the stereo. He leaned out the window and said with the mock seriousness of a radio announcer, "Rock on, rock fans."

"I keep trying, but it isn't getting any easier."

He sighed. "I know what you mean, buddy, I know what you mean."

He put the car in gear and roared off down the driveway.

11

The plant manager for Capitol Records's M And E division was named Weiner, and he told me some heavyweight vice-president whose name I didn't catch had called him and told him to expect my call. It took him a couple of minutes to look up the *Maricopa* LP and find out that all the copies had been pressed at the Capitol plant. None had been farmed out. I thought of Carey and counted my blessings as I stepped out of the phone booth; that only left sixteen more to go that day.

The address the phone book listed for Sound Tek was in a fin-gernail-hanging area of Culver City filled with commercial enter-prises as small and varied and tattered as the lives that ran them. Cheap motels shared blocks with ethnic restaurants exuding Ori-ental smells, liquor stores leaned against auto upholstery shops, chiropractors and dentists advertised discount family rates on hand-painted signs. Sound Tek was a graying, windowless, stucco trapezoid wedged in between a film-processing store and a bar called Shady's Alibi Room, and from the looks of that place, I was willing to bet every one of its patrons had one for every night of the week. I parked in front and locked up the car.

The picture in my pocket had not been taken in front, so I walked around back. A narrow alley ran behind the stores, the other side of which was residential. It looked like the place. A van similar to the one in the picture was parked by the back door. All the other parking spaces behind the stores were filled. I studied the picture and tried to figure the angle. It looked as if the pho-tographer had probably parked down the alley in one of the other spaces that ran behind the buildings and taken the picture from there. All the other spaces were filled now, and with Shady's, probably were most of the time. A car parked there would not be that noticeable; with a telephoto, it would be no problem. That was the most logical, anyway; I doubted that the people who lived across the alley would have been receptive to a peeping Tom with a camera camping in their yards.

There was a cheer and an explosion of raucous laughter from the Alibi Room. I went around to the front door.

It was one large, warehouse-type room inside, filled with machinery and the acrid smell of burning plaster. Along one wall in front, a glassed-in partition that did not reach the ceiling had been slapped together to serve as offices. In the first one, a woman who looked like a runner-up in the Beast from 20,000 Fathoms Beauty Pageant sat at a desk, eating a ham sandwich. She looked as if she needed it; she only weighed 250 or so. Her brown hair was pulled back and fixed with a comb and she wore almost no makeup, which was probaby smart on her part. It would've been a waste of money.

She held the sandwich daintily, with pudgy little pinkies extended, as she proceeded to take half of it into a mouth that looked like the entrance to Carlsbad Caverns. Her eyes were shut in ecstasy as she savored the sandwich, and my cough seemed to startle her. Her eyes jumped open and she said, through a mouthful of ham, lettuce, and whatever, something that sounded like, "Whhhuh?"

"I'm looking for the owner."

"Who're you?" Friendly, too.

"The name is Moody," I said, smiling. "Golden Eagle Records."

"I'm one of the owners," she said. "Whaddya want?"

"Dean Cuthburton told me to come by. But he told me to talk to a man."

"My husband."

"Short man? Gray hair?"

She nodded and swallowed the last of the sandwich in her mouth.

"And his name is?"

111

"Ainsworth. Sid Ainsworth."

"That's the name Dean gave me, right."

"Sid's in the back right now. Maybe I could help you."

I gave her a dubious look. "Dean told me to talk to your husband, but seeing as you're an owner, I guess it's okay. I need some records stamped."

"How many?"

"Ten thousand."

"Kind of a small order."

"If the job is good, the next one will be bigger."

"Wait here," she said. "I'll go get Sid." She grunted as she pushed herself out of her chair with a monumental effort. Her designer jeans made crisp, rasping sounds as she walked by me and I watched her go, amazed that they made pockets that big.

I looked the office over. The record-pressing business didn't seem to be booming. Besides the ham sandwich, there was nothing else on the desk. Clear desk, clear mind, they say. Except this one was a little too clear. I went to the electric typewriter that sat on the rolling stand beside the desk and ran my finger across the top of it. Dust.

She called me and I went out of the office and past a row of bulky, boxy machines maybe twelve feet high that stood in a line down the middle of the room. She was standing with the man from the photograph, who was emptying a bucket of black vinyl pellets that looked like rabbit turds into a big vat. An elastic tube ran from the vat into an overhead network of pipes that crisscrossed in the high ceiling and emptied into the open tops of the machines. It was very hot back there and the damn plastic fumes were suffocating. The man's face was florid and covered with sweat. He put down the bucket.

The corners of his eyes slanted down toward his round cheeks, giving him a slightly Mongoloid appearance, something that wasn't noticeable in the picture.

"You're a friend of Dean's, huh?"

"That's right."

He nodded, then held out his black palm. "Excuse me if I don't shake hands."

112

He went to one of the sinks along the wall behind him and began washing his hands with soap and water. "Holly says you want some records stamped."

"That's right. Dean said you were the one to do it."

"You got the mother?"

I nodded.

"Ten thousand?"

"Yeah."

"Kind of a small order."

"These are just extras. We've already pressed our major run. And as I was telling your wife, if the quality is good, there will be more jobs."

He turned off the water and wiped his hands on a towel.

"Where do you know Dean from?"

"He's done some sessions for me at Golden Eagle."

"Golden Eagle, huh? Never heard of it."

"We're a small label, and new. But we're comers. Got some acts signed that are going to be hot." I hesitated meaningfully. "The labels on this ten thousand won't say Golden Eagle, though."

He raised an eyebrow. "No? What'll they say?"

"Elektra."

His expression soured. "Why would they say that?"

I ran a hand over the back of my neck, then flicked the perspiration off my fingers. "Golden Eagle is a small company. I've got to be concerned with my costs. A friend of mine—where would we be without friends, right?—gave me a whole lot of Elektra labels the other day, and I figure I can save on my cost per unit by using them."

"Get out." It was the woman.

I turned to her. "Pardon me?"

She put her hands on her gargantuan hips and snarled, "What do you think we are here, counterfeiters or something? We run a legitimate operation here."

"And one that doesn't seem to be doing all that well. These pressing machines are awfully quiet. I'm offering you a chance to give them a little workout."

"We don't need your kind of business," she said.

The man winced. "Now, honey—"

"Keep quiet, Sid," she snapped.

"But Dean—" he whined.

She scowled at him. "You think Dean's going to send somebody over here without calling first? This joker didn't even know your name."

"He told me. I just forgot. Call him right now and ask him. He'll tell you. I helped him unload the *Maricopa* albums."

She took a step toward me. "I don't know what your game is, mister, but you'd better get out of here before I call the cops."

She was on my heels all the way out. As we passed the office, I paused and pointed at her desk. "Be careful of those ham sandwiches. You know what happened to Mama Cass."

I got out before she decided to sit on me.

12

The business license on file at the Culver City City Hall stated that Sound Tek was owned by Sound Tek, Inc., and had been in business at the same address for the past seven years. A trip downtown to the County Corporations Commission Office might have told me who the principal officers and shareholders of Sound Tek, Inc., were, but it was almost three, and that trip would guarantee my getting stuck in the rush-hour snarl. I decided to let it go until the next day and headed home.

On the way, I stopped by my office to check the mail. It was not far from Sound Tek, but it had a Marina del Rey address, which carried a little more prestige than Culver City. The place itself was hardly prestigious; it was a tiny, dusty walkup with almost enough room for the desk and two filing cabinets in it, as long as nobody was in there with them. Aside from being close to home, I had picked it for two reasons: the rent was cheap, which was a primary consideration, as I only used the place as a mail drop, and two, it was upstairs from Charlie Chan's Accounting Service. All I had to do was see that and the landlord had me.

The venetian blinds were shut tight over the inscrutable Mr. Chan's windows as I started up the outside stairs, and I stopped for a moment and listened. Not a sound inside. There never was. No typewriter clacking, not a cough or a sneeze. I didn't know when the elusive Mr. Chan did his tallying, unless it was three in the morning. I had never seen a client go in or leave, I had never gotten so much as a glimpse of Chan or his sons. I could have knocked on the door one day and walked in, I suppose, but that would inevitably put a halt to my imaginative peregrinations, so I never had. Mr. Chan was one mystery I found I enjoyed perpetuating; he gave me things to wonder about on long, boring afternoons.

The office was hot and stuffy and I went through the mail quickly so that I could get out of there. Aside from two letters, the mail was the usual assortment of junk fliers advertising specials on pickled pig's feet at Ralph's and a reminder from the Southern California Gas Company that the cost of natural gas was going up and that we all had to cut back on consumption. The reminder did not say that it was printed on expensive foil paper that must have cost at least a quarter and that that cost would be tacked on my gas bill at the end of the month. Schmucks.

One of the letters was from a Thelma Tort, with a Skid Row address, who wrote in a palsied hand that she suspected that the Rescue Mission was poisoning bums with their free soup. She suspected this because three of her friends had died in the past year—of cirrhosis of the liver—and all three had partaken of the Mission's gourmet repasts. She had picked me to uncover this nefarious plot to rid the world of the unfortunate because she had seen my name in the phone book and "liked it." The other letter was from a manufacturer in Seattle who wanted me to call him collect about a plant security matter. I put that one in my "To Answer" pocket and filed Ms. Tort's letter in the wastebasket, then got an idea and fished it out. This was a case worthy of the famous Charlie Chan. The letter had been written in pencil and it was nothing to make the proper substitutions and make out a new envelope.

Before I left I tried Blackburn again, and this time he was available. I told him everything, and he sounded pleased.

"Sounds like you're making headway."

"Some."

"At least it throws some other possibilities into the pot. The D.A. is smelling blood. He's found out about the enmity between Cooney and Fred and he's going to ask the grand jury for an indictment for Murder One."

116

"Murder One? Hell, he could never prove that."

"Maybe not, but he'll get his indictment, unless we can come up with something that'll make him change his mind. Can you get me a report written by tomorrow?"

"Tomorrow? Jeez, Ed, I don't know. I've got a lot to do tonight and tomorrow I wanted to see what I could do with Walton—"

"You're right. Time is of the essence here. You just keep digging. Tell you what—make a tape and drop it by the office and I'll have Lynne transcribe it."

"Fine," I said. "One more thing: the cop in charge of the case—Exley—has been trying to get in touch with me. I think he might be pissed that I held back on the statement I made. What do I tell him?"

"Segal hasn't been indicted yet, so you have no grounds to withhold information, even as my agent. Just tell him exactly what happened at the party, no more, no less."

"What if he starts threatening?"

"Tell him to go piss in his hat. There was a lot of confusion that night; you were busy saving lives and you forgot a few details, that's all. Don't worry about it."

I told him I would drop the tape by the next morning. We said good-bye. I went outside and locked up. Downstairs, I tiptoed up to Charlie's door and put my ear against it. Nothing. I slipped the letter under the door and left.

At home, I popped the tab on an Oly and took it into the bathroom to keep me company while I stood under a hot shower. I guzzled the beer in an attempt to keep my mood from plummeting out of control. After all, I couldn't very well go out there in the throes of a crippling depression and deal with a bunch of vicious, degenerate punk rockers. The depression could wait until later; right now, I had to have an *edge*, a little artificial stimulation to lift the spirits and the will. I wished I had some of that coke right there; since I didn't, I pulled the bottle of whites down from the medicine cabinet, shook out two, and washed them down with another beer. The crash would be worse, but at least it would be postponed.

I spent some time in the closet searching for appropriate garb

117

for the evening, and decided finally on a long-sleeved black shirt, a pair of brushed-denim blue jeans, black loafers, and a black imitation-leather sports jacket. I looked more like a Newark junkie than a punker, but it was the closest I could come and I had no hopes of being able to blend in with the crowd anyway. I just didn't want to stand out too grossly; the communication gap between us was going to be big enough without letting tweed get in the way.

By 6:30 the whites had kicked in and I felt my mood sharpening as I drove over the Cahuenga Pass into the Valley. I was actually feeling pretty good.

Golden Sound was on Ventura Boulevard in Van Nuys, a street that has been called by some the "most interesting street in the world," and I had to admit it achieved a kind of pinnacle. Ten unbroken miles of storefronts selling everything from bassinets to waterbeds, chateaubriand to chicken knishes, camper vans to karate lessons. You could buy anything you needed there, supplies from the cradle to the grave; and it achieved this without one tasteful piece of architecture. The block Golden Sound occupied seemed to be specializing in furniture. It was a freestanding, boxy building, painted gold, of course, and there were two girls standing outside talking to a man when I passed, ogling the curb for a parking space.

The girls were still there when I walked up, but the man was gone. They were two cloned, miniskirted bubble-gummers with stick legs and teased hair that looked like straw. Between them, they wore enough makeup for a mime troup.

"What an asshole," one of them said, snapping her gum.

"For sure," the other said.

Their eyes were on the door of the studio, so I assumed they were not talking about me.

"Whaddya wanna do?"

They stopped talking as I tried the front door and found it locked. I knocked and it opened and a large, bouncer-type stuck out a head the size of a watermelon. "Yeah?"

"Dean Cuthburton in there?"

"He's busy, man."

I handed him a card. "Give him this, will you? Tell him I met him at Fred Segal's party. Ask him if he can spare me a couple of minutes when he gets the time."

He didn't look happy about it, but he took the card and closed the door. One of the bubble-gummers minced up to me. "You a friend of the band's?"

"What band is it?"

"Black Friday," she said, in disbelief, knowing now she was dealing with a retard.

"No."

She made a face. "They won't let you in."

"We've been trying to get in for an hour," the gum snapper whined. "It's a total drag. The engineer says he doesn't want any more people in there. There must be fifty girls in there already."

"For sure," the other one said.

The door opened and the bouncer said gruffly, "Okay."

I started in and one of the clones grabbed my sleeve. "You gonna see the engineer?"

I nodded.

"Tell him we got coke."

"I'm sure that news will thrill him," I said, and followed the doorman inside.

We went through a series of paneled offices and down a narrow hallway, and then I heard the band. Actually, I felt the vibrations more than heard. We went past several doors and at the end of the hallway, the bouncer opened the last one and we went up some steps and through two more doors and we were in the control booth. The bouncer pointed at Cuthburton, who was sitting at a control panel between two men, intently working dials and switches, then went back out, closing the door behind him. Cuthburton didn't look up; he was concentrating on the pulsing columns of colored lights on the board that were rising and falling like mercury in a thermometer.

The glass front of the booth looked out onto the floor of the large, high-ceilinged studio in the center of which the band was set up on a carpeted section surrounded by sound baffles and microphones of every description and amplifiers the size of small buildings. It was a heavy-metal band of five pieces—two guitars, a bass, drums, and a synthesizer—and at the moment the lead guitarist, a tall, skinny kid with long hair and skin so pale he looked almost albino, was working on a solo that would have drowned out a Concorde flyover. The two dozen or so people that stood behind the baffles watching didn't seem to mind; they had ecstatic looks on their faces as if in the throes of a religious experience.

The albino finished his solo and the three string players stepped up to their mikes and sang in unison:

> "You don't know
> You don't know
> You got no idea, baby—"

It sounded like they didn't either.

Cuthburton hit a switch and his voice filled the studio: "Cut it, cut it."

The band stopped playing and looked up at the booth questioningly. Voices scrabbled as Cuthburton rewound the tape. "Chauncey," Cuthburton said, "you're coming across too heavy on the falsetto. You're taking over the chorus."

"I can't go much weaker on it," the albino said. "If I do, it'll fade completely."

"Dave and Jer, try standing a little closer to the mikes," Cuthburton instructed. "I'll sweeten the rest later."

The man next to Cuthburton, heavyset and swarthy, with a big, sweaty face, leaned over and spoke into the mike: "And Dave, try to clip that rhythm guitar more, drive that sucker, you know, chuckah, chuckah, chuckah—"

The guitarist nodded, but he seemed to be concentrating more on the bottle of Jack Daniel's that he had materialized from behind his amp. Most of the spectators had already taken the opportunity of the break to whip out joints and several of the girls were helping out by scooping fingernails full of toot from paper bindles and holding them under their noses.

The swarthy man in the booth let go of the mike switch and said to Cuthburton in an irritated tone, "This is fucking *costing*, Dean. I want all these people out of here."

"You're the producer," Cuthburton said, unruffled. "*You* tell 'em."

The man hit the switch and said, "Chauncey, you're going to have to clear these people out of here."

"They're *friends*, Harry," the albino said as a chorus of complaints erupted from the crowd. "We asked them here."

"Goddamnit, Chauncey, time is money. We've only got the studio until one and we've got to get down three more sides. Every time there's a break, it takes twenty minutes to get started again."

More jeers and complaints from the peanut gallery.

"We *need* them here," the albino insisted. "They're our support."

"Support, my ass," the producer bellowed. "They're a distraction."

"Let 'em stay," Cuthburton cut in. "You're just going to piss off Chauncey and then they'll tighten up even more and we'll never get a side down."

"We'll never get one down the way we're going."

"We'll get it," Cuthburton said confidently. "They'll loosen up. Relax, Harry."

"Relax, hell," the heavy man said. "It's only the tension that's holding me together." He hit the mike button: "All right, they can stay."

The moaning changed to cheers and Cuthburton said to them, "All right, everybody, we're going to take ten. When we come back, let's quit jacking off and get serious."

The albino gave him a raised fist and unstrapped his guitar, and there was a whoop from the crowd, and the drugs and booze began to flow in earnest. Cuthburton stood up and stretched, then turned to me.

He wore a pale blue T-shirt that said "EAGLES THE LONG RUN," a pair of Calvin Kleins, and brown penny loafers, with white socks. He was shorter than I remembered, only five-eight or so, but then I realized I didn't remember much about him at all, except how his breathing had sounded. I took a better look.

He had a long wedge of a face, with a narrow, hooked nose with pinched nostrils, and a full mouth with a protruding lower lip. His black hair was shaggy and his washed-out, greenish-brown eyes looked happy, although not in any pharmaceutical way. He gave me a relaxed, amiable smile and held out a hand. "You must be Emergency One."

"You don't look quite as blue as I remember you."

"I've been meaning to call you. Thnaks for the save."

"We all do what we can."

He glanced at the manila envelope in my hand but didn't say anything about it. "Hey, you guys," he said to the other two men, "this is Jake Asch. He's the one who played paramedic over at Freddie's the other night."

We all exchanged greetings, then the producer and the other man, who was Cuthburton's assistant, said they were going outside for a smoke and went out. "Maybe you know I'm working for Segal now," I told Cuthburton as the door closed, leaving us alone.

"Freddie told me. He called this afternoon and said you might be coming by."

"You two are still on speaking terms, then."

He wrinkled his face and waved a hand in the air. "Hell, yes. I never thought for a second that Freddie would do anything like that on purpose. Hand out skag at a party or use it himself? I've been tight with the man for eight years. No fucking way, man."

"I didn't realize you two were that close."

"Oh, yeah. We go *way* back. Hey, I felt like a complete fink fessing up to the cops where I'd gotten dosed, but what was I going to say? That I'd found some white powder in a vial along the side of the road and I decided to put it up my nose to see what it was? They already knew what happened anyway. They'd talked to the others in the hospital; they'd figured it out."

122

Somebody whooped excitedly in the studio. Two of the musicians were on the floor, alligator wrestling. At the edge of the crowd were the two clones from outside; I wondered if the bouncer's nose was white. "Looks like you've got your hands full here," I said to Cuthburton. "I'd go nuts."

"This isn't so bad. I've worked sessions that were fucking bedlam, man. This group can't work without a little chaos around them. They need it to function. Harry doesn't realize that. He hasn't been around them as much as I have."

"These guys personal friends of yours or something?"

He shook his head. "No, but I've spent the last week or so hanging around with them, going to their practices. An engineer, if he's any good, has to spend a lot of time with any group he's going to record. If you go into a session blind, not knowing what the group is, what they should sound like, how they work, it'll create a lot of confusion. You've got to understand the music so you can know what's wrong when you hear it. If an engineer is insecure, it'll come out in the grooves."

I stepped over to the board and shook my head in awe. "And everything is controlled right through here, huh?"

He nodded and smiled indulgently. "Every one of the mikes on the floor out there is a track, and each of those tracks is mixed onto that tape through the sound board. It's my job to adjust levels and coordinate the mix to capture the way the producer and I think the group should sound."

I pointed to the reel-to-reel tape. "And that's called the master, right?"

"It will be when we're done. Depending on what we wind up with, we might have to dub in some additional tracks later."

"You'll have to forgive me, but I'm really fascinated by the whole process. How long does it usually take to do all that extra dubbing and stuff?"

"That depends on what needs to be done."

I ran a finger around the edge of one of the reels. "And you have to have access to the master while you're working on it, obviously." I looked at him steadily. "With the amount of money tied up in one of these sessions, the company must keep pretty tight security on these suckers. Especially with all the piracy going on today."

"It does." There was a hint of uneasiness in his tone now.

"Of course, there's always a way to beat the system."

He returned my smile, but it was as dry and brittle as a potato chip. "I guess." He patted me on the arm and said, "Look, I don't mean to be rude, but as you point out, these sessions cost a heap of scratch, and I've got to get the train back on the track. . . ."

"I understand," I said. "I know you're on a tight schedule. But I would like to ask you a few questions about your recollections of the party. It could be important to our case."

He bit his lower lip and sighed. "All right, if it won't take too long. I've got to get a Coke first, though. I'm dying of thirst."

We went out of the booth and through the first door in the hallway and we were in the studio. You didn't have to smoke in there to get high; the air was so heavy with pot that you could get ripped to the tits just walking through the place. The wrestling matches were over and the crowd was breaking up and drifting out the door to get some fresh air or to their cars to replenish supplies. Electrical cables covered the concrete floor like black snakes and I stepped gingerly over them as we skirted the band setup, to the back of the room. In the corner stood a Coke machine, next to a young kid who sat with his back to the wall, holding a blood-soaked towel to his head. Three feet away stood two young gum-chewing girls, one wearing leather leopard-skin tights, the other wearing an oversized army jacket with campaign buttons all over it. Apparently oblivious to the man beside them who was bleeding all over the floor, the girls were immersed in a copy of *Showtime*.

"Listen to *this*," Leopard Woman said excitedly. "'Moon Children: This is a good week to review your priorities, especially in matters of finance. Budget your money wisely and you will be able to attend that concert you've been wanting to see.'"

"Oingo Boingo," the Campaigner said.

"Def Leppard," Leopard Woman said.

I bent down and asked the bleeding kid what had happened.

He said he'd cracked up his bike in the parking lot, but he was okay and didn't want to go to the hospital. I looked at Cuthburton questioningly, but he just looked bored as he ripped off the top of his can of Coke and I said to hell with it, I wasn't going to be the only one to worry about it. The kid must have had better friends than I there. Let them take care of him.

The two astrology queens moved off and as they did, the one in leopard pants looked down at the kid and made a face. "Eeeuu. How gross."

They joined the others and drifted off. I asked Cuthburton, "Were you in the room when the bottle of smack was broken out?"

"Yeah. Freddie told me to come into the back room, that he had some real good whiff that was too good to share with everybody."

"Who else was there?"

"Him, Wanda Fleming, myself, and Ross Stillwell."

"How about Julia Roth?"

"She came in later."

"When?"

"After Segal brought out the bottle. It was in his pocket. Julia knocked on the door and told him he was wanted in the living room and he left and said to go ahead and enjoy ourselves, that he'd be right back."

"And Julia stayed?"

"For a couple of minutes. Then she left, too. Said she had a nature call and would be back to partake."

"Did she handle the bottle?"

He thought for a moment. "She might have. Yeah, in fact, I remember her picking up the bottle and looking at it."

"Who else handled it?"

He shrugged. "I think I did. Wanda Fleming. She was chopping lines. Maybe Ross, I don't know. It's hard to remember exactly. I mean, who was paying attention? I'd already had about six or seven drinks by that time and half a dozen lines. Things were a little hazy."

"Then what?"

"Then you and Carey came in, and the rest you know." His left eye squinted slightly. "You think somebody switched the bottle?"

"Yeah, that's what I think."

"Julia?"

"I thought that for a while, but now I'm not so sure." I paused and gave him a hard stare. "I found something at her place that started me wondering."

"What?" he asked, truly curious now.

"Some photographs."

The Coke balked on the way to his mouth. His eyelid twitched. "What of?"

I opened the envelope and picked out the one that showed him the most clearly and handed it to him. He took it stiffly and when he saw what it was, his eyes darted around to see if anyone else was watching. When he determined we were completely alone except for the motorcycle casualty, who was probably too preoccupied with his own injuries to be eavesdropping even if he wasn't out of hearing range, he asked in a voice that was supposed to sound bored, "So?"

"I got kind of curious because they were in an envelope Cooney had sent to himself, registered mail. I've heard of writers doing that to protect themselves from being plagiarized—it dates the material, see?—and it got me wondering what could be so important about establishing the date these were taken. So I did some checking and you know what I found? I found that the album in your hand there hadn't been released at the time this was taken."

He shoved the pictures back at me and said in a taut voice, "If he—or you—had bothered to check, you would have found out I was the engineer on that LP. That was an advance copy."

"What were you doing with it over at Sound Tek?"

"I don't remember. Sound Tek does some pressing for Capitol every once in a while—"

"I checked with M and E at Capitol," I said not letting him finish. "All the *Maricopa* albums were pressed there. None were farmed out."

"I might just have stopped by to talk to somebody and had it with me," he snapped. "Who remembers?"

126

"What was in the boxes you and your partner were loading into the van?"

He lifted one shoulder. "Sid was short of help that day. He asked us to give him a hand loading some stuff, so we did. I didn't ask what it was."

"You pretty chummy with the Ainsworths?"

"I wouldn't say chummy, no."

"But you schlepp boxes for him," I said doubtfully.

The glint in his eyes turned stony. "You got something to say? Say it."

I ignored the challenge. "Did you know about the photos?"

"How would I?"

"I don't know," I said. "I thought maybe Cooney told you about them."

He lifted an eyebrow. "Cooney?"

I nodded. "Yeah. He was talking about putting together a new album. I thought maybe he had approached you to arrange for the session."

"Cooney couldn't put together shit," he said, his voice rising in both volume and pitch. "His fucking brain was stir-fried."

"Then he didn't approach you about engineering an album for him?"

He took a swig of Coke. "No."

"Good. Because if he had, that would make you a prime suspect for his murder."

For an instant, I thought he was going to lose the Coke in his mouth. "What the fuck are you talking about?"

I turned up my palms. "I'm perfectly willing to believe everything you've told me, Mr. Cuthburton; I mean it all makes perfect sense to me. But you know how the cops are; they don't believe *anybody*. Let's just say that they found these pictures and started nosing around and they found out that there was something funny going on at Sound Tek—something like, oh, say, counterfeiting records. Not that anything like that is happening. I'm just throwing this out as a what-if."

He licked his lips and stared at me.

"Say they jumped to the erroneous conclusion that you had an

127

arrangement with the Ainsworths that Cooney found out about and that's what these pictures were proof of. They would probably suspect—because this is how their minds work—that Cooney had a plan to use them to blackmail you, either for money or to get you to arrange for and engineer a session for his new material—"

"Man," he said, waving a scoffing hand, "I don't think you're wrapped too tight."

I put both hands on my chest. "It's not *me*, Mr. Cuthburton. It's the *cops*. They can twist everything all around so that it sounds bad, when it's really not. And once they'd gotten to that point, it wouldn't be a quantum leap in logic to conclude that you secretly invited Cooney to Segal's party in order to O.D. him—"

"And took a dose of the stuff myself," he said, taking a step away. "Now I know you're out of your mind."

I threw my hands toward him helplessly. "I know it sounds crazy. It sounds crazy to me, too. But that's the way they think."

"That I killed Cooney and nearly died myself because of *those*?" He pointed in disbelief at the envelope in my hand. "Those pictures aren't worth shit. They don't prove a fucking thing; I don't care if they were mailed in 1956." He stopped and thought for a moment. "How did you get them out of the envelope without breaking the seal, anyway?"

"I didn't."

He smiled. "Then they *really* aren't worth shit."

"You might be right about them not being proof, Mr. Cuthburton," I said, "but what they are is a loose thread. One of those that you have to cut because if you don't and somebody starts pulling on it, the whole sweater can come unraveled."

He squinted, searching my eyes for clues. "What are you after, anyway?"

"I'm trying to clear my client, that's all."

He looked over my shoulder at the people who were starting to drift back into the studio, and said, "I have to get back to work now. If you have any more questions, don't bother to drop by."

He started away. I waited until he'd gone about five paces before I added, "By the way, Mr. Cuthburton, there were *two* envelopes. The other one is still sealed. I don't know what's in it, but I'm assuming it's the same thing."

He put a finger in the air and twirled it in a whoopee gesture, and walked back toward the control booth.

The injured kid on the floor groaned as I walked by, and I told him, "I know how you feel, buddy," and went down the hallway. The two astrology queens were still there, absorbed in their *Showtime*, and I stopped and peeked over the shoulder of the one holding the magazine. She recoiled as she looked back at me. I asked, "What does it say in there for Capricorns?"

The Leopard Woman looked me up and down and didn't seem too displeased by what she saw. "You a Capricorn?"

I told her I was and she ran a finger down the page. "Let's see, Capricorn, Capricorn, yeah, here it is. 'Capricorn: It is important to understand every phase of the work ahead of you before you tackle it. Relax tonight.' "

"Just what I thought," I said.

The Campaigner batted her false eyelashes at me. "What?"

"The stars suck," I said, and left.

13

S tack was waiting for me at the bar when I got to the Rainbow. "Have a drink, son," he said as I sat on the stool next to his. I ordered a vodka-soda. "Find out what you wanted to know today?"

"I found out that I should understand every phase of the work ahead of me before tackling it."

"Sounds reasonable to me." He drained his glass quickly and signaled to the bartender for one more. "One for the road. I'm going to need it for the freak show. A bracer to face the monsters of the midway as they attempt to burn rock and roll on the funeral pyre."

Our drinks came and he started to pay, but I reminded him it was my turn and he demurred. He downed his entire drink by the time I had taken two sips of mine, and looked at his watch. "We'd better split. We don't want to miss the bass player bite the head off the bat."

"You're kidding," I said.

"What's with you, boy? It's 1984. Get with it."

I paid for the drinks, and we went outside. Stack told me to leave my car there and had the valet bring up his Mustang. It was a three-speed and the throaty purr of the big engine was soothing as Stack moved through the gears. He pushed in a cassette. The beautifully haunting sounds of the Flamingos' "I Only Have Eyes for You" filled the car, filling my head with a fragmented flood of long-lost images—Laurie Rolly's black Chevy station wagon and the clumsy grappling over gearshifts on convertible-top nights and carefree beach days sweetened by the smell of greasy hamburgers frying. I closed my eyes and gave myself over to it, let myself drift back, then it was over, and the Diamonds were telling their "Little Darlin'" that they were wrong to love her, and I surfaced again.

"Was it only in us?" I asked Stack. "Or was there really something special in that music?"

"The music was full of something then. All those doo-wops and shoo-wahs were the blushing innocence of youth."

"You think things have changed that much?"

He grinned sardonically. "Hey, you can't stick safety pins in your cheeks and remain in Eden. With the pain, comes the Fall."

"But people still relate to your music," I protested. "They must. You're three with a bullet this week."

He nodded out the window at the New Wavers lined up outside the Whiskey, waiting to gain entrance. "Not them, and they are the future. There is no common ground of communication between us. No, I'm finished, Jake; it's just a matter of time. But that's okay. I wouldn't want to survive in a time when the heroes of the day are groups called the Dead Kennedys."

"How did you start songwriting, anyway?"

"It's an inspirational story. I had this friend Barry in high school back in Vineland, New Jersey, who played the piano. Barry was a big hit with the girls. I was kind of shy and still a virgin and I couldn't help noticing how the girls ate up on that piano playing. So I decided to take up the guitar. You might actually say my beginnings were a musical score."

"Boo."

"Right." He grinned. "Anyway, I found out that I had a feel for music, especially as a lyricist, and a year later, Barry and I formed a little band. We played odd gigs here and there, bar mitzvahs, private parties, real heavy gigs, but then Barry went to college and the band broke up."

"And you packed your guitar and headed for the bright lights?"

"Not quite," he said, signaling and turning left onto Crescent

131

Heights. "Actually, I knocked up the girl I'd been going with and everybody's parents decided I should do the 'right' thing, so I got married and got a 'responsible' job working in a factory. But the songs wouldn't leave me alone. I kept writing, but I didn't like anything I'd done and I knew I needed to get out and experience more, to soak up more of life than working on an assembly line days and coming home to meat loaf and a whining wife nights. I had bigger dreams than Sears prints and polyester carpet. The marriage was already coming apart anyway, so after the baby was born, we agreed to file for divorce and I hopped the first freight west and never looked back."

"What was your first hit?"

"'Ride the Big One,'" he said, shaking his head and laughing. "I'd been bumming around a bunch of little dives where musicians hung out and got to know a couple of guys and we formed a group called the Surf Stompers."

"That was you?" I asked, surprised. "Hell, I saw you in Newport one summer."

"And your eardrums are still intact? You're lucky. Boy, were we bad. But we hit. Only for one record, but we hit."

"What happened?"

"What happens with a lot of groups. You get a hit and everybody gets big-headed and the internal fighting starts. Our range in those days was pretty limited and I was tired of songs about cars and surfing. I wanted to write other things, so I wrote a song for a group called Sparrow that turned out to be a monster for them. The rest of the guys got pissed about that; they thought I should have kept the song in the group, but it wasn't Surf Stompers stuff, it was a love song. They asked me to leave the group, so I did. I never performed again, but I didn't have to. I wrote three songs that turned gold that year."

"Truly hard-bitten cynics don't write love songs," I said.

"Deep in the breast of every hard-bitten cynic beats the heart of a slobbering romantic. Only I learned a long time ago, the world makes very short work of romantics, especially in this business, so I built a wall to protect myself. I only let down the drawbridge in my music." He glanced over. "How about you? How'd you get into this racket? Don't tell me you picked up a Raymond Chandler novel and were immediately struck with a vision."

"Hardly," I said. "I happen to be good at digging up information. And I've picked up this nasty habit of eating that I can't seem to shake."

"You were always a private detective?"

"No." I gave him the whole sad story in a nutshell—about how my career as a reporter had come to an abrupt and bitter end when I'd been jailed on contempt charges and about how upon my release six months later, I'd found I'd been fired and labeled a shit-stirrer all over town by my former employer. It would have sounded better with a violin in the background playing "Hearts and Flowers."

"You'd think the goddamn paper would rally behind you, instead of dumping you on your ass," he said indignantly.

"There were some personal things going on between the owner of the paper and myself," I said, shrugging. "He saw an opportunity to ream me, and he took it."

"Ever think of getting back into it? Reporting, I mean?"

"Funny. For a long time, that was about all I thought about. I never considered this as anything other than a way to keep eating until I could land a job writing copy again. But the longer I'm on the outside looking in, the less I miss it. When you're in it, all you can smell is ink. You'll do anything for a story and justify it by telling yourself you're performing some great social service, but really you're just a whore for ink. I may live off other people's problems now, but at least a few hundred thousand other people aren't getting their jollies off because of it." I thought about it. "Maybe that was what I was doing in the county jail—expiating past sins."

He nodded as if he understood. "Payback is a bitch. Me, I don't know of any past sins I've committed that I'd be willing to give up six months for. That's the difference between us, Jake. You've got integrity. That's one reason I like you."

"You're saying you don't have any?"

133

He shrugged. "I might not be willing to do some things other people would to peddle their asses, but that's only because I've made it and don't have to. But it's just like at your newspaper—you can't live in a whorehouse for any length of time and not have some of it rub off on you." He pointed through the windshield. "Here we are. Welcome to Punk City."

The place was a rambling wood monstrosity, the outside of which was covered with a mural of women's faces, some space-age savage with blackened eyes and jet-propelled eyebrows, and some remnants of the late '60s, psychedelic flower children, their big eyes filled with vacuity and their long hair and gauzy diaphanous gowns blowing in the wind.

Nothing else in the area seemed to be open, which was because when the O.N.O. opened its doors at night, the surrounding retail merchants and residents closed theirs. Tight. Every once in a while, like once every other month, some of the O.N.O.'s more spirited patrons would kick up their youthful heels and go on a foray through the neighborhood, breaking store windows and peeing on front lawns, and the local constabulary would close the place down as a public nuisance. The dozen or so punks milling about outside the place as we passed, with T-shirts and red bandannas wrapped around their spiked hairdos, looked as if they were getting ready for another expedition.

We found a parking space on a residential street a few blocks away and walked back past the group of punks and punkettes, who eyed us as if we were recent arrivals from Arcturus. The admission to Valhalla was five bucks apiece; I paid for both and marked it down on my expense pad before we went inside.

The place was not exactly the Stork Club. The cement floors were sticky with spilled drinks, the plywood walls were covered with rock posters. There was a sunken pit in the middle of the room surrounded by a wooden railing, like an English dog-fighting pit, and in it, kids were jumping up and down to a record, wildly bashing and smashing into each other. The wraparound dark glasses a lot of the men wore made it look like the frenzied mating dance of a swarm of night-flying bugs.

We went through a room filled with video games and a large bar, and into the barnlike back room, the walls of which were painted black. There were some tables, but they were already taken, as was most of the standing room in the place. The stage was on the right, a wooden platform elevated six feet off the floor, loaded with huge amplifiers and surrounded by a bank of spotlights suspended from the high ceiling. We went to a stoolless bar at the back of the room and ordered drinks.

The man on my right had a green Mohican haircut and barbed wire wrapped around the sleeve of his army jacket. The woman on Stack's left looked like a featured player from *Night of the Living Dead*, and wore a studded leather dog collar around her neck. I was beginning to feel a trifle uneasy, as if I'd wandered into the middle of a Fellini nightmare.

A stir went through the crowd, and I turned to see the band climbing onto the stage. Wanda was up first, wearing a zebra-skin jumpsuit that was only skimpy laces across her naked stomach and nothing above that except for a black push-up bra. There was plenty to push up. Over that, she wore an unzipped pink leather jacket and, to complete the ensemble, red, knee-length boots with spiked heels and black leather gloves. Her hair was pink-and-bleached-blonde now and fluffed up to look like cotton candy.

The blue-haired bass player was up next, dressed in a blue tutu and white, high-topped Keds, followed by a black man with paper-white hair shaved into a cross over his otherwise bald skull. Next was a burly man with butched hair and wearing a zoot suit two sizes too small. The drummer was the last up. His black hair was combed in a black jelly roll and he wore black wraparound sunglasses, jeans with the knees torn out, and a T-shirt with fuzzy letters that said "FUCK YOU." His small, delicately featured face contained a pale, ethereal kind of beauty that was only slightly marred by the green and red warpaint striping his cheeks.

Restlessness ripped through the crowd as the band tuned up; then Wanda stepped up and grabbed the microphone, and the guitars blasted into a dissonant jumble of cacophony loud enough to warp the wood on the walls.

Fleming's voice was a nasally, robotlike monotone, punctuated with occasional grunts and groans, but the lyrics were unintelligible as she gyrated all over the stage, making obscene gestures with the microphone. She seemed totally unbothered by the screeching feedback from the amplifiers, but all I could do was put my hands over my ears to salvage any internal parts that were still working.

The black guitarist started on a deafening solo and the man in the zoot suit went behind one of the amps and brought out a portable television set, put it on the front of the stage, then picked up a sledgehammer and buried it in the seventeen-inch screen. Cheers from the crowd. Wanda picked up a six-inch .38 and put the barrel in her mouth and began mocking fellatio to delighted cries from the audience, then whirled and fired a round into one of the amplifiers, which exploded into flames. The crowd screamed its frenzied approval, but the screams turned panicky and there was a frightened surge backward as she turned on the audience and emptied the gun into their horrified faces. Some people up front fell, but the band played on, their faces demonic in the spots, and slowly, the screaming turned into nervous laughter as the people got up, checking for blood, and realized she had been firing blanks.

The number ended finally, and they went into a second song that sounded very similar to the first, except this time I made out one line, "I've got nothing to say." I was willing to believe that. During that number, the bass player in the tutu put his instrument on an easel and Wanda cut it in half with a chainsaw. But the topper came at the end of the set, when the drummer opened a box and set loose a bunch of live bats. There were female screams all over the room as the little leathery critters dive-bombed the crowd, trying to echo-locate a way out of the madness. The drummer apparently liked bats, because he saved one of them. He sat there stroking it lovingly, then put its head inside his mouth, bit it off, and swallowed it. The crowd went completely bananas.

"Well," Stack asked, as the applause died down and the band came off the stage. "What do you think?"

"The music was godawful, but I have to admit, I was mesmerized by the violence."

"That's the purpose of it. Takes your mind off the fact that they haven't learned a third chord yet." He pointed at Wanda Fleming, who was off the stage now and heading toward the back exit. "We'd better catch her before she gets outside. Otherwise, you'll have to wait until one tomorrow afternoon."

Interference was being run for her by two burly men who looked like off-duty cops, but even they weren't making much progress against the thick throng of fans crowding around her and I reached her before she got to the door. "Ms. Fleming." She turned and I shouted over the shoulder of a leather-jacketed punk, "My name is Asch. I talked to you this afternoon on the phone—"

"That's right!"

One of the advance blockers turned, and she said to him, "It's okay, babe. Bring him."

We fell in behind the human wedge jostling and shoving toward the door and, after what seemed like twenty minutes, we made it outside.

A gray Caddy limo was parked in the alleyway by the door. The driver, a man of the same general dimensions as the two interference runners, leaned against it with his arms folded, waiting.

"Hey, guys," Fleming said, "this is the guy who pulled my fat out of the fire at Segal's party the other night. What's your name again?"

"Jake Asch." There were some hi's and a few waves. Nobody attempted to shake hands, but I didn't sense any hostility from them. They all seemed quite jovial, in fact. "This is Carey Stack."

"The songwriter?" the bass player in the tutu asked. A trickle of blood ran down the side of his face from a cut on his forehead he had opened during the set, when in an apparent state of rapture, he had bashed himself in the head with his instrument. He materialized a bottle of amyl from beneath his tutu, took a good whiff, and had to steady himself against the limo.

"WHHHOOOOEEE! Dirty socks!" He laughed and offered the bottle to Stack, then passed it when he turned it down. "So, Mr. Songwriter, what'd you think of the set?"

"The choreography was interesting," Carey hedged.

"What choreography, man?" the drummer asked scoffingly. "This ain't *Stayin' Alive*. What we do is a release, man. We got all this violence in us we gotta get out."

Carey's face contorted into a skeptical grimace. "You're not going to try to shuck me with that usual shit about punk being a 'spontaneous expression of youthful frustration and rage,' are you? I didn't see much on that stage that was spontaneous. You're doing the same thing the rest of us are—trying to get money from those kids' pockets into your own—only you're doing it in an even more contrived, self-conscious way than the rest of us." He waved a hand at Tutu. "I mean, come on. Look at yourselves."

"Everything we do relates to one overall attitude," the bass player said.

"Really?" Carey asked. "What attitude is that?"

"If something has been standing long enough, tear it down."

The black guitarist seemed to have other things on his mind than his partner's profundities. He took a hit of amyl and shouted, "I want a burger, goddamnit! You want a burger around here and all you can find is fried fucking chicken!"

I tried to signal Carey to cool it, but he was having too much fun playing antagonist to pay attention. The drummer was looking as if he would like to start gnawing heads—human this time—and I wanted to get Carey out of there before some of that contrived violence fell on us, choreographed or not. "I'm a private detective, Ms. Fleming," I said hurriedly. "I'm working for an attorney named Ed Blackburn and I'd like very much to ask you some questions about what you remember about the party, if you wouldn't mind. Can we talk someplace?"

The perspiration that covered her face had caused one of her huge false eyelashes to come loose and her green eye shadow to run. "Who's the attorney working for?"

"Fred Segal."

She shied away. "I don't know. My attorney might not want me to talk to you. I'm considering suing for damages." Her voice was low and gravelly, sexy in a husky kind of way.

"Wouldn't you like to collect from the person responsible?"

"Segal's responsible," she said. "He handed out that shit."

"I don't think so."

"I *saw* him."

"That's what I want to talk to you about, what you really did see. Look, I don't want a deposition or anything. I just want to ask you a few questions to see if together we can determine exactly what went on in that room. This isn't just a civil case. Two people died."

"Two?"

I nodded. "Julia Roth. Segal's secretary and Cooney's girl friend."

Her look grew troubled. "I didn't hear about that."

I was distracted by the drummer's raised voice. "And what would you call that commercial bubble-gum shit you write, man?"

The band had encircled Stack, except for the black man, who was still bitching about wanting a burger, but Carey seemed unconcerned. He just stood there with his arms dangling loosely at his sides and a nasty smirk on his face. "I think commercial bubble-gum shit about covers it," he said. "Some of them even have a melody line and more than two chords."

"You think we've got time to create works of artistic significance?" Tutu snarled. "Think again. We're running on Doomsday time, Jack." His tachometer was approaching the red line now as he bounced up and down on the balls of his feet.

"Hey, man," the guitarist with the butch chimed in, "I've been playing guitar for twelve fucking years. I studied classical music. I can play Mozart's Fifth with my dick tied around the fretboard, so don't hand me any of the two-chord crap."

"Why don't you, then? It might sound better. And it'd be a crowd-pleasing addition to the freak show you've got going."

It looked like the ending scene in Tod Browning's *Freaks* as Butch, Tutu, and Batman closed in on Stack, primed for the kill. What had me concerned were the driver and two bodyguards. They were uncoiled and ready to strike as Carey took a step back, fists doubled and the same smirk on his lips, waiting for the first one in.

"Cool it, you guys!" Wanda shouted and everyone stopped and turned. They started to grumble and she continued sharply, "I *mean* it, goddamnit! Haven't you assholes had enough trouble for one day?" They obeyed her like scolded children, muttering as they veered off the target. The black one started talking about hamburgers again and everybody relaxed a little.

"Thanks," I said.

She nodded but didn't look happy about it. "Your friend has a problem."

I was angry at Carey for putting me in this position; I had wanted to talk to the drummer, but he didn't look as if he would be in a receptive mood to any friend of Stack's. Maybe later, when he cooled down. "I'd better get him out of here before he gets himself killed. But I really need to talk to you."

"Considering all the trouble you went to for me the other night, I guess I owe you at least that much. I'll be at the hotel in an hour."

"I'll call you."

Carey must have picked up the irritation in my voice when I called him, because as we walked out of the alley, he said, "I'm *really* sorry, Jake. I should've kept my mouth shut, but I just couldn't help myself. A bunch of fucking geeks like that passing themselves off as musicians and trying to get me to swallow it!"

"Never mind. You're just lucky Fleming has those animals trained."

He waved a hand disparagingly. "I've never been up against a man in a tutu I couldn't take."

I had to laugh; he was a hard man to stay mad at. "That guy *was* a piece of work. It was the bodyguards who worried me. They get paid to protect those assholes. They would've stomped you flat before you did much damage."

"We could've taken 'em," he said, as if he really thought so.

"Right."

We pulled into the parking lot of the Rainbow and he asked if I wanted to go in for a drink. I told him no thanks, that I had to call Wanda Fleming in an hour. He said he was glad he hadn't botched things up completely and apologized again and I told him to forget it, that I'd call him the next day.

14

I took my time driving to the Holiday Inn and, not feeling like getting hit by any flying bodies that night, I let the valet park the car. In the downstairs bar, a few touristy-looking couples were listening to the piano player and I bellied up to the bar and joined them. I ordered a greyhound and let the soft, smooth version of "Girl Talk" the man was playing work soothingly on my scarred eardrums. I ordered another greyhound, then almost regretted that decision when a fat man in a red-and-green-checked coat and maroon pants and a white belt requested "Rhapsody in Blue," in a loud Midwestern twang and the piano player obligingly proceeded with the mutilation by starting in the middle of the piece and working backward and forward, whichever struck his fancy at the time, hitting every crack he could along the way. He probably never would have attempted it except for the five-dollar bill Mr. Whitebelt dropped into his tip glass. Wanda would have had a legitimate reason to use her chainsaw at that point, but at least the piano player knew he was in over his head and mercifully wrapped the massacre up quickly and dropped back down to the minor leagues where he was comfortable.

There was a house phone just outside the lounge door and I picked it up and asked for her room. "Hello," she answered.

"Ms. Fleming? This is Jake Asch. I'm downstairs."

"Come on up."

I went back into the bar and downed the rest of my greyhound, tipped the bartender, then took the elevator up to the seventeenth floor.

142

She answered the door in a long green silk dressing gown with flamingos lighter than the pink in her hair all over it. She had removed most of her makeup and I was mildly surprised to see that her features were actually quite attractive, both individually and in the way they were arranged. Her eyes were large and green, her nose short and straight, and her mouth small. She waved me inside with the cigarette in her hand. "Excuse the mess, but I'm a slob."

The living room of the suite was large but plain. Magazines, newspapers, and articles of clothing were scattered over the floor, on couches, and over the backs of chairs. A fifth of Jack Daniel's stood half-empty on the television set, which was tuned in to an old black-and-white movie. The curtains were pulled back from the sliding glass doors that opened onto the balcony. The city glowed out there, hot and cool at the same time, like a banked fire not quite through burning.

"Would you like a drink?" she asked. "All I've got is bourbon."

"Are you having one?"

"I'm laying off for a while," she said, taking a last drag and mashing her cigarette out in a square ceramic ashtray on the coffee table. "*Everything.* I'm not into that artificial stimulation anyway—I'll have a drink or a toot every once in a while—but it kind of freaked me the other night, how close I came."

Her speech quelled any temptation I might have had and I said I was fine. She picked a newspaper and a copy of *Scientific American* from the seat of a chair and told me to sit down. That was hardly the kind of magazine I would have expected a girl with pink hair to be reading; maybe she just liked the pictures.

She sat down on the couch and crossed her legs. The leg that was crossed was naked up to the thigh and it was a good one. I tried not to stare at it too obviously. "Listen, I want to apologize for tonight," I said.

"What for? If Terry didn't want an honest answer, he shouldn't have asked. Actually, most of what Stack said was right on. Hey, all you have to do is look at us to see we *are* this year's freak act. But that's the way things are now. You can't make it on the stage anymore just *performing.* If that were the case, it would be toilet

143

time for us, because none of us has that much talent. But as long as we can cash in on it, I'm not going to bitch."

The almost serene smile on her lips and the calmness in her voice made me wonder if her boycott of drugs was total. It was hard to believe that this was the same bundle of destructive energy strutting the stage an hour ago, chainsaw in hand. "I admire your candor," I said.

"Listen, after twenty-seven years, I'd be stupid to start bullshitting myself." She fidgeted with her robe and said in a low, dusky voice, "That's something you've got to be careful of in this business. It's easy to make yourself believe that all those screams mean something, but when they stop, the fall is twice as high and twice as hard. I've known a lot of poeple who duped themselves, and they're still bouncing."

"Like the girl this morning?"

Her face remained calm. "You heard about that, huh?"

"I saw it. I was coming over to talk to you and got here just after it happened."

She leaned forward and picked up the pack of Carltons beside the ashtray, plucked one out and lit it. She took a drag, then shook her head slowly. "That poor, sick chick. I knew she was goofy, but to go and do something like that—"

"You knew her?"

"Let me put it this way: I had contact with her."

"Who was she?"

She draped a relaxed arm over the back of the couch, and the robe opened, exposing a good bit of cleavage. If she was aware of it, she didn't seem to care. "A demented little groupie who'd hung around the Starlight. She had a thing for Tommy, our drummer. I guess he balled her once or twice and after that, he couldn't get rid of her. She'd send him love notes and come to his room and beg through the door to be let in. Once, she blew the bellboy to get him to let her into the room. Tommy came back from the set and found her naked in the bed and he tossed her out. She wound up hiding in the laundry closet for an hour before Tommy tossed her clothes out."

144

I was starting to get that old adrenal feeling again. "What was her name?"

"I don't know her real name, but she called herself Star. Star E. Knight. Catchy, huh?"

"*Real* catchy."

"That was why everybody was so uptight tonight. Until five-thirty we weren't even sure we were going to have a drummer tonight."

Somewhere I had slipped out of sync and was not tracking. "Why was that?"

"The cops were really raking Tommy over the coals. She went off our floor, y'know, right off the balcony at the end of the hall. They found her purse there. They started asking around and they found out she'd been hanging around like an unwanted house cat and they thought Tommy might have gotten pissed off enough to see if she could land on her feet. Tommy has been known to get a little weird, especially if he's dusted, which he wasn't."

"Weird? What could be weird about a guy who likes to gnaw the heads off bats?"

"That bat wasn't *real,*" she said scoffingly. "It was chocolate."

"I'm glad to hear it."

"He did do a real bat once, but it turned out to be rabid, and he had to go through the whole treatment. He'll do birds now, but not bats."

"Birds," I repeated.

Her smile turned amused and she nodded and took another drag from her cigarette. "It's all a big show-off thing with Tommy. He has to be one up on everybody all the time, be the most freaky, punked-out guy around. He gets off on that rep and it can get out of hand sometimes, but I have to admit, it hasn't hurt the band any. Like a few months ago, we were signing a recording contract with Polydor Records and we were in the president's office and Tommy calmly opens up his briefcase and pulls out a live white dove and bites the poor thing's head off. I mean, it was totally disgusting and none of us knew he was going to do it, but that's

Tommy. You just have to take him whole or not at all, which was what the president wanted to do. He was so freaked, he wanted to cancel our contract right there, but luckily our manager convinced him that Tommy had been under a lot of strain lately and wasn't himself. In the meantime, some New York rock critic heard about it and did an article about us for the *Times*, and then AP picked it up and our attendance doubled."

"There's no business like show business," I said. "The cops think it was murder, then?"

"The girl jumped. She was laying a big guilt trip on Tommy by coming here to do it. Tommy was in his room asleep when the cops knocked on his door. They just didn't like punks and were trying to push their weight around."

"Did the girl leave a note?"

"No."

"Did she try to see Tommy before she stepped off?"

"No."

"I don't blame the cops for thinking nasty thoughts," I said. "I would, too. Anybody who chews the heads off birds is not your normal, run-of-the-mill person."

"Neither is anybody else in this business. Tommy may be a little crazy, but he wouldn't hurt anybody. Not like that. The cops don't understand that to be in this business any length of time, you have to be a little crazy, otherwise you don't survive."

"Why is that?"

"The road is a punked-up place," she said. "You travel three days to go onstage for one hour. You don't eat right, you don't sleep right, you take little helpers to get you up for a show and to bring you down afterward, and all the time you're up on that stage, the audience is screaming for you to be crazy. They *demand* it because that's what they paid their money to see, and the crazier you are, the louder they scream. Anybody seeking sanity and balance in his life doesn't survive in the rock scene. Those people either get out, get kicked out, or die."

"You don't seem so crazy."

She grinned. "I'm a short-termer. I haven't been in long and I

146

don't have the talent to stay in it much longer, which might be a blessing in disguise, actually. But I have a streak of it in me, too." She let out a short laugh. "Hell, sometimes I feel like I'm twenty minutes to meltdown. That's why this job is good for me. I can work out a lot of that craziness on stage. I have a lot of pent-up rage in me I probably wouldn't be able to get out any other way."

"Rage against what?"

Her grin was bitter now, and she shrugged. "The usual assortment: life, parents, ex-boyfriends, the system. See, this was all a fluke. I've seen chicks with really great pipes not be able to make it in this business and here I am, making considerable bucks, and I can't sing worth shit. The only reason I'm in this is because I happened to graduate at the wrong time."

I was out of sync again. "Sorry?"

She got up and turned off the TV, then bent down and got a Coke from the refrigerator. "I graduated from NYU during a recession, when there wasn't too great of a job market for women with degrees in theoretical physics. I worked my way through college as a cocktail waitress and bottomless dancer, so to make the rent, I kept dancing. St. Jacques, the black guitarist you met tonight, used to come into the club and we'd talk and he persuaded me to join the band. He said it didn't matter if I wasn't Beverly Sills, that the instruments would take care of that. I was in a pretty antisocial mood at the time and rock is basically antisocial anyway and it couldn't be any worse than what I was doing, so I said what the hell." She came back and sat down sideways on the couch. "I haven't regretted it. I've managed to store up a little nest egg and by the time this fad passes, who knows? Maybe NASA will be hiring again."

I felt empathy for the girl; her history did not sound totally dissimilar to mine, except that I had no degrees in anything except the street and that the only job I could ever hope to get at NASA would be in the janitorial department. Maybe she'd be the first punk in space. I couldn't picture her at the controls of the next moon mission. I kept seeing her already on the planet.

She tore the tab off the Coke and dropped it into the ashtray.

"Why not? Because I have pink hair and wear spiked-heel boots? You grew up in the sixties, right? When everybody grew their hair long and sat around whining when the cops beat the shit out of them that hair doesn't make the man? Hey, it doesn't sound as if you learned your lessons well.The first thing I learned in physics lab was that everything is illusion. The whole universe is nothing but a big con. Appearances can only deceive."

"You're probably right, and I'm sorry, but I'm just having a little difficulty pulling the images together."

"Why? I know who I am, that's all that matters. I know what color my hair really is. You want to discuss the relativity of mass or the existence of gravitons or the role of intermediate vector bosons on radioactive decay? I can still do that without putting on horn-rimmed glasses and putting my hair up in a bun.

"Hey, a few years back, after the Apollo shot, the papers were filled with horror stories about laid-off NASA physicists and engineers who were working as dishwashers just to feed their families. I'd say I was doing a little better than they were. Academia isn't what I want right now, and believe it or not, I like what I'm doing. I like the money and access it gives me. I like the oddball hours and the tumult and the craziness. Hey, what kid—or adult—hasn't at one time wanted to run off and join the carnival? This is my time and I'm enjoying it."

I couldn't help thinking of the college professor in *The Blue Angel* who gets seduced by Marlene Dietrich and runs off to join the circus and in the end, loses everything—Dietrich, his money, his integrity—and winds up a half-crazed buffoon to a stage magician. Only in her case the movie would probably end with her billed as "The Stripping Scientist," dancing in some greasy, smoke-filled bottomless bar, wearing a mortarboard and nothing else. I hoped that wouldn't happen, because I liked her. Beneath her spiky façade was an honest, intelligent, tough young cookie, one that would have made P. T. Barnum proud. But it was none of my business, and discussing the possible pratfalls of her future was not what I was there for.

I took the picture I had picked up at Cooney's house from my pocket and held it out to her. "Recognize her?"

148

She leaned forward and studied it. "No. Who is she?"

"I'm not sure, but I think her name was Lisa. Unlike you, her big aim in life was to be a rock singer. Only she wound up another victim of the Cooney Curse."

Her head jerked up. "She's dead?"

"So I've been told."

"How?"

"Overdose. I can't verify it positively until I come up with a last name, though."

"I wish I could help you, but I've never seen her before. Why do you want to find out about her? Has she got something to do with this?"

"She lived with Cooney for a while. She also knew Star. From what I've been told, Cooney liked a little kink to straighten out his day and had them do scenes together."

Her eyes widened a bit. "Are you saying Star's death is somehow connected to the others?"

"I doubt that. She's probably just another self-destructive. But I would like to talk to some of her friends to see if any of them knew this Lisa. Would you know who she hung around with?"

She shook her head and handed back the picture. "She always came in with other groupies, but I wouldn't know them if I saw them." She leaned toward me. "Was that for real, what you were saying before about Segal, or were you just saying that because he's paying you?"

"It's for real." She listened with interest as I told her about the other attempts at sabotage.

"Do you have any idea who's behind it?"

"A lot of ideas, all of them different, and very little to back up any of them. Tell me what you remember about the party."

Her recollections were about the same as Cuthburton's, but she definitely remembered Julia handling the bottle before leaving the room. I couldn't think of anything else I wanted to ask her, so I stood up and she walked me to the door. I looked both directions when I stepped into the hall. At one end, beyond the elevators, was a double steel door with panic bars. "Is that where she went off?"

She nodded.

"Thanks for talking to me, Ms. Fleming. You've been a pleasant surprise."

"Wanda," she corrected me. "*That's* not part of the act, by the way."

"Pardon?"

"My name. It's real."

"It's great. I love it."

She nodded and smiled. "My father was a Rhonda Fleming fan. He was probably more in love with her image than he was with my mother. Not that I blame him."

We shook hands. "We'll be in town another four days," she said. "If you want to come back and discuss W particles, feel free."

"The carny would be more my subject."

"Whatever," she said, and closed the door.

The double doors at the end of the hall pulled me to them. They opened onto a small balcony, eight or nine feet long and maybe four wide.

I looked down at the street and shuddered as I tried to imagine what that final terrifying plunge had been like. A shooting Star. Why did she do it? Because her adolescent love had been spurned by a geek drummer? Because years of taking drugs had turned her young brain to Swiss cheese? Because she had been rejected by her father or pissed off at her mother? None of those seemed reason enough, but then people don't just jump for big reasons; more often, they do it for the littlest ones, ones that would never show up on any psychological autopsy. Death due to boredom. Death due to being born when Mars was in Venus. Why the hell not? That was probably as good a theory anyone could come up with to explain why some of them can be coaxed back inside to watch the "Monday Night Movie" while others, uncoaxable, give up the ledge.

Born under a bad sign. Maybe someone should have sent that in to *Showtime* for Star's obit.

I gave up the ledge, but in the other direction, to take the slower way to the street.

15

The service had four calls when I got home: two from Sturgis, one from Sergeant Exley returning my call, and one from Segal, who wanted me to call him no matter how late I checked in. It was nearly one, but I guessed one fell into that category, so I called. He sounded wide awake when he picked up the phone.

"You wanted me to call."

"Yes. How is it going? Are you making progress?"

"I think so, yeah."

"Good." There was a pause. "I got a call this evening from Dean Cuthburton. He was quite upset. He said you barged into his recording session tonight and accused him of operating some kind of counterfeiting operation. Is that true?"

"Not completely."

"What do you mean, 'not completely'? Did you or didn't you?"

"I may have hinted in that direction, but I don't think I accused him in so many words."

"Hinted," he said scornfully. "And do you have any proof to back up those 'hints'?"

"I have a photograph of Cuthburton outside a record pressing plant called Sound Tek loading boxes into a van—"

"Am I hearing right, or is it just late?"

"I have another picture of him at the same plant holding an album that had not yet been released at the time the picture was taken."

151

"And how do you know that?"

"Because Cooney, who had taken the picture, mailed the pictures to himself registered mail. The date is on the envelope and the envelope was sealed."

"Look, what, for fuck's sake, were you trying to accomplish?"

"I was fishing."

"*Fishing?* The only thing you're going to hook with that line, my friend, is a nice fat slander suit." I could hear him breathing heavily. "Listen, Jake, you've put me in a bad position. Dean Cuthburton is a good friend of mine and has been for years, which is probably the only reason he called me before he called his lawyer. He was hot and he wanted to know what's going on. It took some talking to convince him I had no idea. He's talking about taking legal action if he even hears the word 'counterfeiting' again, against you and against me, as your employer—"

"You're not my employer."

"No judge would buy that technicality."

"I didn't say anything in front of witnesses."

"I don't give a shit about witnesses, goddamnit! It doesn't seem to be sinking in. I don't want to lose Dean's friendship and I certainly don't need another lawsuit right now, so stay the fuck away from him and forget about any pictures or Sound Tek or counterfeiting."

"Look, Mr. Segal, if Cooney was blackmailing Cuthburton with those pictures, then he could have—"

"There is absolutely *no way* Dean Cuthburton would be involved in something like counterfeiting," he said sharply. "What for? Money? He happens to be one of the best engineers in the business. He makes plenty." He stopped, and his voice sounded calmer when he started back up again. "In the morning, I want you to take those pictures over to Ed's office. He'll determine what they mean, if anything."

"Yes, sir."

"And stay away from Dean. Otherwise, I'm going to have to fire you. You read me?"

"Yes, *sir*," I said, and as soon as I heard him hang up, slammed the phone down. Fuck him. Who the hell was he to talk to me as if I were some goddamn houseboy? I considered quitting, but remembered that pride was one of the seven deadly sins and decided not to give in to it. So was avarice, but if you give in to avarice at least in the end you have more to show for it. To hell with it, buddy. If he wanted to tie my hands and go to jail for murder, let him. Anyway, there were more approaches than just the direct one.

The phone rang. I debated whether to answer it, then picked it up.

"I've been trying to reach you all day," Sturgis said in a peeved voice. "Didn't you get my messages?"

"I got them."

"You didn't return my calls."

"I've been busy."

Her voice softened. "Busy now? I'll come over."

"I won't be here."

"Where are you going at two o'clock in the morning?"

"That," I snapped, "is none of your business."

"Well, excuse me all to hell," she said in a hurt tone.

Part of my reaction may have been from the bad taste Segal had left in my mouth, but part of it was her, too. Lately, Sturgis had been trying to insert herself into my life with a desperation, dropping by at odd hours, phoning, asking questions about where I'd been and how I'd spent my day, and I was beginning to feel distinctly claustrophobic. She was fun to be with and a superb lay, but I certainly was not in love with her—a fact of which I had apprised her many times, but which she seemed decidedly reluctant to accept—and even if I had been, there was no room in my life right now for another person. I'd gone through too much in the past year and I needed space and distance. Still, I didn't want to hurt her feelings. "It's work. All right?"

"I doubt it. What time are you going to be home? I'll come over and rub your back."

I rolled my eyes upward in exasperation. There she went again. Attack, attack, and attack again until you've got your enemy down. "Rain check." I tried to get her off the subject. "Did you shoot your commercial?"

"No, but I met the director today. He liked my feet. Said they were just like Garbo's. And guess what?"

"What?"

"I have a screen test Friday for a lead in a movie."

"Great."

"It's set after a nuclear war and all these motorcycle gangs have taken over the highways. The part I'm trying out for is the leader of a women's biker gang. The costume I have to wear is really kinky—heavy-duty leather-and-chain stuff. You'd love it."

"A Jewish Princess biker? What's the name of it going to be? *Born to Raise the Rent?*"

"I'll suggest that to the director when I take the test," she said, laughing. Her voice turned coquettish again. "You're sure you don't want me to come over? I could suck your toes."

"It sounds great, but not tonight."

"How can you turn me down? If you really loved me, you wouldn't act like this."

"Probably not," I agreed.

"You're going to blow it, Jacob Asch. You're going to pass up this fabulous deal and it'll be too late and the sale will be off. This is a limited offer here. Only one model left."

"I couldn't afford the payments," I said, and yawned so she could hear it.

"All right, I can take a hint."

"Since when?"

"You can be such a putz," she said. "Sometimes, I don't know why I bother."

"I thought it was because I made you hate men so much that you can go out and do anything you want and not feel guilty."

"I may have come closer to the truth when I said that than I realized."

We said good night and I went into the bedroom and grabbed my little Polaroid from the shelf, and a dark jacket that was warmer than the one I had on, got my set of picks and a heavy screwdriver from the kitchen drawer, and I was ready to go a-burgling.

I wasn't particularly surprised that there were still signs of life in Shady's Alibi Room, but I was hardly expecting to see the lights still on inside Sound Tek at two-ten in the morning. Either the Ainsworths were an industrious couple, or the janitors were working late. I pulled around and parked down the block and went to the alley on foot, figuring I'd better find out which before I stayed out there all night.

As I reached the mouth of the alley, I was startled to a stop by shouting behind me, but it turned out to be just a Shady couple having a domestic tiff as they stumbled out of the bar to their car. I went on down the alley.

A Dodge van, dark blue, was parked behind Sound Tek, alongside a silver Seville. The back doors of the van were open, and one of them was blocking my view inside. I started to move away from the cover of the building to see if I could get a better look, but ducked back into the shadows when the back door of the building opened and a short, swarthy man came out, pushing a dolly loaded with four cardboard boxes. He wheeled the dolly around to the back of the van as if he was in a hurry and began loading the boxes inside. As he was loading the last box, Cuthburton's tall assistant from the photos came out of Sound Tek, pushing a dolly loaded with four more boxes. He and the other man tossed the last one inside and the tall man said, "I think that's all of them, but I'll check with Sid and make sure."

He disappeared inside Sound Tek, then came back out a moment later saying, "That's it."

They threw both dollies into the back of the van with the boxes and shut the doors, and the swarthy man said testily, "I still don't see why the fuck this couldn't wait until morning."

"You don't have to see. Just take my word for it."

"Tell that to my old lady," the man grumbled. "She's gonna ream me a new asshole. I was supposed to be home two hours ago."

"Stop by the graveyard on your way home and pick her up

some flowers," the tall man said. "She'll get over it." He laughed and got in the driver's seat.

I was back in my car, scrunched down in the front seat, when they pulled out of the alley and headed east on Washington. I left my lights off as I made a U and followed, turning them on after half a block or so. This was not a part of the city famous for its nightlife, unless you were into smudge-stained industrial buildings and trucking yards and dark, brooding warehouses, and traffic on the street was virtually nil, making the van easy to follow, but at the same time forcing me to let them get far ahead to keep from being spotted. I had to gun it several times to make lights, then slowed down afterward to keep my distance. Half a mile or so later, they crossed the Southern Pacific railroad tracks and made a left. I goosed it to keep from losing them, but by the time I got to where they'd turned, the van's taillights were nowhere in sight.

My lights caught a sign that said Hoke Street before I dowsed them and turned.

The dark, narrow street was one block of dirty, brick warehouses that dead-ended into the railroad tracks. I shut off my lights and cruised down it slowly. The only place I saw where they could have possibly disappeared was a driveway that ran between two of the warehouses. I parked behind the Dempsey Dumpster in the trash area by the railroad tracks, and trotted back down to the driveway. The driveway provided access to three dingy brick buildings, each separated by a small parking area. The van wasn't in the first, and I was beginning to think one of them might have been a nose-wiggling cousin of Samantha in "Bewitched," when I heard voices. I tiptoed to the corner of the building and stuck out an eye.

The two men were loading the boxes from the van onto the dollies and wheeling them with dispatch through the front door of the last building. They seemed to have the routine down, one going in with a full load as the other came out empty, avoiding collisions with mechanical mindlessness, and in less than ten minutes the job was done. As the tall man locked the front door of the building, I went down the alley to the first parking lot and hid around the far corner of the building until the lights of the van made a left onto the street and sped off. On my way out to the driveway, I noticed a sign in the grimy window of the second building: FOR RENT 275-1934. I jotted the number down on a piece of paper and trotted back to my car to fetch some tools.

The front door of the building had a dead bolt in addition to the simple Schlage tongue lock, and picking it would have taken more time than I wanted to spend. The dirt-streaked window beside the door was secure, and I could probably have jimmied it or, if worse came to worse, broken it, but I wanted to check out other options first and went around back.

The back door that led out to the garbage area also had a Schlage lock, but no dead bolt; it took about half a minute working with a screwdriver and credit card to open it. I slipped inside and waved my flash around the room.

The place was one open storeroom less than a thousand square feet. Except for the thirty or so boxes that were stacked in one corner of the concrete floor, there was nothing, not so much as a chair. I went over to the unmarked boxes and peeled the tape off the lid of one of them.

The box was full of Sammy Hagar LPs called *Metal Madness*, and it didn't surprise me much when I pulled one out and found that Cuthburton had been the engineer for the session, which had taken place at Golden Sound six weeks before. I set that box on the floor and opened the next box down. Sammy Hagar's face stared up at me with a crazed glint in his eyes. I leaned over it with my Polaroid. I popped off two flashes and laid the prints out on the boxes to develop. When I was satisfied they were going to come out all right, I stepped back and shot a couple of the entire shipment, then pulled out two more LPs to add to the one I'd already removed, and resealed the boxes. I hit the lights and went out the back door. I stopped out front to take two more pictures of the outside of the building and went down the driveway to the car. Washington was deserted as I pulled out, and my rearview mirror was clear all the way home.

16

Sammy Hagar's blond locks greeted me from the breakfast table when I went into the kitchen the next morning. I wondered what to do with him while I put on the coffee, then went outside to get the paper.

Carey had been right about Star rating a column, but it was only a small one, on page four. Esther Knight, AKA Star E. Knight, 17, had lived in Beverly Hills and had attended Beverly Hills High. Although her mother, Edie, denied that her daughter would have had any motive for committing suicide, and the police were not "ruling out the possibility of violence," LAPD investigators were leaning toward the theory that the girl had jumped. According to a police spokesman, the girl had been depressed over an unrequited love affair she had going with rock drummer Tommy Balin, and they were assuming she had jumped from the floor of the hotel in which Balin was living as a "final suicide gesture."

I reached Carey at his home. Although he was awake, he sounded as if he'd had a rough night. He confirmed that fact, saying he'd tied one on the night before after he'd left me, to celebrate the new contract. He asked if there were any new developments and I said no, but I wondered if he could do me another favor and find out from whomever he knew at EMI whether the *Metal Madness* LP was out yet and, if not, whether there were any advance copies floating around.

"Counterfeiting again?" he asked, perking up.

"I don't know."

"Not fair, bucko. You want me to do all this legwork for you, but you won't give anything back."

"Sorry, Carey, but I really can't. Not yet."

"Okay," he relented, "but you owe me. I want you to remember that. And when you solve it, I'm going to collect. You're going to have to sit down and fill me in on all the details."

I told him he had a deal and dug out the number that I'd got off the FOR RENT sign on the warehouse. The woman who answered said that I would have to talk to her husband, Mr. Friedlander, if I wanted to know about the property on Hoke Street but that he was out of town and wouldn't be back until the next day. I left my name and number and told her I would call back then.

By the time I had finished dressing, Carey called back with the news that the Hagar album wouldn't be out for another three weeks, and that there were no advance copies available yet. I made him promise he would keep my inquiry to himself, and he made me promise once more that once I'd put the case together, he would be the first to know what it was all about.

Since I couldn't come up with any ideas better than Cooney's, I sealed the Hagar LP and the Polaroid snapshots in a large manila envelope, donned a jacket appropriately dark for visiting grieving mothers, and left.

My first stop was the post office, where I mailed the envelope to myself, registered. Then I went over to the DMV and ran a check on the plates on the van, which turned out to be registered to Bud Jorgensen, 1235 Vanowen, Reseda. Since I had no idea who this Jorgensen character was, I stopped by the West L.A. office of the Computer Credit Corporation, and ran his name and Cuthburton's.

Credit reports can be a gold mine of information; very often, the distillation of a person's life. Aside from being able to tell if someone would be a good risk for a loan, you can get addresses, social security numbers, spouses' names, and names of employers. You can tell what a person owns, what he owes, where he shops, and what he drives. Both Cuthburton's and Jorgensen's credit ratings were clean as a whistle, and I already knew what Jorgensen drove. What I hadn't known, and what I found interesting, was that his present employer was listed as Hot Wax Records, Encino, and that his former employer, from 1980 to 1982, had been Segal Productions. I thought about calling Segal and asking him exactly what Jorgensen had done for him, but decided against it. He hadn't been thrilled the night before by my accusations against Cuthburton, and I doubted his reaction would be any milder this morning. Even though I had some proof that there was chicanery going on at Sound Tek, I still didn't know if it had anything to do with Cooney's death, and I didn't want to get fired before I found out.

Wilshire Boulevard divides Beverly Hills like a set of railroad tracks. The address the western directory had for Edie Knight was on Maple, on the nonmansion side. The street was lined with trees and two-story Spanish revival houses, a lot of which had been divided into half-address duplexes by the owners to help with the property taxes. Edie Knight's address was one of those, upstairs.

The puffy-eyed brunette who answered the door was carelessly dressed in a baggy, green V-necked sweater, a pair of jeans, and sandals. She was early fortyish and might have been fairly attractive if she worked at it, but now, anguish lay on its surface like an oil slick on water. "What is it?" Her voice was flat, expressionless.

"My name is Jacob Asch. I'm a detective—"

"What is it with you people?" she asked shrilly. "Can't you understand? I don't want to talk to you or to any other detectives. All you're interested in is smearing my daughter's name so that you won't have to bother finding out who killed her. Go away and leave me alone."

She started to close the door, but I held up a hand.

"I'm not a policeman, Mrs. Knight. I'm a private detective and I happen to be *very* interested in finding out what happened to your daughter."

The door stopped before it reached my hand. "Why? Why would you be interested?"

"Because I think you may be right about her death. And I think it might be linked to a case I'm working on."

"What case?"

I took Lisa's photograph out of my pocket and held it up to her. "Can you identify this girl?"

She looked at the picture, then scowled. "No. Who is she?"

"She was a friend of your daughter's," I said. "She's dead, too."

"My Esther's death had something to do with that girl?"

"That's what I'm trying to determine." I was counting on the probability that she would be willing to latch onto anything I said that would make her daughter's death not a suicide. At least she would not have to shoulder the responsibility for murder.

"If I could just have a moment . . ."

She hesitated, then pulled the door open. The place had a neat homy look, filled with inexpensive Mediterranean furniture, laden with a lot of embroidered pillows. I smelled coffee brewing.

"Would you like some coffee?"

"I'd love it, thank you," I said, smiling.

She led me into a small breakfast nook and I sat at a Formica-topped table while she poured out two cups. She gave me one and sat down opposite me, then brought out a half-destroyed wad of tissue from her pocket and daubed at each side of her nose. "You said that girl was a friend of my daughter's?"

"Her name was Lisa. You didn't know her?"

"No."

"You never heard your daughter mention her?"

She shook her head. The morning sunlight that slanted through the kitchen window threw aging shadows under her eyes and across her face. "Who was she?"

"She was a girl friend of a rock star named Phil Cooney who died a few days ago."

Her eyes grew animated and she leaned forward expectantly. "Esther knew him. She got really upset when she heard about his death." Her hands started to work, making tiny, quick, explanatory gestures. "She knew a lot of rock stars. That was all she talked about—concerts, rock groups. She was too wrapped up in that whole scene, with those people. I tried talking to her about it, but she wouldn't listen. She was always a little wild, hard to handle, especially after her father and I got divorced. Maybe I just wasn't strict enough, but it's hard when you work nights. As soon as I'd leave for work, she would sneak out with her friends. I couldn't control her." Her mouth hardened into a resolute line. "But she wasn't a bad girl. Wild, but not bad. The police insinuated that she was one of those groupies who hang around rock stars to have sex with them. They wouldn't come right out and say it, but I know that was what they were thinking. They said that was what Esther had gone over to the hotel for—to meet some rock musician. They didn't say, 'have sex with,' but it was obvious what they meant."

Her voice trembled with grief and rage, and the knuckles of her hands whitened as they murdered what was left of the tissue. "The dirty bastards. First they make me look at her—like that—" A sob caught in her throat. "Then they make *her* out to be the villain. What right do they have? What right to make my seventeen-year-old baby into some kind of whore who went crazy on drugs and killed herself? Why don't they ask that punk-rock monster how many drugs he takes and how many young girls he has seduced and how many innocent minds he has helped destroy? They *know* a friend of his called her and asked her to ditch school and come up there. So how do they know he didn't go into some kind of rage when she turned him down and killed her? Why? Because they want to wash their hands of it, and it's easier this way. What right do they have, the bastards? *What right?*"

Her voice cracked and I was startled by the primal, animal-like howl of pain that welled up from deep inside her and spilled out into her tissue. She sobbed uncontrollably for what seemed to be an eternity before she managed to get herself under control again. "I'm sorry."

"It's okay."

"Esther's sister doesn't even know yet," she said thickly.

162

"It'll hit her hard. They were close, in spite of how different they were."

"Where is she?"

"In Europe. She's taking a year off before she goes to college. She starts next fall at Stanford."

I felt a lot of sympathy for the woman. I knew how brutal and uncaring cops could be, and she was probably right to an extent about them not being anxious to take on any extra work if they could file it suicide. Hell, I'd once seen a death listed as suicide in which the victim had been shot in the head with a .44 caliber revolver—twice. But the image of the punk-rock Baal eating up little children was probably stretching things a bit. Any girl willing to blow a bellboy to get into somebody's room knows what she wants. Her daughter probably hadn't been an innocent since she had turned eleven. Still, the woman's outburst of naked, unashamed grief made me uncomfortable, and I felt silly at the same time, like a Peeping Tom who gets embarrassed at the sight of nudity. "You said the police know a friend of Balin's called her. How do they know that?"

"Charlene told me and I told them."

"Charlene?"

"Charlene Wilde. Esther's best friend."

"She live around here?"

"On Reeves, a few blocks over." I took it down. She sniffled, and wiped her nose, then remembered. "You haven't said yet what that Cooney and the girl in the picture had to do with my Esther's death."

"I'm not absolutely sure they had anything to do with it, but your daughter's name came up in my investigation of Cooney's death. I was trying to locate her to ask her some questions when it happened."

Her eyes widened. "My God, you think Esther could have been killed as part of some sort of conspiracy?"

"I don't think so," I said, trying to quench the fires of her imagination before they got too hot. "There's no evidence that any of these deaths were anything more than accidents. It's only a hunch I'm working on. Did you ever hear your daughter mention the name Julia Roth?"

She thought, then shook her head. "I don't believe so. Who is she?"

"Nobody," I said. "Were the police over here?"

"Yes."

"Did they look through Esther's things?"

"They went through her room."

"Did they take anything away?"

"No. They just spent a few minutes in there. They wanted to know if Esther kept a diary. I guess that was what they were looking for."

"Did she?"

"No."

"Have you looked through her things?"

Her lips trembled. "No. I haven't been able to bring myself to do that yet. I, I—"

Her face contorted, but she managed to turn away and temporarily stave off another outburst.

"Would you mind if I looked through her room?"

She shook her head. "I don't think I want anybody violating her anymore. I know it doesn't make any difference to her, but I don't want it."

"I understand," I said, digging out a business card. "I'm sorry to have bothered you at this time. If, when you do go through her things, you find any reference to the names I mentioned, would you please contact me?"

She promised she would, and I asked if she had Charlene Wilde's address handy. She stood wearily and took a leather-bound address book from the kitchen counter and read me the address and phone number. I thanked her and apologized again for intruding during her time of grief, and went to the door. When we got there, she touched my arm and said, "If you find out something . . ."

"You'll be the first to know."

I stopped at a House of Pancakes on Olympic and ordered

164

some bacon and eggs and while it was being cooked, I used the pay phone in the back to call Charlene Wilde's number. Her mother answered. I told her I was a friend of Charlene's from school and that I had to return some books that I'd borrowed from her. I must not have sounded much like a seventeen-year-old because there was a hint of skepticism in her voice when she told me that Charlene would be home from school around three, and I said good-bye quickly, before she could ask my name again.

Walton's secretary put me right through to him when I gave my alias, but he sounded something less than thrilled.

"Yeah."

"J. D. What it is, brother?"

"I ain't your brother, chump."

"It's just an expression, J. D., to remind you of our common goals. You've thought about my offer?"

"You've overpriced your act, man. I could never book you for that much." He was being careful, just in case somebody was listening in.

"I'm sure we can work something out. Why don't we get together and discuss it?"

"I don't think so. I don't see you got that much worth buying."

This was not the way the game was supposed to be played. If he was as unconcerned as he was trying to sound, why did he take my call? I tried to think fast.

"What if I sweeten the deal a little?"

He didn't say anything. Finally, I said, "J. D., you still there?"

"Sweeten with what?" he grunted.

"With what Legrand was looking for in Julia's apartment when I interrupted him." There was a pause, then his voice turned sly. "What might that be?"

"Pictures."

He didn't react but I could almost hear him thinking. Then he asked, "Pictures of what?"

"Let's get together and I can show them to you."

"All right," he said gruffly. "My office, nine o'clock."

"I'd prefer someplace a little less private, if you don't mind."

165

He chuckled. "You are a suspicious motherfucker, aren't you?"

"Yeah, well, I have this thing about my bones. I've gotten used to the way they're arranged and I can't see any reason to change things now."

"I told you, man, that isn't my thing. But you want someplace public, fine. You name it."

"Tiny Naylor's on La Brea. Same time, nine o'clock. And come alone, J. D. Otherwise the deal is off."

I hung up and went back to my booth where my breakfast sat, looking cold and lonely. The over-easy eggs were already semi-congealed, but I was too preoccupied to taste much anyway, and forked them into my mouth without complaint. I'd made a lucky cast and Walton had taken the hook, but I had no idea why. Why would he be willing to spend money to tie Cuthburton into a counterfeiting operation? Did he think he could benefit in some way by exposing the whole thing, or did he plan to use the pictures to get his claws into Cuthburton? Or maybe there was another reason. Maybe he was part of the operation himself. I left the restaurant with a case of indigestion and a head swimming with tadpole possibilities.

It must have been a slow crime day because nobody seemed to be doing much in the detectives' room of the West Hollywood station when I came in, except Momaday. What he was doing was sitting at his desk against the back wall, practicing his walnut routine again. On the wall behind him was a large photograph poster of a motocross rider standing up on his bike. The rider's pants had fallen down to his knees, exposing his bare ass. The caption below read: "Never look back; there may be somebody gaining on you."

"I know how he feels," I said, pointing at the poster.

He disregarded the admonition and glanced behind him, then turned back and nodded. "Don't we all?"

On the desk I spotted the framed color photograph of an attractive, blondish woman sandwiched between two teenage boys with Momaday's dark features. "Yours?"

"Yeah."

166

Lesson Number One about how to win friends and influence people: comment on their family pictures. "Nice-looking family. How old are the boys?"

"The oldest one is fourteen now. He was twelve when that was taken."

I picked up the picture again and looked at it, surprised. "Jesus Christ. He looks like a tight end for the Forty-niners."

He sighed. "You don't have to tell me. I know. I pay the bills. Fourteen years old and he's already six-one and one-ninety. Every day, I catch myself looking at his hands and feet, to see how much they've grown. Seems like every week I gotta go out and buy him a new pair of running shoes. You know what they get for a pair of running shoes today? Thirty, forty dollars. They make the fucking things out of old tires, slap on a lightning bolt and a fancy name and they get forty bucks for them."

With a nod, I commiserated with him about the state of the world and asked where his partner was.

"He'll be back in a few minutes. Why? You want to see him?"

"No, no. I don't think he'd be too thrilled to see me."

"He had nothing personal against you. It's just the way he is."

"Uptight."

He rummaged through his palm looking for meat, his curiosity under apparent control as to why I was there. Finally, he brushed the shells into a chrome ashtray on the desk and looked up.

"What's on your mind?"

"Anything official on Julia Roth yet?"

"Yeah. I had an official-type inquiry about her from an LAPD sergeant named Exley yesterday. He was very interested to learn that you were the one who called it in. He sounded kind of annoyed. Said he wants to talk to you about some things you left out of the statement you gave to the investigators at the Cooney scene, but he feels like you've been avoiding him."

"I've called him back a few times, but he's always out."

He nodded. "I figured it had to be something like that. I told him *you* wouldn't do something like withhold information from the police, that it had to have been an oversight. You didn't hap-

167

pen to have any lapses of memory in the Roth apartment, did you?"

I tried to remember exactly what I'd told him. "Not that I remember."

He tossed up a huge paw. "Good. Let's talk in circles."

"Are the autopsy results in yet?"

He nodded. "Electrocution. It took a while for the breaker to trip. She slow-fried."

"What about the toxicology report?"

"Alcohol, Percodan, some phenobarbitol." He took another handful of walnuts from his coat pocket and played manual trash-masher. He picked out a fat one, popped it in his mouth, and said casually, "Something interesting about that." He didn't follow up, but munched away on the nut.

I leaned forward expectantly. "Like what?"

"No residue of any kind of capsules was found in her stomach."

"What about needle marks?"

He shook his head and tossed another nut into his mouth.

"Don't you think that's kind of peculiar?" I asked.

He shrugged. "Maybe a little. Not much. The dosage she had taken was not that much—maybe a couple of capsules—and you can't build a castle out of that. Who knows how long before she died she took the pills? Maybe she passed them or threw them up, although there wasn't any trace of vomit in her mouth or esophagus." He brushed the shells into the ashtray, then studied me with a sleepy-eyed slyness. "I'll tell you something that is god-damn peculiar, though."

He did it again and I bit again: "What?"

"The M.E. puts the time of death between seven and eight-thirty."

"But the clock radio said—"

He nodded slowly. "Ten-ten. Which means either she set the clock to the wrong time or somebody else did it for her."

"Somebody trying to get tricky," I said.

He nodded again.

"Have you determined where the radio came from?"

168

"Maybe the bedroom. At least there wasn't one in there, and most people keep alarm clocks by their beds."

My mind was tripping now. "If she unplugged it and brought it in from there, it would have *lost* time, not gained it."

"*If* she unplugged it," he said. "Maybe it wasn't running for days."

"That's not likely. She would have needed the alarm to get up for work."

"Maybe she was one of those people who got up at the same time no matter what and didn't need an alarm. Or maybe she was one of those people who always set their clocks ahead so they won't be late."

"An hour and a half?" I said dubiously.

He leaned back and put a shoe that looked like the *Queen Mary* on the edge of the desk. "Who knows? Maybe she was so fucked up that night that when she reset the thing, she got the time all screwed up."

"You can try to explain it away any way you want, it's still peculiar."

"Peculiar, yes. Evidence of crime, no."

"You're not going to file this as an accidental death?"

He emitted a world-weary sigh, took his foot off the desk, and opened his desk drawer. He took out a snapshot and tossed it across the desk at me. It was a color photograph of the nude body of a girl lying on a pile of broken glass on the floor of a room. Her kneecaps were shredded and her face was an unrecognizable pulp of red meat. "Three weeks ago," he said, "a packaged photocopier arrives by mail at an accountant's office on Sunset. It's addressed to the boss, but the boss is out to lunch so his secretary, thinking he's ordered it for the office, opens it up and plugs it in and *kablooey*! The fucking thing explodes, removing her face and most of her legs." He leaned over and looked at the picture again. "Damnedest thing. It blew off her clothes, but didn't seem to damage the torso much at all. Nice body, too."

I handed him the picture and he put it away. "Now, the package had a phony return address, but it was addressed to the boss, so we're assuming the bomb was meant for him, as he would have been the person most likely to use it first—"

"Does this story have some relevant point?" I interrupted with undisguised annoyance.

"The point is, Asch, that we've got somebody out there who mailed a bomb. Now he may have mailed it because of a personal grudge or he may have mailed it because he's some fruit loop who has been a little off-center ever since he got fired for using the Xerox machine wrong and who picked the boss's name out of a hat. Which means that as soon as the guy saves up enough to buy another Xerox machine, somebody else might wind up human hamburger. Now what do you want me to do? Drop that investigation to make a murder out of something that in all probability wasn't?"

"You forgot to mention your retirement."

His face hardened. "What's that supposed to mean?"

I said through a sneer, "That this is one you can tie a nice red ribbon around and put away on the closet shelf before you cut out."

"You really believe that?"

"Fucking-A I do," I said in a tone intended to sound nasty. "You know, that's what really pisses me off about you guys. You all bitch and moan about the lenient judges and the D.A. plea-bargaining away cases by the bushels and you're into the same goddamned thing. Only you do it before it gets to a courtroom."

He said in a voice that almost sounded bored, "Don't try to lay that line of bullshit on me, Asch. Some of what you say may be true, but if you expect me to feel guilty about it, forget it. It's called having priorities. Hell, you want us to take on cases like Julia Roth, fine. You and the rest of the righteous taxpayers out there ante up so the department can put on a thousand new men to do it."

I leaned toward him. "The case smells and you know it."

"It doesn't smell *enough*," he said. "You have a girl dead in her own bathtub with no signs of violence except some bruises you say she had a couple of hours before. The only prints on the radio are hers. The scrips for the pills are hers and only her prints are on the bottles, as well as the glasses and the vodka bottle from which she'd been drinking. Nobody is seen coming and going from her apartment except one suspicious black man, who can't be identified, but that doesn't matter anyway if the M.E.'s time of death is correct, because the dumbest fuck on the street wouldn't kill someone and then hang around for a couple of hours waiting for somebody to find him."

"What if he left and came back?"

He guffawed. "You've been watching too much late-night TV, Asch. *Nobody* returns to the scene of the crime."

"What if he came back to look for something?" I tried. "Maybe he was looking when the lights went out and he had to leave to go get a flashlight."

His eyes narrowed. "Looking for what?"

I smiled. "I don't know. Why don't you listen in tonight and find out?"

His dark eyes remained implacable. "Listen in to what?"

I let him in on what I knew about Walton, lying enough about how I'd found out to make it sound like intrepid detective work rather than evidence tampering.

He watched me steadily and said, "You wouldn't be trying to shit me, just to try to cloud up the case against Segal? Because I wouldn't like it much if you were."

I shook my head. "I wouldn't try to pull anything like that on you. My scalp may flake a bit, but I like it where it is."

He ignored my comment. "We found a bottle of cocaine in her purse, identical to the one at the party that had the heroin in it. We managed to lift a few partials from it."

I started to get excited. "Did you check them against the prints of the guests at the party?"

"They were smudged and there weren't enough points of identification to match anything positively, but I sent them over to the LAPD lab anyway, just to see if we could get any kind of match on the two bottles. I haven't heard back yet."

"If they do match . . ."

"It won't mean a fucking thing. I told you, there aren't enough points of identification. If you're right about Walton, a better bet is this Legrand character. You're sure he's the one who ran you over?"

"I didn't see him in Walton's office, but he fits the general description."

"We can pick him up."

I shook my head. "If he was in the apartment, you'll need something stronger than my say-so to make it stick."

"Like what?"

"Maybe I can sucker Walton into dropping the net on him. And maybe I'll have a wire on when he does it."

"If you're right, and they whacked the girl to shut her up, they might try to do the same thing to you."

"I've thought about that," I said. "What do you think I'm doing here?"

He rubbed his chin pensively.

I tried again. "Look at it this way: you can wipe this off the books tonight and go dig in the dirt with the satisfaction that you ended your career with a good collar. You might never find the Xerox bomber. I'm handing you this one on a platter."

He scowled. "I'm not sure I like that platter bit. You make me feel stupid that I missed all that stuff connecting Walton and the girl."

"I had a reason to look for it, you didn't." I paused. "I'm only saying that to make you feel better and show you how truly magnanimous I can be."

"Fuck you."

I grinned. "Don't look back, somebody might be gaining on you."

The corner of his mouth lifted sourly.

"How about it?"

"If you're scamming me . . ."

"I'm not. You can check out everything I've told you."

He thought for a moment, then sighed, "I guess I could tag along for an hour or so. I suppose you want me to bring the wire?"

"That would be very thoughtful."

We picked a location to meet a few blocks from Tiny Naylor's, and I said, "One favor. The jumper at the Holiday Inn yesterday—I want to find out if there was any evidence of foul play."

"She connected to this?"

"She did scenes with Cooney and Julia, but that's the only connection so far. It just strikes me as a pretty disastrous group."

"I'll make some calls," he said. "I wouldn't want to be gained on twice in the same day."

17

The Wilde house was a small, one-story Spanish stucco with a large arched window in front covered with ornamental wrought iron bars. It was only four blocks over from the Knights', on a similar shady street, and I had been parked outside for almost an hour and a half when a blue Accord loaded with young girls pulled into the driveway, Foreigner blasting out of the open windows. A girl with short, coppery-colored hair, her arms loaded with books, climbed out of the backseat and thanked the blonde driver for the ride. The other pasengers waved good-bye and the driver backed the car out of the driveway and took off.

I got out of my car and cut off the girl's angle to the front door. "Charlene?"

She stopped, looked at me questioningly, then glanced nervously at the house. "Who are you?"

She wore tight-legged jeans and a white sweatshirt that had been purposely shredded at the neck and sleeves, and golden pyramids that dangled from her earlobes. She was short and small-boned, and there was an insolent, yet somehow still innocent sensuality packed into her slim-hipped, almost boyish body that is found only in girls of that age. She would not have it long, though; it was already fading in her heavily made-up eyes. The color was there—blue, like imitation aquamarines—but there was no sparkle in them. How could they look so tired and jaded at seventeen? They had shortcuts for everything these days. It had taken me thirty years to get that look in my eyes.

"My name is Asch," I said, whipping out my license so that she could see I was not a cop or a child molester. "I understand you were a friend of Star's."

She stopped working on the gum she was chewing and puckered her lips. Her mouth looked like a ripe strawberry. "Yeah? So?"

"I'm looking into her death and I thought you might be willing to answer a few questions for me. Star's mother told me you two were very close."

"Is that who you're working for? Star's mom?"

"No."

"Who, then?"

There was challenge in her tone and I tried to think of something that would hit a responsive chord with her, bridge the generation gap. "My client wishes to remain anonymous and if I told you his name, you'd know why. If word got out, the publicity wouldn't do him any good. All I can tell you is that he's a big recording star who was close to Star for a while and who wants to find out what really happened to her."

She blinked. "What do you mean, 'what really happened to her'?"

"My client doesn't believe she committed suicide. Neither does Star's mother."

"Neither do I."

"Why not?"

"She would've told me if she planned to do anything like that," she said. "Star told me *everything*."

"Then she never talked about suicide?"

"No."

"Was she depressed lately?"

She shook her head. "Not at all."

"I hear she was pretty hung up on the drummer from Jiz."

"Tommy?" She wrinkled her nose as if she'd smelled something bad. "That's not who you're working for, is it?"

"No."

"Good, because if anybody pushed Star, it was him."

"Why do you say that?"

She looked toward the front door and squirmed uncomfortably. "Look, mister, I have to go in now."

"I'll give you a hint," I said thinking fast. "The name of the man I'm working for starts with a 'B.'"

Her head snapped back toward me. "Bruce? Bruce Springsteen?"

I shrugged noncommittally, but that was good enough for her. Her eyes grew feverish with excitement. "Gee, I didn't even think he'd remember her. I mean, they were only together a couple of times. She hadn't seen him since his Greek theater concert last year."

"He obviously remembers, and he cares much more than you thought."

She nodded, misty-eyed. "I guess so."

"And he would really appreciate your help on this thing."

Her eyes were hopeful. "You think he remembers me? I was with Star at one of his shows. We were in his dressing room."

"I'll ask him when I see him."

"You can give him my number, if you want." She looked away dreamily, as if she thought dying might be a small price to pay for Bruce's attentions.

"Why did you say that about Tommy pushing her?"

"He was the one she was going to see," she said. She was still hedging, but I decided to let it slide for now.

"When did you last talk to Star?"

She pulled her books tighter to her chest. "Yesterday morning. We have a lit class together."

"Did she say something about going over to the Holiday Inn?"

"She said she was going to ditch school and go over there. I guess somebody called her the night before—some friend of Tommy's—and said Tommy wanted her to come to the hotel at noon. She was all hyped up about it. She dug Tommy. I could never understand why. I mean, he's far-out looking and all that, but he's a little too freaky for me."

"Freaky how?"

"In every way you can be. He's just totally weird."

I wasn't going to argue with her on that score. "Did she say who the friend was who called her?"

176

"Uh-uh."

"How long have you and Star been friends?"

"Since grade school."

"Did you know Phil Cooney?"

"Sure. He was another weirdo."

"Why do you say that?"

She winced. "Well, maybe not that weird. He was just fucked up all the time. And I mean *all the time*. And he likes scenes, y'know?"

"What kind of scenes?"

She said unabashedly, "Whatever he could put together. He wasn't too particular. I went over to his house a couple of times with Star, and they tried to get me involved in some things, but I never went for it." She paused. "Besides, he was nothing anymore."

I wondered if she would have gone for it if Cooney had been a chart buster at the time; I had a feeling that if Bruce Springsteen had told her to get into a chicken suit and bark like a dog, she would have gladly done it. I took the picture of Cooney and Lisa out and showed it to her. "Did you ever meet this girl?"

"Lisa," she said. "She lived with Phil for a while."

"Would you happen to know her last name?"

"Trent," she said. "But if you're looking for Lisa, you can forget it. She's dead."

"Do you know when exactly?"

Her eyes rolled up to the sky, as if she expected the answer to be written there. "It was around Thanksgiving sometime. Yeah, I remember because we went to my aunt's house up north and when I came back, Star told me that they'd found her body up in Topanga, that she'd O.D.'d."

"Where did you meet her?"

"With Star, up at Phil's place. That was when she was still living there, before Phil kicked her out. I guess she turned into a real junkie and stole some things from him to buy dope."

"Did you ever hear her mention anything about her father?"

Her brows bunched together. "Her father? No, but then I didn't really talk to her that much. Things were going on over there all

177

the time when I was there, and nobody was much in the mood to talk, if you know what I'm saying."

"How about a woman named Julia Roth?"

She shook a finger at me. "I remember her. She was at Phil's one of the times I went over with Star. She and Lisa and Phil were in bed, naked, and he wanted Star and me to get undressed and join them, but, like I said, I don't go in for group scenes, y'know, so I split."

"Star did?"

She shrugged. "I really loved Star, I really did. I mean, I can't believe she's gone. But she did have some problems to work out. She was always getting herself into weird shit with the biggest jerks. Real loadies or weirdos like Tommy. You know what I think?"

"What?"

Her face grew serious. "I think she was looking for her father in all those guys. He was a loadie, too. A real alky. Every time I saw him, he was stoned out."

I nodded as if interested, then tried to divert her attention from her amateur psychoanalysis of Star's ex-problems to more concrete matters. "What kind of thing was she into with Tommy?"

"What do you mean?"

"Why did you say he was the one who pushed her, if anybody did?"

She shifted her books around and bit her lip, trying to make up her mind.

"I promise anything you tell me will be held in the strictest confidence."

She really wanted to tell me and that iced it. "Star thought she might be pregnant," she said quietly. "That was one reason she went over to the Holiday Inn. She wanted to talk to Tommy about it."

"It was his?"

"She wasn't even sure she was pregnant. She was only a week overdue. She was pretty regular, but a week's nothing. Anyway, that was what she was going to tell him. She wanted to see what he'd say. She thought he might give her some money for an abortion."

178

"She was going to try to extort money from him?"

"She was going to tell him about it and see what he said, that's all. She was playing a head game with him."

"Have you told that to the police?"

She shook her head. "I haven't talked to the cops at all."

"Does her mother know?"

"Oh, no. I'm sure Star didn't tell her and I sure wouldn't. Are you going to tell her?"

"No, but the cops might."

Her expression grew fearful. "But you promised you wouldn't tell anybody any of this—"

"Look, what if Star went to Tommy and laid a trip on him about being pregnant and he flipped out and killed her? Would you want him to get away with it?"

She hesitated. "No." Her eyes widened. "You think that's what happened?"

"I don't know. But I do know that the information could have a bearing on the way the police handle the investigation."

She looked down at the ground and said grudgingly, "I guess so."

I patted her on the arm. "Good girl. Bruce will be proud of you."

She looked up, hopefully. "You really think so?"

"I know so."

I gave her a card and asked her to call me if she heard anything or thought of anything else that might be pertinent. She said she would, then asked me for another card. I gave her one and she wrote her phone number on the back of it and said, "Give this to Bruce when you see him and tell him to call me. If he doesn't remember who I am, tell him I'm the one with the butterfly tattooed right here—" She pointed to a spot on the inside of her thigh.

Anticipation had crowded thoughts of Star to the back of her mind now, her celestial light washed out by the blaze of Bruce. It was very cold in space.

"I'll tell him," I said, and left.

18

The case was ready to crack; I could feel it. As a little pre-wrap-up celebration, I stopped by Valentino's and treated myself to an early dinner of veal piccata and pasta, before heading home.

The anticipation was building by the time I got there. I tried watching the news, but was too antsy to handle that, so I took a hot shower, got into some more comfortable clothes—jeans, a blue windbreaker, and my Ponys, in case I had some moving to do—and drove over to the airport. I rented a new Subaru from a Budget office there, just in case Walton had the bright idea to try to trace my plates, then killed some time in one of the terminal bars, sipping vodka and watching the planes take off. That only made me more antsy, thinking about all of the wonderful, far-off lands of incense and mystery those planes were headed for; so I left. I had my own mystery going. I didn't need to go to Istanbul for one.

I spotted the unmarked car as soon as I pulled into the restaurant parking lot; it was the only Dodge car with a head the size of a basketball behind the wheel. I pulled into the empty space beside it and got out. Rhodes was slumped down on the passenger side, his cowboy hat tilted over his eyes.

"Good evening, gentlemen," I said, sliding into the backseat.

Momaday said hello, and Rhodes grunted under his hat.

I said to Momaday, "He's in his usual good spirits, I see."

"What have we got to be in good spirits about, Asch?" Rhodes growled, pushing up the front of his hat with two fingers. "I could be home right now, kicking back with a brew in front of the tube. Instead, I'm out here in this piece-of-shit parking lot providing backup for some jerky gumshoe so he can milk a few extra bucks out of a client. It's bullshit."

"Maybe," I admitted. "But look at it this way: you probably couldn't have gotten home early enough to catch 'The Flintstones' anyway."

Momaday chuckled. Rhodes's face reddened, but before he could verbalize his vexation, Momaday headed him off. "Relax. And don't give me any of that 'home' crap. If you weren't here, your ass would be warming a bar stool in that shitkicker bar you always hang out in."

"Yeah, well, that'd beat the shit out of this," Rhodes grumbled.

"Consider it a retirement present for me," Momaday said.

Rhodes turned away with a disgusted look and I asked Momaday if he had found out anything about Esther Knight.

"They're looking into it, but nobody is going to get eyestrain. The girl was apparently on her way to some punk rocker's room. She'd been bugging the guy for some time, I guess, trying to get into his pants, but he wasn't going for it. Anyway, he claims she never got there that day, and they found no violence in there, or in the hall or on the balcony where she went over, and nobody staying there heard anything resembling a struggle or arguments. They found her purse on the balcony, set down neatly by the railing, and they found a couple of her palm prints on the railing where she climbed over. They figure it was just another teenage suicide—one pill and two disappointments too many."

"Her mother doesn't think it was suicide."

"So what's new?"

"Have they done an autopsy yet?"

"They're working on what's left, I guess. If toxicology finds any drugs, I guess that'll ice it."

"Tell them to check for pregnancy, if they can."

His heavy lids lifted a little. "Pregnancy?"

181

I related Charlene's story and he shook his huge head. "So what if she was pregnant? What's it got to do with Julia Roth?"

"I just thought whoever is handling the Knight investigation might be interested."

"I'll pass it on."

"Still," I said, "it *is* kind of weird."

"What?"

"The chick and her groupie girl friend used to do scenes with Cooney and Julia Roth and within six months, they're all dead."

"I don't find it particularly weird," Momaday said. "These people live in the fast lane, Asch. Drugs, sex, and rock and roll. Casualties run high."

Rhodes yawned and slid the cowboy hat back over his eyes and slumped back down in his seat. "Wake me when it's over."

Momaday thought about it and shook his head again. "In most pretechnological Indian societies, the punishment of a murderer was the responsibility of the victim's family. There was no socially imposed punishment. The victim's family could demand from the family of the murderer either the death of the murderer or retribution in the form of payment. Things were a hell of a lot simpler: just let them sort it out."

"Did they have Indian private eyes then? Hell, for a case like this, I could have gotten a goat and six cowrie shells."

Rhodes mumbled something else I couldn't understand, but which I automatically took to be derogatory. Momaday reached over him and opened the glove box and took out a recorder-transmitter, about the size of a pack of cigarettes. "Where do you want to put it?"

"Somewhere they won't find it if they decide to look."

From beneath the cowboy hat came, "Tape it to your balls. They won't look for it there unless they're fags."

Actually, that wasn't a bad idea. Momaday handed me a roll of adhesive tape and I unzipped my pants. "You're sure this thing works?"

"It works."

I went about taping the recorder into position, trying not to think about what it was going to feel like taking it off, and Rhodes sat up and looked over the back of the seat. "You're shittin' me. He's actually doing that?"

I smiled at him. "I wouldn't shit you, Rhodes. You're my favorite turd."

Rhodes's face crinkled in disgust. "All I know is, I'm not touching the fucking thing afterward."

After I was satisfied the bulge wasn't visible through my pants, I took out my wallet, pocketed a couple of dollars from it, then handed the wallet to Momaday.

"What's this for?"

"In case Walton wants to double-check the name I gave him."

He nodded and dropped the wallet into his coat pocket, then checked his watch. "If you get into trouble, say, 'I'd better be going now,' and we'll move in."

"Right," I said, and got out of the car.

"And Asch . . ." Momaday said.

I turned. "Yeah?"

"Watch your ass."

I grinned. "I'll be sitting on a mirror the whole time."

They pulled out and I gave them a couple of minutes' head start before I followed. It was a couple of minutes before nine when I pulled into the parking lot of Tiny Naylor's. The lot was almost full and I didn't see either Momaday's Dodge or Walton's Lincoln. I had to hand it to them; when they went undercover, they went undercover.

I parked in an empty slot and sat there peering through the restaurant windows, but could not pick out Walton among the patrons. I got out of the car and was on my way inside to check things out when a car horn honked behind me. Walton's Lincoln pulled up and stopped and he stuck his head out of the window and signaled to me. His engine was still running and I approached the car cautiously. "Get in," he said when I got up next to the door. He appeared to be alone.

I glanced back at the restaurant. "What's wrong with inside?"

"I don't discuss business in public. Too many ears to pick up things. And then there's the fact that I don't know who the fuck you are or who you came here with or what you want."

"I didn't come here with anybody and I told you what I want," I said, checking out the backseat. "Dinero."

"Uh-huh," he said dubiously. "You can tell me about that while we take a nice scenic drive around the block." He caught the hesitant look in my eyes and said, "What you nervous about, chump? You think I'm that bad? Even if I was, I'm driving the fucking car, which means I'm going to have two hands full of steering wheel."

Walton flipped up his hand in an impatient gesture. "Look, man, you said come alone, so I'm alone. You said you wanted to deal, I'm here and ready to deal. But make up your mind, because this is it right here. I don't fuck with you anymore after tonight. No more calls, no more office visits. Whatever shit you got to peddle, you peddle it elsewhere after tonight."

I didn't have much choice. If he drove off now, even if I managed to talk him into another meeting, I would never get Momaday and Rhodes to tag along. I'd just have to trust in their skills at surveillance.

I went around to the passenger side and, as I got in, I was hit by the strong musk scent of his cologne. He had on a black suit and gray silk shirt with no tie. The collar of the shirt was flared over the lapels. He backed up and turned right on La Brea. As we drove, he kept his eyes on the rearview mirror, which I purposely tried not to look into.

"You bring the pictures?" he asked as he switched lanes without signaling. His eyes were like Stick Ups on the mirror.

"You bring the money?"

"Wait a minute. I don't even know yet that I want to buy. What are these pictures supposed to be of ?"

"You don't know?" I asked.

He shook his head, then switched back into the right-hand lane and turned on his blinker for Santa Monica.

"Julia didn't tell you?" I asked, fishing.

"No."

"You should have kept Legrand on a tighter choke chain and maybe she would have."

"You back on that? How many times I gotta tell you I had nothing to do with Julia steppin' off?"

I put both hands on my chest and looked down as if I was inspecting for mustard stains. "Are there turnips growing on my shirt or something?"

"Look, motherfucker, I don't give a shit whether you believe me or not, but just for the record, the junkie-ass bitch was already dead when Legrand got there."

"He just pop over for a cup of tea at eleven at night? Is that what he was taking her drawers apart looking for?"

A skinny black hooker wrapped in a fur coat that looked like it had been made from forty-two Chihuahuas that had died of Parvo stood on the corner of Santa Monica, eyeing us as we slowed for the light. She must have thought we were slowing for her, because she showed us a mouthful of piano keys and started toward the curb. The piano keys retracted when Walton turned the corner and hit the gas. "Runty-assed bitch," he mused, glancing at her as we passed.

I wasn't about to let him get sidetracked by a moth-eaten fur. "Legrand was looking for something. Julia called you shortly before she died. You knew about the pictures. It doesn't take a genius to put together what he was doing there."

"Julia called me, yeah. She told me she had something she thought I might be interested in buying, some pictures. I asked what they were and she said to come over with five grand and I could find out. She said she needed the scratch to get out of town, that everything had fallen apart and she had to get away. I thought she was just pumping air castles into my skull, just to get her hand on the bread. She was totally wasted when she called and the bitch was a freak for scratch."

"But you sent Legrand over anyway."

"Hey, Julia and I went way back. She was going through an emotional time. I was more than happy to help her out."

"And yourself at the same time. You could hardly have her running around loose in her condition. She'd become too squirrelly. Too many drugs, too much booze, and too much guilt make for a bad security risk. Hey, in a way, I don't blame you for taking care of business like that. The bitch was greedy. I told her so when she told me she was going to put the bite on you. I said, 'Hey, babe, that's not right, not after the man laid all that bread on you over the past year.' I told her she was just buying herself trouble, that that sort of shit always comes back at you, but she wouldn't listen. She just kept saying that she had it coming after everything that had happened, that it was your fault Cooney was dead. She said you owed her."

A little knot of muscle rose on his smooth jawline, just beneath the ear. His eyes looked angry in the rearview mirror as he slowed for Fairfax. He didn't say anything as he turned right on Fairfax and headed back in the direction we had come. "I owed her shit. Every fucking thing she owned, I bought."

"Well, don't worry, J. D. I'm not Julia. I'm not greedy and I have no ax to grind. This is a one-shot deal with me—in and out."

"How much?"

"Tell you what: since I want to get this whole thing cleaned up tonight, and since I hate dickering, I'll give you the whole package—the pictures and my disappearance—for the same five grand Julia was asking."

He looked into the rearview mirror, but his eyes remained unexcited. Momaday must have been doing a crackerjack tail job. Or he wasn't there. Two miniskirted working girls with teased hair stood on the corner of Sunset, either looking for phone change or counting up their quarter tricks for the evening. Walton stopped on the signal and turned to me. "You still haven't said what these pictures are supposed to be of."

I watched his face closely. "A little counterfeiting operation."

Both eyebrows jumped. "Segal's into counterfeiting?"

I stepped back in the pocket and started looking for my secondary receivers. Since he was the only one there, I tossed him the ball and hoped he would hang on this time. "That's what Julia told you? That Segal is involved with Sound Tek?"

He looked as if he were having some fun now. "I don't know shit about Sound Tek, man. All Julia told me was that once those pictures were made public, Segal wouldn't be able to book a square dance in Lodi."

I tried to decipher something out of the barrage of thoughts that rushed at me, but there were too many. One of the two hook-ettes bent down and smiled, and when I looked up; I realized why. The light had changed, but we were not moving, and she must have mistaken that for prurient interest. I turned to tell Walton that the light was green, when the car door was yanked open and a forty-pound trip-hammer slammed into the side of my neck, turning the night into the Fourth of July. Powerful hands grabbed the front of my jacket and shoved me over the seat, and then a body squeezed against me and the car door slammed. Somebody yelled, "Go!" and we took off. My vision was starting to clear when a forearm was jammed into my throat, cutting off my air supply, and when I tried to protest, it pressed harder. I hoped Momaday would interpret the meaningless gurgling sounds coming out of my mouth as "I think I'd better be going now," but I wasn't counting on it. I clawed at the arm and tried to twist away, but all that bought me was less air, and then I was floating above the seat watching myself struggle against the bullet-headed black man who was trying to kill me, until the fireworks fizzled and died along with the city lights outside.

I surfaced through a blurry, pain-filled haze. I seemed to be breathing again, which meant that unless this was a scene from *Sunset Boulevard*, and I was Bill Holden explaining by voice-over how I got to be dead in the pool, I was still alive. I tested out the theory by trying to swallow, then decided I wouldn't attempt that again for a while. I felt as if I'd just swallowed two bottles of meat tenderizer.

The black face that stared at me when I opened my eyes wasn't Walton's. It was big and beefy, with fat, fleshy lips and the yellow, menacing eyes of a Rottweiler. A diamond was stuck in the side of his wide nose, and his smooth, shiny head was smaller than the neck it flowed into.

"I believe you've met Legrand before," Walton said. He was still driving and I was wedged between them in the front seat.

I sat up and tested my vocal chords: "I recognized the fist, but not the face. It was a little dark that night." I glanced at Legrand. He *did* look like a Rottweiler in spite of the diamond and the brown leather coat. "Is that his lower lip or is he wearing a turtleneck?"

"Let me jack the motherfucker's head up," Legrand snarled, his right hand clenching and unclenching in anticipation. It was the hand of a surgeon—the kind who removed hearts and other vital organs in back alleys without benefit of an anesthetic.

"Be cool, brother," Walton told him in a warning voice, and Legrand settled down into a pouting silence and transferred his glare out the window. It was my turn to be warned: "You shouldn't fuck with Legrand. He don't like white people too much."

"Really? Some of my best friends are white."

"Let me jack the motherfucker's head up," Legrand repeated.

"He's a regular Chatty Kathy," I said. "Is that all he says, or does he have a whole repertoire?"

My dislike of being manhandled was overcoming my prudence. I was 0 for 2 against the guy and there was no reason to think things were suddenly going to turn around. I was relieved when Walton held up a hand and said, "Easy, brother." Legrand obeyed the command grudgingly, and Walton said to me, "I ain't jivin' about Legrand. He did a dime in the joint for carving up some white boy's booty finer than a cat hair."

Not trusting my tongue to comment appropriately on Legrand's prejudices, I skirted the subject. "This doesn't exactly show good faith, J. D. You were supposed to be alone."

"Good faith has to be tempered by good judgment," he said, smiling. "And what about yourself? You come waltzing into my life uninvited and threaten to put my business in the street unless I pay you and you won't even give me your right name. Shit. You're so afraid I'm gonna find out your name, you don't even carry a wallet. You call that good faith?"

They had gone through my pockets while I was out. A wave of panic hit me and I wanted to grab my balls to see if they had found the transmitter, but I stopped myself. I thought I could feel it when I pressed my legs together, but I wasn't sure. "Why should I carry a wallet? I know who I am."

"But I don't."

"You don't need to. I'll be out of your life as soon as we conclude our business tonight. Consider me a ship passing in the night. A foggy night."

At La Brea, he turned right again, without acknowledging Tiny Naylor's with so much as a backward glance. "Oh, I consider you a lot more than that, Mr. Asch," he said in a voice like satin. "I consider you a potential motherfucking iceberg."

The sound of my name set off a smoke alarm in my head. I was beginning to like this entire scenario less and less. "I've known who you were from the day you came to my office. Julia told me Segal had hired a detective named Asch to sniff out the traitor in his ranks. It didn't take a lot to find out he was none other than our mysterious no-name friend."

Legrand was smiling now. He seemed finally to be enjoying himself. My eyes darted uncontrollably to the rearview mirror, but if Walton had been watching all this time and not spotted a tail, it wasn't likely I'd see anything comforting in a two-second glance. Then it hit me like a glass of ice water in the shower— Rhodes. Walton couldn't see them back there because they weren't there. That prick Rhodes had convinced Momaday that this whole thing was bullshit and they'd gone home to their nice warm houses to watch "Dukes of Hazzard." Son of a bitch.

"I didn't do anything about you," Walton said, "because I didn't know exactly what to do. I was waiting to see how big a problem you were going to be. I was hoping I could ignore you. But when you called and said you had those pictures, I got intrigued."

"You've got other problems besides me, J. D. The cops found the coke vial from the party in Julia's purse. They've got the scent. It won't take them long to find your door. Look how long it took me."

"Ah," he said, holding up a finger, "but you've obviously got a devious mind. You also had a reason to find me. They don't. They got what they need—Segal—and as long as you don't go around with your jib flapping in the breeze, they'll probably be real happy to keep him. *That's* what we got to deal with."

Traffic was thinning as we crossed Olympic, heading toward the freeway. I thought about trying to jump out at a stop light, but we were hitting them all. If I had been alone, I wouldn't have made one. Not that it would have mattered; I was wedged in too tightly to have any chance of making it out without Legrand being awarded both ears and tail.

"How do you propose to do that?" I asked, not sure I wanted to hear the answer.

"That'll depend on what you want to do, and on whether those pictures exist and are what you say they are."

"They exist." I looked around. "Where are we going?"

"That'll depend on you, too." His tone became prosecutorial: "Who's in them?"

"Dean Cuthburton and Sid Ainsworth, the owner of Sound Tek, and another man I don't know."

The oncoming lights deepened the crease in his brow. "What do they have to do with Segal?"

"I didn't know they had anything to do with him until you mentioned it."

"Does Segal know about them?"

"No," I lied.

His mouth turned up into a sly smile. "Why not? He's your client."

"No reason to," I said, trying to gauge what it was he wanted to hear. "I figured I might be able to make a little bread on the side with them."

If that wasn't what he wanted to hear, it was close enough. He nodded and smiled. "Who were you planning to hit up? Cuth-burton?"

"Maybe," I said, purposely hedging.

"Then you shouldn't mind sticking to the original deal. Except

190

this time, it's my turn to sweeten the pot. If the pictures are what you say they are, and you can prove Segal is tied into it, I'll give you ten thousand."

"*Ten* thousand?"

He nodded.

"And if I refuse?"

He shook his head sadly. "Baby, let's not even get into that. There ain't no need. You and I can reach an agreement without all that bullshit gettin' into it."

His changes were bewildering. Like a confused chameleon trying to change color on a plaid coat, his dialect flip-flopped constantly between Cambridge and the ghetto, and I wasn't sure whether it was all contrived. Below the calm surface, there was something powerful and feverish and out of control.

"I don't know," I said uncertainly. "I don't want to get mixed up in murder. . . ."

"There you go again," Walton said, tossing up his right hand in a frustrated gesture. "It ain't bad enough you go stirrin' up shit that's true, you gotta go around and stir up a bunch of fantasy shit. What murder you talking about?"

"Julia."

His palm came down on the steering wheel. "How many times I gotta tell you, man, I had nothin' to do with Julia's death. She was dead when Legrand got there, just like I told you. I had no reason to want to kill her."

He was worked up now. I threw it out and held my breath. "You gave her the heroin that killed Cooney."

He made a face. "I didn't tell the stupid-ass bitch to *kill* anybody. It wasn't my fault she switched the shit pure. I only wanted to piss a few people off. I wouldn't have trusted her with the job if I'd known what a flaky fucking pillhead she'd turned into. That honky motherfucker Cooney did that to her. Far as I'm concerned, he did it to himself. And Julia couldn't have brought me into it unless she wanted to flush herself, too."

There it was. We had him. The only trouble was, he still had me.

191

There was only one set of headlights fairly close behind us and they turned off as I watched the rearview mirror. If Momaday was tailing us, he must have been using a telescope to keep us in sight. I concentrated on converting my anxiety into an appearance of hesitancy; I didn't know if Walton was trying to sell me a lie with this offer, but I wanted to make him believe I would accept, and he wouldn't if I caved in too readily. I shook my head and bit my lip. "I'd be dumping Segal in the shitter. . . ."

"He's going in the shitter anyway," he said, waving a hand. "*I'm* taking over. A few more moves and this town is mine. You got to go where your bread is being buttered, baby. I'm the one whose interests you got to look out for, not Segal's. I'm the one who's gonna be able to do you some good. I'm your future, baby." He seemed to be working himself up into some kind of megalomaniac rapture and he grinned demonically as he ran a private screening of his visions inside his head. He threw a glance at Legrand. "Legrand, give me a toot, man."

Legrand pulled a small paper packet and a skinny plastic straw from the inside pocket of his leather jacket. He carefully unfolded the paper, dipped the straw in it, and held it out across me, to Walton. He held the straw up to Walton's nose and J. D. took a noisy hit in each nostril without ever taking his eyes off the road. Walton offered me some and shrugged when I declined. Legrand took a couple of toots and put the stuff away and Walton said, "You got to learn to seize your opportunities, Asch, otherwise you're fucked. How do you think I got to where I am? By being nice? Shit, man, I grew up in Compton, the blood-leakage capital of the world. I made up my mind when I was eight years old I was going to get out of there, but you don't get out of there by being nice. You get out of there by getting your shit down and doing *what is necessary*. You pimp and you steal and you hustle your way out. I knew what I wanted—what the white man had—and I did what I had to do to get it. I knew that I was going to have to deal with white people, so I educated myself and learned to speak white and pretty soon I found I had a jump on any white man I met. You know what that jump is? The ghetto. It was a survival course, man. You learn as a kid, you get into a fight, you move first, move fast, and go for a vital part. You honkies have had it too soft too long. Your lag time is too great. That's why I know Segal's ass is mine. You want to stick by him, go ahead. You might be able to squeeze a couple of bucks out of it. But stick with me and I'll take you to the fucking moon, baby."

I didn't want to be the one to break the news to him that there is no air on the moon. The overpass for the Santa Monica Freeway loomed up ahead and I said, "Get on the freeway going west."

He looked at me curiously. "Where we going?"

"Playa del Rey."

"What's there?"

"Your pictures."

He beamed. "That's my man. Now you're getting smart."

Legrand folded his arms and grunted, unhappy he was not going to get to jack my head around.

As we got onto the freeway, I asked Walton, "Just out of curiosity, if I hadn't taken your offer, what would you have done with me?"

He smiled and said casually, "Ever see that movie *The Warriors*? Where a white gang gets caught on the wrong side of town and they have to fight their way through a bunch of other gangs to get back to their own turf?"

"Yeah."

He nodded. "I would have driven you over to Compton and dropped you off in front of a place I know and split."

"I get the picture," I said, and settled back, trying to forget it.

Walton and Legrand spent about eleven of the fifteen minutes it took us to get to the beach with their noses in the paper packet, while my mind was absorbed in plan and prayer. By the time we were a block from my apartment, I'd abandoned the plan and was totally converted to prayer. Walton pulled into the driveway and parked, and we got out of the car. I might have thought about rabbiting if Legrand had not had a viselike grip on my upper arm. I talked to my crotch. "I think I'd better be going now."

"What you say, boy?" Legrand asked.

"I said, 'I guess I better be going now.' "

He looked at me as if I were nuts. "You goin' all right, mother-fucker, don't worry 'bout that."

"Which one is it?" Walton asked.

"Upstairs," I told him and glanced back hopefully at the driveway.

"What you lookin' for, motherfucker?" Legrand growled suspiciously and tightened the grip on my arm.

"The Little Big Horn," I said, and then the grip on my arm was released as Legrand froze in his tracks and blurted out, "Holy Jesus."

The vision was not in the driveway, but stepping out from behind a car, and it was straight from a De Sadean horror movie. It stood six-four, and wore black-leather football shoulder pads, a chrome-studded, black-leather bra that crisscrossed underneath and around ample breasts, a ribbed corset of black leather, and black leather boots that went halfway up the thigh. Blond spikes of hair stood out like a thorny halo around the black hockey-goalie's mask that covered the face, and it held a wicked-looking spiked mace in one black-gloved hand. "I am Leah, Queen of the Highway," the vision announced, holding up the mace menacingly. "You must pay me tribute to pass."

Legrand dipped a hand into his coat and I yelled, "No!" and shoved him when I saw the gun he held. The shot went wild and as he turned it on me, the automatic was spotlighted by the headlights bouncing into the driveway. He wheeled around to confront the sound of screeching tires, but froze when he heard the shout, "Police! Freeze, asshole!" and saw the two magnums staring him down from behind the open doors of the car.

"Drop the fucking piece and put your hands on your head," Rhodes's voice said.

Legrand complied with the command, and I let out the breath I had been holding and looked at Walton, who was smiling affably at the two cops as they approached. He held out his hands in a supplicating manner and said, "I can explain all this, officers—"

"Not yet," Momaday said, holding up a hand, then proceeded to read him his rights.

I scanned the parking lot frantically for Leah, Queen of the Highway, but she was nowhere in sight. A chill of fear ran through me and I sprinted over to where she had materialized, She was hunkered down behind the back fender of the car, shaking uncontrollably. "You all right?"

Sturgis ripped off the goalie mask and looked up at me, bewildered. "That guy tried to shoot me," she said disbelievingly.

I reached down and helped her to her feet. "Yeah, I know."

She blinked at me with wide, vacant eyes. "I could've been killed."

I took my apartment keys out of my pocket and put them into her hand. "You'll be okay. Go upstairs and let yourself in and make yourself a good, stiff drink. I'll be up in a minute."

She obeyed docilely and went up the stairs a bit unsteadily, which was probably due more to the six-inch platforms on her boots than the mild state of shock she was in. I tossed the hockey mask into the back of her Mercedes and went back over to the car where Walton and Legrand had assumed the position. "This is just a misunderstanding, officer," Walton was saying. His voice was completely Cambridge now. "What am I being charged with?"

Momaday brought Walton's hands behind his back and snapped on the cuffs. "We might start with discharging a firearm in public and attempted murder."

"This man lives here," Walton said, nodding his head toward me. "We were coming over to his place when that girl going up the stairs there stepped from behind a car and threatened us with a club. Legrand's my bodyguard and he reacted, thinking I was in danger. Asch here can verify it. It's all a misunderstanding."

Momaday looked at me with sleepy eyes. "That right, Asch?"

I looked Walton in the eyes. "That's right. A misunderstanding. You can add assault and battery and kidnap to those other charges. I'll sign the complaint."

Walton's entire face melted. "Honky motherfucker—" and re-formed into a mask of fury.

"If I have but one life, let me live it as a blond."

"Your white ass is dead meat," he snarled.

195

"Look on the bright side, J. D. You can sew up all the concerts in Q for the next twenty years or so."

Momaday put him into the backseat, but on the other side of the car, Rhodes seemed to be having some difficulty with Legrand. The bullnecked black man had a few more things to say about the Caucasian persuasion, and Caucasian cops in particular, and he was not about to get into the car until he said them. Rhodes was starting to get hot, and was trying to keep Legrand under control while he reached for his sap. Momaday was around the other side of the car in three giant strides. "None of that now," he said, grabbing Legrand by the back of his collar and slamming his head into the roof of the car three times. Legrand went limp and Momaday tossed him into the backseat as if he were a rag doll.

Rhodes was still hot, and was trying to match Legrand's racial remarks under his breath. I went behind the car and removed the transmitter, along with three months' growth of pubic hair, and tried to hand it to him. He shook his head adamantly and said, "Fuck you. I told you there was no fucking way I was going to touch that thing."

"Put it in the glove box," Momaday said.

I did, and asked, "You get it all?"

Momaday looked surreptitiously at his prisoners and walked me out of their hearing range. "We got it, but I don't know how much we'll be able to do with it. He didn't confess to murdering Julia Roth."

"He confessed to dirty-tricking Segal," I argued. "That should be good enough to get him for Cooney. There was also a stabbing at one of Segal's concerts you might be able to pin on him."

The massive shoulders shrugged. "I'll give it to LAPD. Say, what was all that about counterfeiting and photographs?"

"Nothing. Just bullshit."

He took out a handful of walnuts. "Uh-huh."

"Really."

He nodded sleepily. "He seemed to be going for it."

"That's because I'm such a convincing actor." I tried to change the subject. "I'm glad to hear you were listening. For a while there, I was beginning to wonder if you guys were ever going to show up."

"We got hung up at a light," he said, splintering the walnuts with a loud *crack*.

"You don't have to stop for lights. You're *policemen*, goddamnit."

"Yeah, but only for three more weeks," he said, and got into the car. "I'm assuming you wouldn't have sent that girl up the stairs if she wasn't okay."

"She's okay. A little shook up, but not hurt."

"We'll have to take a statement from her."

"I'll bring her down tomorrow, when she calms down."

He nodded. Rhodes looked at me over the roof of the car and grinned nastily. "She live here?"

"No. Just a friend."

"Looks like the kind of girl you'd want to bring home to Mama. What does she do, hang you up in a harness and spank your ass?"

"Naw," I said, grinning nastily myself. "I have to go over to your house for that kind of treatment."

He called me a few names he had previously reserved for Legrand, and Momaday laughed. "Catch you later, *doctor*," I said, and the Indian smiled contentedly and backed out of the driveway.

By that time, several other tenants of the building had gotten brave enough to venture outside to see what all the commotion was about. I took the opportunity to score a few points for my flagging tenant rating with Mr. Jablow, the building manager, by telling him that the whole thing was nothing, that I'd spotted two suspicious-looking men lurking around the building and had called the cops, thinking they might be burglars, then had gone down to confront them. When I'd demanded to know what they wanted, one of them drew a gun and in the ensuing struggle, it had gone off. He smiled, patted me on the back, and went back inside feeling warm and safe now that the building had its own security guard, gratis. On the stairs, I ran into the big-eyed American Airlines stewardess whose panties I'd wanted to get into ever since she moved into the building. Her eyes got even bigger when I hinted vaguely of murder and conspiracy, and she told me she would be flying out tomorrow, but would be back the day after and that she would just love to hear all the lurid details then. I told her I would bring a bottle of wine and went up to my apartment, thinking it was funny what a little gunfire can do for your sex life.

Sturgis's state of shock had worn off and she was pacing the room like a wild-eyed timber wolf when I came in. She stopped pacing long enough to look at me and nearly shout, "I could have been *killed*, for chrissakes."

"That's what you get for running around dressed like something from *Friday the Thirteenth.*"

She looked down at herself. "This is what I'll be wearing in *Highway Hell.*"

"You got the part. Congratulations."

"Thanks. I thought I'd drop by and surprise you with it. If I'd known you were going to have friends over, I would've worn a bulletproof vest."

"They weren't exactly friends."

"That's good to hear," she said. "If you hadn't hit that man's arm, I'd be dead right now."

I had no doubts that she was genuinely upset, and rightfully so, but whether it was an outgrowth of her profession or she'd chosen her profession because of it, she had a tendency to let the scene run away with her, and I didn't think I'd be doing either of us any favors by playing to her hysteria. "We don't know that. He could have been a lousy shot."

"Funny," she said, offering a purposely fake smile.

I went into the kitchen and poured myself a vodka, and she said, "You have any Librium?"

"No. Have a drink."

"I already had one."

"Have another. Scotch?"

She said all right, and I fixed her a stiff one, and came out and

198

handed it to her. I sat on the couch and she remained standing. "So what was all that about out there?"

"A case I'm working on," I said. "Run-of-the-mill stuff. Murder, extortion . . ."

"And those wonderful men downstairs?"

"Primary suspects."

"You usually bring them home with you?"

"I didn't bring them home. They brought me."

"They kidnapped you?"

"Not exactly, but that's close enough to a definition that I'm not going to bicker about shades of meaning."

She threw up a gloved hand and resumed pacing. "Jesus Christ. How can you live like this?"

"Like what?" I asked, imbibing a little vodka.

"Like *this*," she said, following my example and taking a sip. "Having the sanctity of your home violated by thugs. Being kidnapped, beaten up, shot at—"

"I think you're getting me confused with Magnum, P.I.," I said, wondering how she stayed balanced on those boots. "This isn't the way I live. Believe it or not, ninety-nine percent of my day is spent sifting through credit reports and court records. The detective you're thinking about is on Channels Two, Four, and Seven, five nights a week."

She stopped in front of me and struck a combative pose, with her legs spread apart and one hand on a leather-sheathed hip. "Yeah? Well, I got news for you, buddy. That gun down there wasn't from the prop department. Those were real fucking bullets I was dodging—"

"And amazingly well, considering the handicap you were under," I said, pointing at her boots.

She turned away and her voice grew strident. "I'm *serious*, goddamnit."

The back of the leather corset ran up through the crack of her ass, exposing a good portion of her nicely rounded buttocks, and I felt a twinge of arousal. "So am I. I think I could really get attached to that outfit."

She turned and smiled wickedly. "You find me interesting,

scum-sucking male trash?" She made a fist and jabbed a thumb into the air. "Up."

I put down my glass and stood up, and she pointed imperiously to the bedroom. "In there."

She left her boots on, which was a nice touch, and for the next forty minutes, she called me names and scratched and bit and pinched, seemingly trying to hurt me, while we made love until we were exhausted, inert lumps of sweaty flesh. Her exhaustion dissipated before my breathing even returned to normal, and she swung the boots off the bed and sat with her back to me. "I thought that would help, but it didn't."

I propped myself up on one elbow. "What?"

"I can't relax here. I keep thinking somebody is going to kick the door down and spray the room with machine-gun fire."

"Don't be ridiculous, Syd."

She shook her head, then got up and started to get dressed. "I'm going to go home, Jake."

"*Now?*"

"I want to be in the warm, quiet safety of my own little house."

"Look at it this way," I said jokingly, "the percentages are with you here. We've already had our one attack for the evening. It's really rare that I get more than one in one night."

She pulled on her bra. "I'm serious, Jake. I can't handle this. My life is precarious enough without adding random gunfire into it." She paused and looked at me. "That shot, it changed something in me tonight. I saw how tenuous everything is. You're in the wrong place at the wrong time and it's all over. I can't live like that."

She was nuts; there was absolutely no doubt about it. "Who's asking you to live like anything? I thought we were talking about one night."

She shook her head, and said, as if she were intoning a line from "General Hospital," "I don't think we should see each other anymore, Jake."

I waited for the follow-up.

"If tonight is an example of one percent of your life, I don't think I could handle it."

"You're being totally silly, Syd. I know you're upset about tonight, but there's risk in everything. You take a risk every time you step off a curb, but you'd never get anywhere if you refused to cross a street."

I told myself to shut up. For weeks, she had been trying to insert herself into my life with a vengeance, and for weeks, I'd been trying to discourage her in various subtle and unsubtle ways, hoping she would get either tired or smart and depart. Now she was ready to take the hint and make for the high ground, and there I was arguing like a schmuck.

"Maybe," she said, sticking to her guns, "but you don't cross dark streets on blind corners. Find a crosswalk with a light. I'm sorry."

She went out of the bedroom and the front door opened and closed. I lay there, still propped up on one elbow, soaking up the silence of the apartment, trying to figure out what had just happened, and what I was feeling. I should have been feeling relief— I liked the best of her, but not enough to take the craziness for very long—but I wasn't. But that was the story of my life. It seemed as if I was always waiting around for a phone call, but the phone never rings until I step out for ten minutes, and there I am, fumbling with my keys to get the door open, and when I finally get inside, it's still ringing, but when I pick it up, I get a dial tone. It made me angry sometimes, sad others, but then I always thought about what would happen if I got to the phone in time, and felt better.

I padded out to the kitchen and made myself another drink and took it back into the bedroom. I lay there in the dark, and thought about how it was for some of us, that loneliness itself was a kind of comfortable companion.

19

My registered package arrived with the morning mail, and I stared at it over the rim of my coffee cup as I called Mr. Friedlander, whose number I'd gotten from the FOR RENT sign at the warehouse. He was back from his trip, and his wife had told him I'd called before. I told him I was very interested in leasing one of the buildings on Hoke, the one at the end of the driveway, to be exact, and he said he was sorry, that was already rented, but that he had another one next to it that was identical. I told him no, that for my specific purposes (about which I was very unspecific), I had to have the one on the end, and that I'd already talked to his tenant, Dean Cuthburton, and he had no objection to swapping buildings. Friedlander told me I must be mistaken, that he had no tenant named Cuthburton, that he was renting that building to a Mr. Segal. I told him indeed there must be a mistake and that I was terribly sorry to have bothered him, and hung up.

I looked at the envelope on the table and grinned. Well, Freddie Segal, you nasty little old counterfeiter, you.

There was one more piece of the puzzle that kept bothering me, that I couldn't push out of my mind. I put the envelope into my briefcase, along with Cooney's photographs and the Hagar album, and drove downtown, to the Hall of Records.

Because I didn't have an exact date of death, it took a while, but I finally found Lisa in the index. I gave the clerk the number and he gave me a copy of the death certificate.

Lisa Marie Trent had died on November 21, 1983, at 20:00, in Topanga Canyon. The cause of death was listed as "Acute barbiturate and alcohol poisoning—synergistic," and "probable suicide" had been typed into the "INJURY INFORMATION" box. Her father's name was Carl Trent and her mother's maiden name was Rachel Skerritt, and I assumed they lived at the same address that was listed as Lisa's usual residence, 1170 Ninth Avenue, Twin Falls, Idaho. I wondered when they had moved there from Vineland, New Jersey, which, according to the death certificate, had been Lisa's birthplace. Vineland, New Jersey.

I got the Trents' phone number from long-distance information and spent $2.85 calling it from one of the pay phones in the Hall of Records. A man answered gruffly and I said, "Mr. Trent?"

"Yes?"

"My name is Asch. I'm a private detective from Los Angeles. That's where I'm calling from. I'd like to ask you a few questions about your daughter—"

"My daughter is dead," the answer came back icily.

"I know. That's why I'm calling you. A question about her death has come up and I—"

"*Now* you ask questions?" he asked disbelievingly.

"Mr. Trent—"

"You people told us to bury our daughter and forget. That's what we've been trying to do. We've gone through enough pain. Leave us alone."

"I'm not who you talked to, Mr. Trent. I'm a private detective."

"I don't care *who* you are," he snapped. "I don't want to talk to you. Don't call here again."

He slammed the receiver down and I put mine gently back on the hook. The man had not sounded exactly rational. I thought about calling him back, but decided I would probably just get another couple of bucks in change eaten up for my trouble, so instead I drove over to the Medical Examiner's office, where I spent an hour or so going through the Coroner's report on Lisa. Unlike Julia Roth, a capsule residue had been found in the girl's stomach; and, from the toxicology report, it must have been a colorful assortment. The poor girl's body had to be confused from the cues she'd been trying to give it; aside from the barbs and alcohol, the lab on her blood had come up with codeine, Meth-edrine, and meprobamate.

I made copies of what I needed from the report; then I called Ed Blackburn and told him that I'd pretty much put Segal in the clear for the Cooney thing, but that I'd uncovered some other evidence that they should both hear about. He told me to be in his office at 11:30.

At 11:35, I was sitting in one of Blackburn's cushy leather chairs, inspecting the hangnail on my right index finger that I'd just managed to make bleed, when Segal came through the door, looking perturbed. He said hello to me almost as an afterthought, then said to Blackburn, "I've got a million things to do today, Ed. What's so important that you couldn't explain it on the phone?"

"Jake thought you'd want to hear the good news in person," he said, smiling.

"What good news?"

"You're off the hook on the Cooney thing. I just talked to the D.A. and they're dropping it."

Segal's harried expression turned jubilant. "That's great! What happened?"

"Jake got J. D. Walton on tape, confessing that Julia had been working for him and had switched the vials at the party on his orders. They've got him in custody now."

Segal took a deep breath and let it out in a sigh of relief. "I feel about a thousand pounds lighter." He gave me a warm smile. "Beautiful job, Asch. I have to hand it to you: you had it pegged. I have to admit, when you brought up his name, I thought, No way. I mean, what could a guy like Walton think he could possibly gain by scuttling me? He's strictly small-time shit, a two-bit hustler with a bad rap. He could never have gotten any of the big acts or their managers to go with him."

I looked up from my hangnail and said, "The man had a lot of faith in his hustling abilities. They'd gotten him over bigger hur-dles than that. Then the toot probably did a lot to inflate his

204

megalomania. He was into that pretty heavy; he and his body-guard must have snorted a gram and a half in the half hour I was with them. Everything looks different when you're floating a couple of feet off the ground. He saw himself becoming El Primo Promoter of Southern California, once you were out of the way. And while you were on the way down, Julia could feed him the inside dope on which groups and managers were becoming disenchanted; he figured he could approach them on the sly and jive his way in. But then a fly buzzed into the ointment—Cooney—and fucked everything up."

Segal sat down, and I went on: "From what Johnny Brandt says, Cooney was a kind of modern-day Svengali that certain kinds of women found irresistible. Whether it was some sort of animal magnetism that drew Julia to him, lust, his line of Nietzschean rap, or the lure of the darkness she saw in him—whatever it was, she fell under his kinky spell—"

"If that's so," Blackburn broke in, "why did she kill him?"

"She didn't mean to. The heroin was just another dirty trick in Walton's bag, but nobody was supposed to die. Julia made the mistake of switching the stuff pure. Even then, if Cooney hadn't shown up, everything might have turned out as planned. Julia had no idea he was going to crash the party; all you had to do was see her face when she saw him to know that. When the heroin hit his system and mixed with the booze and whatever else he'd been taking, he went down for the count."

"Why didn't she warn him?" the lawyer asked.

"She didn't have time. Segal pulled her away to talk to her. By the time she found him, it was too late."

Segal leaned forward in his chair. "You're saying Cooney didn't know what she was doing for Walton?"

"He couldn't have," I said. "Otherwise, he wouldn't have snorted the stuff. It makes sense when you consider that she couldn't tell Cooney she was sabotaging you. That wouldn't have set too well with him, seeing what an instrumental part he saw you playing in his future."

He reared back, surprised. "Me?"

I nodded. "Cooney had plans to make a comeback. He wanted to go on tour, but no promoter would touch him as a solo headliner, not with his track record. But he could start off as a starting act for somebody else, and the bigger the act, the bigger the exposure. Who books the biggest acts around? And that would kill two birds with one stone: it would show every other promoter around that you had faith in him, even after all he did to you. He needed you. There was only one trouble: you didn't need him. So he set out to change that, any way he could. First he tried through Julia, but when that didn't work, he started nosing around and somehow found out about Sound Tek and put his talents as an amateur photographer of kink to work."

"What's Sound Tek?" Blackburn asked, folding his hands on the desk.

"An independent record-pressing plant." I took the envelope containing the pictures out of my briefcase and tossed it on his desk. While he looked the photos over, I said, "I found those in Julia Roth's apartment, hidden in an album jacket. The fact that she'd taken the time to hide them made me curious, because whoever was in the apartment when I got there had been looking for something. The other thing that made me curious about them was that Cooney had mailed them to himself, registered. I figured she must have taken the envelope from his apartment the night before."

Blackburn's ferret gaze grew even more ferrety. He spread the pictures out on the desk and said, "What's so special about these?"

"Cooney sent them to himself registered mail because he wanted to be able to prove the date. At the time those were taken, the LP in Cuthburton's hand was not released yet."

"I've explained that," Segal cut in.

I opened my briefcase and tossed the Sammy Hagar album on the desk. "You didn't explain this. It isn't out yet, but there are boxes of them sitting in a warehouse over on Hoke Street that you're renting. They were at Sound Tek until a couple of nights ago, but then I started asking questions, and Cuthburton panicked and called you and the two of you must have decided to get them out of there. You called your ex-employee, now partner, Bud Jorgensen, and he and a buddy did the job."

"I rent a warehouse, sure," Segal stammered, "but I don't know anything about any records. I use it to store things."

"What kind of things?"

He threw a hand up and tried to look mad. "Things. Papers. What is this? The third degree? I don't have to answer to you."

"That's right. But if this gets out, you're going to answer to a lot of people. You think you got trouble with rock-and-roll managers? Wait until the FBI starts looking up your ass."

"I don't have to take this kind of shit from you, Asch. Those goddamn pictures don't prove anything. It's only your word that they were in that envelope when it was sealed."

"I followed Jorgensen the other night. I took some pictures of my own."

Segal was doing a knife-throwing act with his eyes.

I dodged one and said, "You don't really think in your wildest dreams that Cuthburton and the Ainsworths would be willing to take the fall all by themselves, do you?"

"I don't have to sit here and listen to this shit."

"Cooney told you he knew about the counterfeiting operation and he threatened to expose you if you didn't put him back on the stage. That's what the argument at the party was about and that's why you didn't throw him out.

"Julia knew about the pictures," I went on, ignoring him. "She had to, otherwise she would have broken the seal on the envelope to see what was inside. When Cooney died, she took them and called Walton and offered them to him for five thousand dollars. She was panicked and she needed the money to get away on. She blamed herself for Cooney's death and she was afraid of going to jail for his murder, and her one instinct was to run. She didn't tell Walton what they were, just that they would drop Segal into the shitter for good; he sent Legrand over to find out what the story was. He probably didn't intend to pay her for them; otherwise, he would have gone himself."

"You're saying this Legrand killed Julia?" Blackburn asked.

"Walton says she was dead when he got there."

Blackburn raised a dubious eyebrow. "And you believe him? If what you're saying is true, Walton had a prime motive for killing Julia."

"True," I said, "but the woman died hours earlier, according to the autopsy report, which meant that Legrand had to have been hanging around the apartment all that time. He hadn't searched the place well enough for that."

The lawyer leaned back and pinched his lower lip. "If Julia was being paid by Walton, why didn't she tell him about the photographs before?"

I shrugged. "She might have been afraid Cooney would figure it out and get really pissed. Or she might have figured that once Segal was completely out of the picture, Walton wouldn't need her anymore and would dump her. As long as Segal was still on his feet, she was guaranteed two incomes."

"That's it, Asch," Segal said, pushing himself abruptly out of his chair. "You're fired."

"I'm working for Ed," I shot back. "If he wants to fire me, fine."

Segal took the cue and looked over at Blackburn, who was tugging on his ear thoughtfully. "Did you tell any of this to the police?"

"Not yet," I said. "I knew if I did, Segal here would immediately become a prime candidate once more for Cooney's murder. Also Julia's. Right now, she's officially an accident, but it wouldn't take too much to make a publicity-hungry D.A. refile her as a homicide stat."

"I was home all night the night Julia died," Segal snapped.

"Maybe. And your wife would probably testify to that. But that doesn't mean Cuthburton didn't do it, or that you didn't hire someone to do it."

"You're getting onto thin ice, Jake," Blackburn warned.

Segal took a step toward me. "What are you trying to say I am?"

"That's what I'm trying to find out, Mr. Segal."

"What's that supposed to mean?"

"I don't give a shit what's going on at Sound Tek," I said softly. "I've taken money from people who have done a hell of a lot worse things than counterfeiting records, and taken it gladly. But the idea of working for a murderer would upset my sensibilities, not to mention make me an accessory. I don't intend to go to jail or have my right to make a living taken away for you or anybody else."

"I'm not a murderer."

"Convince me."

"I don't have to convince you of anything—"

"True. I just thought you might like to."

"How?"

"Take a lie-detector test."

"What'll that prove?"

"Plenty to me. If you pass, you can have your pictures and we can consider the matter closed."

He turned away, then turned back. "And if I fail?"

"I go to the cops."

He wagged an angry finger back and forth in the air. "Those things aren't one-hundred-percent reliable. They aren't even admissible in court."

I smiled. "Court is what we're trying to avoid, isn't it?"

Segal looked questioningly at Blackburn, who scratched the side of his head. "From a legal standpoint, there's nothing to fear from it. The attorney-client privilege would preclude its admissibility as evidence. And if you don't want to answer anything he asks, don't answer it."

Segal gave the lawyer a penetrating stare. "You don't believe I had anything to do with Julia's death. . . ."

"No, Fred, I don't," he said, picking up one of the pictures and looking at it. "And if there's no truth in any of this, tell me to fire the man and that'll be that."

Segal hesitated and turned his back on me. When he turned around, he glared at me hatefully and said, "Bring in your fucking machine."

I brought the polygraph in from the outer office where I'd left it and set it up on the desk. After twenty minutes of getting levels on him, and twenty minutes more of testing, I unhooked him and went over the results. "Well?" he asked smugly, rolling down his sleeve. "Did I kill anybody?"

"I don't know about anybody," I said, scanning the peaks and troughs, "but you didn't kill Julia Roth."

"Isn't that amazing?" Segal said, his voice dripping sarcasm. "What about those pictures?"

I took the envelope out of my briefcase and tossed it on Ed's desk. Segal wouldn't look at them, or at me, either. I wasn't hurt too much by that. "I'm just curious, Segal. Why?"

He shrugged. "It keeps my wife in hot wax treatments."

"I'm serious."

"You don't think I am?" he snapped back. "My wife has expensive tastes, Asch. She won't shop anywhere but Rodeo Drive. It was the way she was brought up—very rich and very spoiled. I could live for a year on what she spends for clothes in a month."

"But a petty scam like counterfeiting—"

"*Petty*?" He laughed strangely and when he turned around, his lips were contorted into a lopsided leer. "I make four times as much off that 'petty scam,' as you call it, than I do working my butt off promoting concerts."

Segal began pacing and gesturing wildly with his hands. "I'm being bled dry by vampires. A group's production man says they want fourteen spots in a hall where I only need five; I have to have fourteen. If I need sixteen stagehands and the union tells me I need twenty-four, I have to pay twenty-four. There used to be a time when you could make some money in this business. Now you're lucky if you make expenses. Now groups come to you and say, 'Hey, we know what your gross will be, what your expenses are, we don't need you to promote us, but we'll allow you to do all the work and guarantee all the expenses, and here's five thousand dollars for your trouble.' Every concert, I have to listen to some drugged-out, half-literate, no-talent asshole threaten that he's not going to play unless he gets cashew chicken and Orange Julius for six at three in the morning. I'm not in the promotion business anymore; they've turned me into a fucking *caterer*, for chrissakes."

He stopped and turned to me, his eyes suddenly sad. "You know, they've even got a video game out now called 'Journey,' based on the rock group. Maybe you've seen the ads for it. 'Help Journey fight their way from the stage, through crowds of screaming groupies and sleazy promoters, to their limo.' *Sleazy* promoters." The sadness in his eyes hardened like plaster of Paris. "I'll let you in on a little secret, Asch. I've gotten a lot of pleasure out of the counterfeiting business. Just the thought that I was taking money out of the pockets of those egomaniacal, money-grubbbing little monsters has given me an intense satisfaction."

"You people created monsters," I told him coldly. "It seems a little hypocritical to be complaining about it now. You built the industry on hype and hysteria. You dish out the drugs and the adulation, then cry about it when these kids can't handle it and run amok."

That knocked the wind out of him and he stopped pacing, shook his head sadly, then collapsed into his chair. I turned to Blackburn: "All of this stays in the room. I don't want you to worry about that. But I do want one more thing."

"What?"

"One more day's pay, plus expenses, and a plane ticket to Twin Falls, Idaho."

He looked at me as if I'd turned into a rubber duck before his eyes. "Twin Falls, Idaho? What for?"

"A hunch. There are some people up there I want to talk to who might help wrap this thing up."

"What thing?"

"Julia. Cooney. And the death of a girl named Esther Knight."

He gave me a puzzled look. "We've wrapped it. You've done the job you were hired to do. Fred is out of the woods for Cooney, and if Julia was murdered—and that's a big if—Walton is the most likely suspect. As far as the Knight girl goes, whoever she is, it's none of our business."

211

"Who is Esther Knight?" asked Segal.

"A groupie Cooney and Julia used to do scenes with."

"What does that have to do with Fred?"

"Nothing that I know of. But I think the three deaths are possibly related in some way."

"How?"

"I'm not sure. We're only talking a few hundred dollars," I said. "Consider it the bonus Segal was talking about."

Blackburn glanced at Segal, who tossed the money out the window with an uncaring wave of a hand. "All right," Blackburn agreed. "One day's pay plus expenses."

I told them I would be in touch when I returned, and packed up the poly. Blackburn told Segal to stick around, that he wanted to talk with him after I left. Neither of them looked terribly unhappy when I did.

20

At 7:35 that evening I was stepping off the eight-passenger Trans Western turbo prop that was my connecting flight from Salt Lake City, onto the runway of Twin Falls airport.

God must have heard about my arrival, because He had arranged a little light show for my entertainment. Spectacular pitchforks of lightning jumped from thunderhead to thunderhead in the quickly darkening sky, and the cool dusk was permeated by the electric smell of ozone and rumblings of thunder.

I grabbed a cab in front of the tiny terminal and gave him the Trents' address. The driver liked to hear himself talk and he didn't seem to care if I was listening to his weather monologue, so I tuned out and watched the lightning. We drove through a wide, flat farming valley, and I rolled down the window all the way and closed my eyes and took in the fresh, sweet smells of the land, and thought about how nice it was not to be in the city, smelling some bus's exhaust fumes, even if I was not exactly on vacation.

After a few miles, we passed a couple of old grain silos, then bumped over some railroad tracks, and we were into town. The downtown core was old and quiet and had a dusty, frontier look to it, most of its squared-off, two-story brick buildings having been built for utility and strength rather than grace and style. But after only a few blocks, those prairie values began to erode and give way to Burger Kings and Taco Bandidos and I was in the home of the Whopper again. Southern California Characterless. Sometimes I felt as if the entire world was becoming L.A. In another couple of years, I'd be able to travel halfway around the world and never leave home.

We passed a park and hung a right at a white-spired church, which looked as if it had been transplanted from New England, onto a sleepy residential street lined with elms and older prairie-style homes. It was the kind of neighborhood in which everyone would sit on their porches sipping lemonade on hot summer nights and wave to their neighbors in the morning as they went to work. There was nobody on the Trent porch when we pulled up in front, but some lights were on inside. I paid the cabbie what I owed him and told him to keep the meter running and wait.

The house was an older gray, two-story, Colonial revival house with a red gabled roof and clapboard sides. The steps leading onto the columned front porch were covered with green astro-turf. I went up them and rang the doorbell.

The craggy-faced man from the photograph I'd seen at Coo-ney's opened the door dressed in a long-sleeved white shirt and baggy gray slacks. He wasn't as tall as he looked in the picture, or as old, either. Maybe forty. He had a newspaper in one hand and a pipe in the other.

"Mr. Trent?"

"Yes?"

I handed him a card. "My name is Asch. I called this morning from Los Angeles."

"I told you not to bother us," he said angrily.

"I know, but I thought I might get better results if I talked to you in person."

"Well, you were wrong."

"Mr. Trent, I wouldn't have come a thousand miles unless I thought it was important. . . ."

"That's your problem, not mine. Have a nice trip back to L.A."

He started to shut the door, and there was nothing I could do about it, short of putting a foot in the door and shoving my way inside, but a female voice stopped him. "Carl."

Rachel Trent stepped into the light framed by the doorway. He had looked tall in the picture because she was so tiny. She had the same short gray hair, but she had lost considerable weight and her yellow dress seemed big on her. Her full face was handsome, without lines, and her hazel eyes large and clear. "The man came all the way up here from Los Angeles to talk to us. If it's that important, maybe we should listen."

"Important?" Carl Trent said to her testily. "What could be important? I won't have him coming in here upsetting you by raking everything up again. What good is it going to do? Lisa is dead."

"So are three others, Mr. Trent," I cut in.

That turned him around. "What three others? What are you talking about?"

"Three other people have died since Lisa. They all knew Lisa and they all died under mysterious circumstances. I think all of them may be tied together somehow."

"How?"

"That's what I'm trying to figure out."

Mrs. Trent stepped forward. "Won't you come in?"

Carl Trent gave her a dirty look, but bowed to her invitation by stepping out of the way. The living room had a homy, rustic feeling to it, even though I wasn't particularly fond of Early American decor. The furniture was all maple Colonial and the brilliantly waxed wood floors were covered with knitted throw rugs. The tantalizing smell of a roast wafted out from the kitchen and a half-finished needlepoint lay wadded up on the couch, completing the picture of Home Sweet Home. The vertical hold on the picture went haywire, however, when I spied the collection of pictures on the mantel over the brick fireplace. They were all of Lisa—standing, sitting on a black horse, standing by the same horse. It looked like a shrine.

Mrs. Trent indicated a red chair by the couch and I sat down. "Can I offer you something? Coffee?"

"No thanks, I'm fine."

They both sat down on the couch. Carl Trent leaned over and tapped the ashes from his pipe into a nearby ashtray. Mrs. Trent cleared her throat and folded her hands in her lap.

"Nice place you have here," I said, hoping to break the ice a little.

Carl Trent looked as if he would like to break the ice over my head. He put his pipe in the ashtray and said, "Let's dispense with the social amenities. Our home isn't why you're here or why I let you in. What's your interest in Lisa? Who are you working for?"

"My client is a man named Fred Segal. Up until yesterday, he was implicated in the death of a rock star named Phil Cooney."

There was no indication in his expression that he recognized the name.

"This Cooney fellow," he said, "his is one of the deaths you were talking about?"

"Yes."

"What does he have to do with Lisa?"

"I'm not sure. She was living at his house for a time. From the evidence I've gathered, he was the one who got her started on drugs."

His eyes tensed. "You mean he murdered her."

"I didn't say that."

"If he gave her drugs, he murdered her," he said with diamond-hard finality. There was pain behind his eyes, but he was keeping it smothered by belligerence. "Do the police know that? Do they know he was the one who got her hooked on drugs?"

"I don't know."

"They told me she'd been sleeping in the woods in that canyon where they found her," he said bitterly.

"Who did? The police?"

He nodded. "She was dirty and she had her sleeping bag and knapsack with her with some food in it."

"From what I can determine, she left Cooney's place a week or so before she died."

He didn't seem to be listening. He looked down at the floor and shook his head.

"Those bastards," Carl Trent snarled. "Lisa was just a case number to them. They didn't care what had happened to her or

216

who was responsible. They talked to me like *we* were responsible. That one sergeant—Verdugo—had the nerve to tell me that they didn't have the time to waste on girls like Lisa, that the streets were full of Lisas, and all the cops in the world couldn't stop them from running away or taking drugs. He said they had to concentrate on crimes that had victims. *Victims.* I blew up then. I asked him what he thought Lisa was, if she wasn't a victim?"

His face was red. For a man who hadn't wanted to talk, he was doing all right. The rage that was boiling up in him was keeping his tongue moving. "You know what that smug, pompous sonofabitch told me? He said Lisa had made a victim out of herself. He said nobody shoved those pills down her throat or held a gun to her head and told her to take them. He told us to take her home and bury her and get on with our lives, that if we stayed around and dug into hers, we'd only unearth things we were better off not knowing."

It sounded cold the way he recited it, but it was not bad advice, all in all. Carl Trent, in all likelihood, would have dug up a whole new daughter, one he wouldn't have liked a hell of a lot. "So you took his advice?"

"What else could we do?" he asked helplessly.

"Did Lisa have any trouble with drugs before she went to L.A.?"

"Never," Mrs. Trent interjected. "She didn't even smoke. She loved nature and her horse and her music. She loved to just go off by herself with her guitar—" Her voice wavered and her eyes grew teary. It was a sight I was getting used to seeing the last few days. "Excuse me," she said, and smiled apologetically.

Her husband leaned toward her and said in an admonishing tone: "I told you this would just upset you. . . ."

"I'm fine," she insisted, and patted him on the leg.

"When did Lisa leave home?"

"March fourteenth," she said. She probably knew the hour, too, but she didn't offer it.

"Did you know where she'd gone?"

"Not right away," she said. "I got up that morning and found a note in the kitchen telling us not to worry, that she was sorry for running away, but she knew we wouldn't let her go otherwise. She said she would call us soon and she hoped we understood, but she had to do what she'd always wanted to do."

"What was that?"

"She wanted to be a recording star. It was her lifelong ambition. Music was always her main love. She wrote beautiful songs and could play three or four instruments by the time she was ten. She was very talented. I guess it was in her genes. I wouldn't know a piano from an oboe, but her father is a kind of musical genius."

I looked at Carl Trent. He looked about as musical as a bull terrier. "Really?"

"Not Carl," she said, catching my expression. "Lisa's *real* father." She smiled at her husband sympathetically. "Lisa always considered Carl her real father, and in a sense he was. He raised her from the time she was two."

"That was in Vineland?"

Her eyes widened in surprise. "Yes. How did you know that?"

"It was on Lisa's death certificate. And I think I might know her father."

"You know Carey?"

I nodded. "Did Lisa know about him?"

"I never kept anything from her," she said sadly. "I probably should have. If she hadn't seen that program, she might be alive today."

"You can't blame yourself for that," Carl Trent said, reaching over and squeezing her hand. She gave him a grateful smile, and I tried to catch up.

"What program?"

"The Grammy Awards," she said. "Carey won one last year and I guess Lisa got the idea in her head that he could help her break into the music business. She never told me that, of course; she knew what I'd say. She'd written to him for several years in care of record companies, but he never answered her letters. He told her he didn't write because he'd never gotten them, and she believed him. But I know better. The man never made any attempt in all these years to contact her, find out if she was alive or dead."

"She saw him?"

"She called from his place about a week after she left. She was staying there. She sounded happy and said they were getting along real well. She said he'd listened to her songs and liked them and that he promised to help her polish them up when he finished this project he was working on. She was devastated when she found out he was just trying to find a way to soften the blow, that he had no intentions of helping her."

"When did she tell you that?"

"He told me that night. After I talked to her, he got on the phone. Let me tell you, it was a shock to hear his voice after all these years. He asked Lisa to leave the room while he talked to me. He made excuses for not calling in all these years by saying that he didn't know where we'd moved to, and said that now he knew what he'd missed, that Lisa was a wonderful girl and they were having a great time getting acquainted. He said he was try-ing to find a way to break it to her gently, but she didn't have the talent or the temperament to make it in the music business. He said it was the rottenest business in the world, full of liars, cheats, and loose women, and that it would eat her alive. He said it would kill everything decent in her and that the best thing she could possibly do would be to forget about music and go back home and finish her education. That sounded sensible to both Carl and me. He said as soon as he found a way to tell her that she would accept, he'd put her on a plane home."

"She never made it," I said.

She shook her head and bit her lip. There were tears in her eyes again. Carl Trent went on for her: "A week later, Stack called and said she'd gone, he didn't know where. Apparently she hadn't taken the news so well and had stormed out, saying he was a liar, that she had the talent to make it and that she didn't need him, that she'd do it on her own. He said not to worry, that if she started contacting in the business, he'd find out about it and track her down, but that in all probability we would be hearing from her first after she beat her head against the wall enough and needed air fare home." Mrs. Trent's lips compressed and her husband said angrily, "I shouldn't have listened to him. I should have gone down there and found her and brought her home, no matter what it cost."

"That's easier said than done, Mr. Trent," I said. "L.A. is a big town. Thousands of teenage runaways get lost in it every year. You might have found her, but the chances would have been against it. You might have hired a professional, but that kind of hunt can run into thousands of dollars and still come up empty."

His shoulders slumped forward, and the anger in his face deflated into resignation. "That's what my lawyer said. He said Lisa would be eighteen in a few months anyway, and that after that there was nothing we could legally do to bring her back. He thought Stack was our best bet."

"I take it that didn't pan out."

He shook his head.

"Did you ever hear from her again?"

"Once," Mrs. Trent said, sniffing. "About three weeks later. It was late. After midnight. Her voice sounded strange—I almost didn't recognize it—and I asked if she was all right. I didn't even think of the possibility that she might have been on drugs. She said she was fine and that she loved us and not to worry, that everything was going great. I asked where she was living and she said with friends, but she was evasive when I asked who they were, saying she was in the process of moving into her own place and she would call and give me the address in a couple of days. I asked if she'd talked to her father and she said she hadn't spoken to Carl. When I said, no, I meant Carey, she got upset, saying she only had one father now. She said Carey wasn't her father, that he hadn't existed for her for seventeen years, so there was no reason he should exist for her now. She said she didn't need his help anyway, that she'd already signed a contract with a big recording company and they thought her songs were hit material. I told her we missed her and asked her to come home, but she said she couldn't, that she had these commitments, and that we should be happy for her." She looked down at the hands in her lap and said in a dead voice, "That was the last time we ever heard from her."

"There was no recording contract," I said.

"No."

Carl Trent slid closer to his wife on the couch and put his arms lovingly around her shoulders. She looked up and smiled and patted his hand and he looked over at me. "How did this Cooney fellow die?"

"Drug overdose, just like your daughter."

"Stack was right about that business," he said in disgust. "It's nothing but dope and perversion. It's in the music, I'm convinced of it."

I was sure he was, and I wasn't up for a debate at the moment. "Have you talked to Stack after that?"

"Briefly, when I went down to claim Lisa's body," he said.

"How did he take the news?"

"He broke down on the phone. He had to hang up. He couldn't even talk." A thought seemed to strike him: "You said something about three deaths. Who were the other two?"

"A girl friend of Cooney's named Julia Roth. I'm sure she knew your daughter. And a friend of Lisa's named Esther Knight."

"What do they have to do with Lisa's death?"

"I'm not sure."

"Then why did you say they did?"

"They all knew each other, and their deaths are all linked by time and circumstance. Julia Roth's death is officially an accident and the Knight girl is being labeled a suicide, but there is a legitimate possibility of murder in each case."

Mrs. Trent clutched her throat. "Are you saying Lisa was murdered?"

"No. I don't think she was. But I think her death might have been a catalyst that set up the others."

"Quit talking in riddles," Carl Trent said, with reborn bellicoseness. "What do you mean, 'catalyst'?"

"Look, Mr. Trent, I know all this may sound vague and cryptic

221

to you both, but I'm not being coy with you, believe me. It's still kind of vague to me. I have suspicions, but I couldn't tell you what they are until I confirm them." I stood up. "Believe me, the trip hasn't been wasted. You've been a great help."

"Wait just a minute here," he said. "You mean to say you just waltz in here and lay all this stuff on us about murder and three other deaths, then waltz on out without telling us what it's all about, what it might have to do with Lisa?"

I didn't feel particularly good about leaving them hanging like that, but there wasn't much I could do about it. "I'm sorry. As soon as I find out something significant, I'll let you know."

"That's not good enough," Carl Trent said angrily.

"I'm sorry, but for now it'll have to be. Good night."

I went quickly to the door and Mrs. Trent followed, looking helpless. I thanked her again for her cooperation and trotted down the walk to the waiting cab, grateful to be out of there.

I asked the driver to take me to a decent hotel and he recommended the Holiday Inn, which I thought was a fitting gesture of closure. But this one had only two stories, so that if I became overwhelmed by despair during the night and decided to jump, the best I would be able to do was break a leg. I checked in and deposited my overnight bag in my room and, heeding the recommendation of the desk clerk, sprinted through the rain, which was now coming down in buckets, to the restaurant across the street.

The restaurant was a woody, beach-type place that specialized in seafood dishes, of all things, and since Segal was picking up the tab, I ordered a shrimp cocktail and a bottle of Chenin Blanc to go with my mahi mahi, and ate a leisurely dinner while watching the lightning dance from my window table.

By the time I paid my check, the rain had eased a bit and some stars were visible in patches through the clouds. I stopped at the liquor store next to the hotel and picked up a half-pint of vodka and took it up to the room, thinking that the combination of a couple of drinks and a hot bath might put a damper on my thoughts and let me get to sleep early. The quicker tomorrow came, the quicker the thing would be over. I'd confronted too much young death and middle-aged grief in the past week, and I needed to take a couple of giant steps back to get some room to breathe.

As I lay in the tub, sipping vodka from a sanitized plastic cup, I wondered how I would handle the next day. I thought I had most of it, but a lot of it was still guesswork, and unless someone filled in the blanks, they would probably never be filled in. No matter; it would be out of my hands. Somebody else could live with it— Stack, Segal, Walton, the cops. What I had to live with was my shoes, which had gotten soaked, and probably ruined, crossing the street to the restaurant. I decided to add them to Segal's tab. That was the only satisfying solution I came up with before my mind signed off for the night.

21

My flight out the next morning was at 7:05, and with the time change, I was back at LAX at 9:35. I called Segal from a pay phone at the Western Airlines terminal and told him I might have something, that I would let him know later in the afternoon, and asked him for the phone numbers of the people who had driven Cuthburton and the other overdosers to the hospital the night of the party. That took him a few minutes to dig up, and after he finally did, he tried to press me again for what I'd found out, but I put him off by telling him there were a few things I wanted to check out first, which was true enough.

Carey was home and sounded happy to hear from me. "Where you been, Sherlock? I called you a couple of times, but kept getting your service."

"I had to go out of town for a day on business."

"All work and no play makes Jake a dull boy. Congratulations, by the way. I heard the news about Walton. How'd you nail him?"

"I'll tell you all about it over lunch. I'll buy this time."

"I won't fight. Name a time and a place."

"Cheerio's on Pacific. Noon."

He said he'd be there and I drove home, unpacked my overnight bag, then checked the service. The only messages were from Stack. I guessed Sturgis had been serious about giving me up as a lost cause. I was still not sure how I felt about that, and to avoid thinking about it, I made my own calls.

I had been at the table for fifteen minutes when Carey came in.

He sat down and looked at the Bloody Mary in front of me and said, "You're full of good ideas today." He flagged down a waitress and ordered a duplicate, then sat back and rubbed his hands briskly together. "So fill me in, and withhold no details."

I spared a few, particularly those about Segal's counterfeiting venture, and when I was finished, he shook his head and said, "I don't know where these people get their ideas. Walton never could have filled Freddie's shoes."

"That's what Segal said."

His drink arrived, and he hoisted it in a toast. "To you, Sherlock. A masterful piece of detection."

I held up my own glass. "There are still a few minor points to be cleared up. For instance, why didn't you tell me Lisa Trent was your daughter?"

The drink paused in front of his mouth, and his eyes darted up at me over the rim.

"I just got back from Twin Falls, Carey."

He drank, then tossed up a hand nonchalantly, but his eyes were uneasy.

"I didn't figure it was any of your business. It didn't have anything to do with what you were doing and I couldn't see any point in sullying her name by linking it to that scuzball Cooney. Anyway, Lisa wasn't my real daughter, not in any way other than an accident of birth. She told me so herself."

"When she came to see you?"

He nodded. "She told me in no uncertain terms that as far as she was concerned, we had no common blood in our veins. She said I hadn't been her father for all these years, so there was no reason I should consider myself that now." His gaze grew distant and he smiled sadly. "She was right. That's why I hadn't answered any of her letters. I didn't feel it would be fair to me to insert myself into her life at this late date. I was scared for myself, too—of assuming the responsibility of having to care. I'd spent all this time building up these protective walls around me; I didn't want anyone coming into my life and tearing them down. Then there she was standing on my doorstep, this . . . this little blonde freckle-faced girl, telling me she was my daughter, and I couldn't ignore it anymore. She was *real*—a walking, talking person— and I had the responsibility whether I wanted it or not."

"It must have been a shock," I sympathized. "How long did she stay with you?"

He stared into his drink on the table and touched the rim of his glass with a forefinger. "Three weeks," he said with false amusement. "I gained and lost a daughter in three weeks. That has to be some kind of record."

"How did you two get along?"

"Great until the end. She was quite a girl. Bright, cheerful, enthusiastic, full of life. She also had a stubborn streak in her that she must have gotten from me. She had her little starry-eyed dreams and she wouldn't let go of them, no matter what. I tried to tell her how easily those dreams can turn into nightmares, but she wouldn't listen."

"You mean her music?"

His expression turned morose. "She had her mind made up she was going to be the next Joan Jett. That was the main reason she just happened to drop by. It was also another reason I didn't answer her letters. It was pretty obvious what she wanted. She wanted me to use my contacts to get her a recording contract. She seemed to think all I had to do was walk into Columbia and say, 'Guys, this is my daughter and she wants to be a rock star. Sign her up, will you?'"

"Her mother said she had talent."

"Every mother whose son plays the trumpet in the high school band thinks her kid is Dizzy Gillespie. Lisa had talent, sure. She had a natural feel for music. But this business is littered with the corpses of hundreds who had ten times the talent. Being able to play a couple of instruments is a long way from having that certain something you need to have to make it. Her songs were nothing and her voice was adequate, but banal. She brought a tape of herself with her and she made me promise to play it for a couple of record people, but I never did. She kept bugging me about it. She wanted me to work with her, but I kept putting her off and putting her off until one day I couldn't anymore. I didn't want to hurt her, but I thought whatever pain I caused her then would save her a hell of a lot more later, so I told her straight out that if she worked real hard and hooked up with a real good group, and if she was real lucky, in a couple of years, she might be making scale in some smoke-filled dive in Hermosa Beach. She didn't take that too well. She said I *owed* her, and she was right. I owed her enough not to let her be destroyed, but she couldn't understand that. The wolves would have eaten her alive and the vultures would have finished off what was left."

"It couldn't have been much worse than the way she wound up."

"It *was* the way she wound up," he said harshly. "Cooney fed her full of drugs and bullshit about how he was going to help her make it, and she went for it. The vicious bastard fanned her dreams into a fire while he systematically destroyed her."

"That was after she ran away from your place?"

He nodded and pursed his lips as if he had just bitten into something bitter, then hailed the waitress and ordered another Mary. "Did you know she was living with Cooney?" I asked.

"Not until it was too late. I ran into her at Madame Wong's one night about two months after she left my place. I couldn't believe the transformation. She was with Cooney and that other little walking cancer, Star. When she'd left, she was vibrant and alive, and two months later, there was nothing in her eyes. Looking into them was like looking into the windows of a vacant house. When she'd been with me, she'd had a kind of rural innocence I found endearing. That was completely gone. She looked like a clone of every cheap little drugged-out groupie whore on the Strip."

"Did you talk to her?"

"I tried, but she was really fucked up on something. I told her her parents and I had been worried about her and asked her to come home with me, but she just giggled. When I asked where she was staying, she turned bitchy and said it was none of my business and who did I think I was, her father or something? She said Cooney was helping her now, and she didn't need me."

"Did Cooney or Star know who you were?"

227

"Cooney knew who I was, but I don't think either of them knew I was Lisa's father. From the way they were talking, Lisa had stuck to her renunciation of me. They seemed to think I was just a dirty old man Lisa had been star-fucking for a while. Cooney and I got into a little scuffle right there because of a couple of remarks he made along those lines, in fact."

"A fight?"

"It was broken up before it got started, but it gave Lisa a chance to slip away." He looked away and his gaze grew distant again. "I never saw her again."

"Did you look for her?"

He nodded. "I called Cooney, but he said she was just some little queenie he'd picked up that night and that he hadn't seen her since. I only found out after she was dead that he'd been lying, that she'd been there all along."

I gave him a purposely skeptical look. "I find the tender-young-innocent-corrupted-by-the-degenerate-monsters routine a little hard to swallow. People don't degenerate that fast unless they want to. It sounds to me like the girl set out, consciously or unconsciously, to become everything you detest in the music business, to get back at you."

His face flushed angrily. "*They* killed her. I don't care what kind of Freudian bullshit you want to try to color it up with."

"Is that why you killed them? An eye for an eye? What were the other two sets of eyes—interest?"

The color left his face. "What are you talking about?"

"Cooney. Julia. Star."

He tried to smile, but he wasn't a good bluffer. "Are you kidding, or what? Julia killed Cooney."

"Julia Roth *thought* she killed Cooney," I corrected him. "She'd switched the stuff, all right, and Cooney was an unintentional victim, but as drunk as he was, the man had a much higher tolerance for drugs than the others at the party, and he started to recover later on. Julia told me that herself."

"So he had a relapse. It happens."

"Yeah, but this time it happened because you were waiting

228

around outside his house. When you saw her leave to go to the store, you went in and mixed up a bourbon bracer fortified with a little of the junk you removed from the bottle at the party, when you went outside to check on Cooney. I don't know how you got him to drink it, but I don't imagine it would have been too hard, especially in his condition."

"You forget, I was at the hospital."

"You took your own car and you disappeared about half an hour after you brought Wanda and Cuthburton in," I said. "You were gone about an hour."

"I can't stand hospitals. I took a walk."

"You took a drive," I said.

His second drink came and he started into it, not saying anything. I nudged him a little: "I'm not interested in busting you, Carey. Segal's in the clear and as far as I'm concerned, those three trashbags are no loss to the world. This is just between us."

He gave me a knowing look. "Us and the cops outside."

"You think I'm wired?" I stood up so he could pat me down.

Carey's face grew somber as he lapsed back into staring silently into his drink. His features contorted as if rallying for some great effort, but all he got out was, "I—"

I leaned forward. "You'll feel better if you tell somebody."

His eyes closed and stayed closed, and he recited as if he were reading cue cards inside the lids: "I hadn't really thought about doing anything to Cooney. In my mind, sure, but I mean in real life. But when I saw him stagger out the door at the party, something happened to me, Jake. When I went outside and found he was gone, the thought that he might live suddenly became intolerable to me. Everybody was in the bathroom when I came back into the den, so I emptied some of the bottle into a glass and hid it. I took it with me to the hospital, then drove over to Cooney's house. Julia's car was there and I waited until she left and went up and made Cooney a good-night drink, like you said."

"And Julia?"

"That wasn't difficult. She was three sheets to the wind when I got over there. I went into the bathroom and took some of her own pills from her medicine cabinet and slipped a couple into her drink."

"Then you put her in the tub, set the time up on the clock, and called me to provide an alibi for yourself."

He nodded weakly. "Funny."

"What?"

His gaze drifted off. "They were playing my song on the radio. 'Bells.' "

"Fitting music for her funeral."

He leaned across the table, his eyes seeking understanding. "I couldn't let her live, Jake. Not after I saw those pictures."

"What pictures?"

"Cooney's personal porn collection," he said, his lips compressing angrily. "I found it in his bedroom when I was there. Lisa was in it, doing all sorts of perverted things with Star and Julia. In one of them, she and that little puss-pocket Star were with a god-damned dog." Tears welled up in his eyes and he quickly daubed at them with a napkin.

"That's why you played Galileo with Star?"

His bowed head nodded.

"What did you do with the pictures?"

"Burned them. But I couldn't get them out of my mind. I kept seeing them. They were like a tumor growing in my brain and I had to cut them out."

"By scissoring them out of real life, you'd cut them out of the pictures."

His head shook jerkily, back and forth. "I'm not crazy, Jake. I'm not some loony freeway killer who has to go out and find a girl a week to feed some warped compulsion. It's over."

I nodded. "Until some voice reminds you that I know about it and whispers my address in your ear?"

"It's *over*," he protested. "I swear it is. I'm not a murderer."

"You could have fooled me."

"They didn't deserve to live. They were cancer—"

"Maybe you can convince a jury of that."

"You're going to go to the cops?"

I nodded.

"They won't do anything about it," he said. "It's your word against mine, and I'm sure they'll find your story harder to buy than the one they already have."

I reached under the table and ripped the recorder from the underside where I'd taped it. I punched the "Off" button and said, "I thought they might want to hear it in your own words."

"You sonofabitch," he spat.

Strangely enough, I felt like one. "Don't worry about it too much until you talk to a lawyer. It might not even be admissible as evidence."

I signaled the waitress and told her we'd changed our minds about lunch and gave her a twenty. While she was off getting my change, Stack stared at me silently. The hard glint was back in his eyes now. "Why are you doing this, Jake? I thought we were friends."

"Come off it, Carey. You were using me."

"Don't you understand? I had to do it. They killed my daughter, my baby girl—"

"You did what you had to do and I'm doing what I have to do," I said.

The waitress returned with my change. I tipped her and left Stack at the table. I drove over to the West Hollywood station and left the tape for Momaday's collection, then drove home, not feeling exactly like the conquering hero. The case was closed and my bank account was flush, but I only felt lonely and hollow inside.

My spirits picked up when I pulled into my driveway and saw the stewardess's Z parked below her apartment and remembered what day it was. The soothing, sympathetic touch of female hands sounded like a healing balm; I could probably even get by with a cheap physical encounter.

I was on my way up the stairs when heavy metallic footsteps clanked behind me, and I turned to see a suit of armor walking clumsily toward me. I started laughing and she stopped and lifted the visor and looked around cautiously. "You alone?"

I stopped laughing long enough to say, "Yeah, I'm alone."

"You mean I can get out of this thing?" she asked, relieved. "It must be a hundred and ten in here."

"I think that might be a good idea."

She clanked over to the stairs and eased down stiffly, and I grabbed a metal boot. "Where in the hell did you get this thing?"

"Western Costume," she said. "Eighty-five a day."

"You're completely gonzo, you know that?"

"You mean you just noticed?" She grinned and made her eyebrows jump, Groucho-style. "It doesn't have to be back until tomorrow. Maybe we can think of some interesting games to play with it."

A couple immediately came to mind. I glanced up at the stewardess's apartment; thought, to hell with it, she wouldn't be moving anywhere tonight; and pulled off the other boot.